MURDER ON THE METOLIUS

A TRAVEL BUG MYSTERY

DELEEN WILLS

COPYRIGHT

Copyright 2021 Life of Riley Publishing

Printed by KDP/Amazon

ISBN: 9798731872171

First Edition

If you have any questions or comments, please contact Deleen Wills through Facebook at Travel Bug Mysteries or deleenwills@gmail.com.

Cover Design by Jessica Spurrier

Cover Illustration by J. Steven Hunt

ABOUT THE AUTHOR

Deleen Wills strives to write stories that entertain, enlighten and educate, hopefully encouraging others to realize how easy and enjoyable it is to embrace new friends and gain new insights while exploring our world.

Her passions are globetrotting and writing. She delights in working from her home as a travel coordinator organizing adventures for groups, family and friends. Living with her husband in Oregon after retiring from her work as an administrator in nonprofit education, she volunteers for several nonprofit organizations.

Murder on the Metolius, is a cleverly plotted cozy mystery set in Central Oregon and the Willamette Valley. Step back in time through this winning combination of embellished childhood memories and a vivid imagination woven together with historical and geographic facts.

Other books by Deleen Wills
THROUGH COLORFUL DOORS
BECAUSE OF COLORFUL DOORS
BEHIND COLORFUL DOORS

Available on Amazon & Etsy or deleenwills@gmail.com

instagram.com/travelbugmysteries

THANKS & ACKNOWLEDGEMENTS

Jay Burcham, Peggy Bruner, Camp Sherman Store-Roger and Kathy White, Maleah Harris, Jefferson County Sheriff's Office, John and Kim, Maralee Knox, Linn County Sheriff's Office, Mike Martin, Oregon Historical Society, Bruce Riley, Mark Riley and Patty Riley.

MURDER ON THE METOLIUS is a collaborative effort and my deepest appreciation goes out to my family, friends and readers who encouraged me to continue writing.

Beth E. Pitcher, for expertly and patiently proofreading.

Jessica Spurrier, graphic designer and photographer. See her work at GreengateImages.Etsy.com.

J. Steven Hunt, cover illustration.

Jennifer Leigh Riley, story consultant.

Kate Boase, story consultant.

Sue Christopherson, the sister I never had, who continues to encourage, support and love me as a true Sisterchick does.

To my cheerleaders for their continued encouragement: Beth, Carol, Cathy, Chaille, Davette, Dorothy, Heather, Jeannie, Jenn, Jessica, Joanie, Judie, Kate, Linda, Margie, Michelle, Nancy, NiCole, Peggy, Russ, Suzanne, and many readers of *Through Colorful Doors*, *Because of Colorful Doors* and *Behind Colorful Doors*.

Mark Wills, for his ongoing exceptional patience helping with technology issues.

For my beloved parents who instilled a vivid imagination and wanderlust. They opened my eyes to travel at a young age as our family of five gallivanted around the Pacific Northwest and Canada in our tiny travel trailer.

PREFACE

He felt like he was going to heave. Did I just kill that guy?

Another wondered, did I hit that guy so hard, I killed him?

A third hoped he'd killed the cockroach.

CHAPTER ONE

I Left My Heart In San Francisco

He didn't remember his mother. She died when he was about three. That's what relatives told him anyway. Throughout the years, he'd overheard whispers about family skeletons that usually included the words, "Her old man did it."

He was the unfortunate by-product of an out-of-wedlock fling between this mother and no one knew for sure, but supposedly his father, Harry, Harold Finch. He hated the name, which regrettably he'd been given, too. Apparently, his father killed her. He didn't know or remember his face. He did remember being hit. He'd been burned with the tip of a cigarette leaving a permanent reminder on his left forearm to prove it. And he could still hear somebody's screams and cries. Maybe his or maybe his mothers. His old man was long gone, he hoped dead.

Someone in the family started calling him Harley, instead of Harry or Junior. He liked his new name. All the relatives meant well, trying to care for him along with their own children. Moving from home to home meant several different schools. Rarely did he get better than a C in any class. He never did his homework. He bad-mouthed his teachers. He got into fights with other students.

He'd overheard plenty of girls talk about him. They called him cute. He learned quickly to use this to his advantage. A smile or a wink went a long way in getting out of some jams early on. His medium brown hair, about the color of a Ghirardelli milk chocolate bar produced down along the wharf of his city, combined with his big brown eyes, made him irresistible to some girls.

At fourteen he drank beer and smoked Lucky Strike cigs. Kids at school called him a Greaser. He settled down for a while during his middle teenage years staying with his mother's mom in a teeny fourth-floor walk-up in the heart of San Francisco. He slept on the sofa in her one-bedroom apartment.

Her little dog Spanky, a mix of a pug and whatever else, slept on his chest. Grandma named him that after one of the boys in a children's television show, "Our Gang." Harley loved dogs and he'd never hurt one. Nobody around him had better hurt one either.

But he didn't love all animals, especially not cats. And birds, he hated most of them, particularly ducks and geese. He remembered one time as a youngster going to Golden Gate Park with whatever family he was living with at the time. They'd taken some dried-up brown bread to feed the ducks. A hungry and aggressive one mistook Harley's brown shoe for a piece of old bread and pecked his shoe really hard and didn't let up. It freaked him out and still did. He couldn't understand why everyone laughed and thought it was cute. The only good duck was a dead duck to him.

If he scrunched down and looked out the lower left corner of his grandma's kitchen window, he could see a section of the middle part of the orangish-red Golden Gate Bridge.

He felt restless. He wandered the streets instead of going to school and hung out with kids that were smoking pot, so he did, too. His life goal—racing fast cars. His grandmother gave up nagging him. She'd tried her darndest to encourage him. The only thing she could do is love him.

Harley told her goodbye when he turned seventeen. He slept on the streets, fending for himself, getting in lots of trouble. When he needed a shower, he stayed a night at the Salvation Army. He felt safe there. He would have stayed more often if he didn't have to listen to some man come in and preach about God. A coming-to-Jesus moment didn't happen for him as it had for others.

Stealing became more frequent. He rarely got caught swiping food from the back doors of restaurants. Or following the milk delivery truck as it drove away, then drinking an entire bottle left on the doorstep. He was thrown in juvie for shoplifting some items from the downtown Macy's jewelry counter. When the salesclerk turned away to help a customer, she left the display case open. He'd almost made it out the doors with three watches and four rings under his coat when some guy grabbed him then called the police. He did two weeks in juvie, instead of calling his grandmother.

Sometime later, he ended up back in juvie for a bolder robbery—cash and jewelry from a ritzy home. When asked why, his response had been, "Well, they left the back door unlocked." He had more and more run-ins with the law. More often than not, though, he didn't get caught. He didn't feel bad at all in his quest to get ahead in the world. He'd do whatever he needed. He knew his grandmother wouldn't approve that he'd become a sweet-talking con man and thief.

Weeks turned into months. About nineteen years old, he encountered some guys in a bar that he'd heard served alcohol to minors. Two guys introduced him to easy money, dealing meth.

San Francisco produced street gangs faster than Ghirardelli produced chocolate bars. Most gangs were based on neighborhoods or by ethnicity. Some were based on family, like crime families. Many were divided by economic lines.

Motorcycle gangs were similar in some regards yet very different in others. He noticed people seemed curious and frightened by the leather-clad mystery surrounding outlaw biker gangs. He wanted people to be afraid of him.

Harley laughed at the ridiculous hippie movement. These flamboyantly outfitted weirdoes hung around Haight-Ashbury and the Golden Gate Park. His turf. He'd heard all about The Merry Pranksters, a large community of crazy like-minded people who took road trips to Oregon traveling in brightly colored school buses while ingesting large amounts of LSD that had been legal until a few years ago. He knew some past acquaintances who helped start the movement. If he had ever looked at a newspaper, he would have read they were known for famous parties and giving out large quantities of LSD. They helped define the long hair and weird fashion that came to signify the American hippie. Some of their events established so-called "acid tests" where large groups would drink Kool-Aid laced with LSD and attempt to experience a community-oriented trip. Harley decided they were the most bizarre people around.

He'd seen a slow-moving psychedelic old bus painted with blue people, tropical fish, jellyfish, sea anemones and underwater plants, a tiger, palm trees, trees, a nude Adonis pointing to the tail of a diving whale, stars, colorful hot air balloons floating over the countryside, swirls, swishes, and curls. If there wasn't a picture or specific design, bright colors filled in the space. The windows were covered with fabric sheets in solid panels of yellow, carrot, jade, scarlet, royal blue and navy. A painted sign on the front top spelled FURTHER. Even the wheel wells were painted in vivid kaleidoscopic schemes. He saw just one side of the vibrant caterpillar as it rolled down a street. At the top of the back of the bus, he saw another FURTHER sign written above a State of Oregon flag flapping in its own bus-generated breeze.

Then protests of students, veterans and hippies started to erupt on the streets. Harley watched as hippies became famous for the widespread Vietnam war protests that helped to define their role in the unruly times. He hated the stupid hippies and now he lived daily smack dab in the middle of it all.

Harley heard young men were being pulled off the streets at night and shipped off to fight in a war they didn't even agree with. He'd heard the rumors and lies so many times, they became truth to him and others.

Harley had enough cash to buy a motorcycle. Not just any motorcycle. He would only ride a Harley-Davidson. He mentioned to several bikers he was on the lookout. A few weeks later a guy told him about a Harley Model KHK 1955 in okay condition. He did some checking around and found new models sold for around $925. He wouldn't be paying that price since it was now five years old.

When Harley laid eyes on the silver bike with black seat and black gas tank, he heard his own heartbeat. He had to have it. It had seen better days, but he'd fix it up. He'd swap out the handlebars for the higher ones like the Breezer or maybe the High Drag. While dreaming of everything he'd modify, the owner kept yammering on about it being a V-2, four-stroke, Flathead 45-degree engine, 4-speed gearbox, tire size, 4.49 gallon fuel capacity, kick starter, 6 volt, as his voice faded into the background.

Harley only heard: Power--5200 RPM. Top speed--95 MPH. They worked out a deal at $50 less than the owner originally had said. Cash talked. Six hundred dollars less in his pocket, Harley rode away on his very own wheels. One bill just happened to be a counterfeit fifty. He thought it pretty cool to pass off funny money.

In his early twenties he stood six-foot, two inches. He probably weighed two hundred pounds easy. Harley turned heads as lots of women who took a second look at him. He had shoulder length medium brown hair, down to his eyebrows with sideburns that morphed into a full beard. He was all hair except for his coal black clothing. He wore a headband. If he smiled, anyone could see his teeth were now a light gray from drug use. He wore several rings on his hands. On the top of both hands were tattoos of different designs of skulls. He wore a black leather jacket over a sooty black shirt with black leather pants. He wore boots, of course, black pearl. No one ever knew he always had a blade in his right boot.

Harley had worked his way up in the number two most infamous motorcycle gang. They had started in the Bay Area about fifteen years earlier. He'd participated in armed robbery, threw a firebomb or two, tried his hand at counterfeiting, sold lots of drugs and some guns, and had several assaults under this belt. He hadn't killed anybody. Well, he wasn't positive. If the grungy flake couldn't swim, he might have croaked. One thing he stood firm on. He wouldn't be involved in prostitution after what his mother probably went through. He didn't know for sure but again, he recalled the whisperings of family members over the years.

Becoming more known to law enforcement, after one particularly bad scene, Harley figured he might have to beat it since he hadn't shown up in court for his latest crime.

The fuzz were cockroaches to Harley. Anyone who cheated him was a cockroach. Outlaw motorcycle bikers from the number one club were all cockroaches. And what did he do to roaches? He stepped on them.

Most motorcycle clubs probably started out innocent enough. Weekend warriors bombing around on their noisy motorcycles. Ever since World War II, California had been strangely plagued by men on motorcycles. They usually traveled in packs of ten to thirty, booming along the highways and stopping here and there to get blitzed and raise hell. The Southern California climate was perfect for motorcyclists. Most were harmless weekend types and no more dangerous than surfers or beachcombers.

But outlaw motorcycle gangs had created an image of brawling buddies, wild behavior, free-spirited in search of fun on powerful, loud machines. They wanted their behavior to be noticed and wanted to upset traditional society. Movies and television were portraying them as seriously dangerous hoodlums.

Magazine articles published in *Time* and *Newsweek* detailed problems associated with the behavior of gangs in California. These articles were the first national media attention directed at the California motorcycle gang subculture. They cast its members in a highly negative, anti-social light. Some did belong to the other gangs called "outlaw clubs" and these were the ones who, especially on weekends and holiday, were likely to turn up almost anywhere in the state, looking for action. They were tough, mean and potentially as dangerous as a pack of wild animals. Some reveled in their notoriety. So did Harley's outlaw biker gang.

———

That summer over one hundred thousand people banded together and relocated to the Haight-Ashbury District. His turf. He'd heard people calling it the "Summer of love." Basically San Francisco had been taken over by the hippie moment where free love, drug use and communal living became the norm. Many called these hippies "flower children." He didn't see any children even though most acted like them.

If anybody or anything intimidated him it would be the unpredictable, crazed guys from the number one biker club. Then the zany hippies invaded. The cops were looking for him. Walls were closing in around him. It seemed the perfect time for him to split.

At age twenty-six, his gang had taken on the number one gang and managed to eke out the territory of Oregon for themselves. Some stories would say they were forced out of the Bay Area and moved north. They all rode Harley-Davidson motorcycles, many modified and souped-up.

After a vicious initiation process, he deserved to wear a leather jacket. The patch on the back had an evil grinning character marching in a red-, gold-, and blue-colored outfit. He never spoke about his initiation. Harley didn't even want to think about what he'd gone through.

Harley had never ridden his bike any great distance. Six hundred fifty miles to Lincoln City, Oregon, would be a long trip and guessed twelve to fourteen hours if he didn't stop much. He packed one bag of his few belongings, jumped on his bike and headed north on the Pacific Coast Highway 101.

He figured it would be fairly easy since the Redwood Highway, actually Highway 101, went right through San Francisco. Winding his way through the city and across the Sausalito Canal, the first of many bridges, to his right he saw the sign for San Quentin. Some of his acquaintances now resided at the prison.

If he followed the Highway 101 signs, he'd be fine he thought. Orchards were loaded with almonds. Heading pretty much due north he came to the small town of Petaluma then climbed in elevation to Santa Rosa, then higher to The Forks. Riding thirty-two miles a spur of the moment decision hit him. He turned left from Highway 101 at Cloverdale onto Highway 128 heading west to the coastline.

Riding through mountainous Placer County, he saw a sign about this area during Gold Rush times. At teeny Yorkville, he read a sign: "Ocean Beaches, Fish Rock 28."

Only twenty-eight miles and he'd be on the ocean. Probably an hour, or an hour and a half at the most, he thought. Why not? He'd avoid the snail-people, whom he

impatiently called anyone pulling travel trailers. He hated
log trucks, too. He'd had nightmares about logs mysteriously rolling off the side and squashing anything underneath. He'd avoid the more popular roads probably loaded
with snoopy cops, too. He exited onto the smaller road
called Fish Rock Road. It didn't matter to him that he had
no map.

There was no traffic on the asphalt road. Soon, when
asphalt became dirt and gravel it became obvious why. He
snaked around forested mountains, flinging up gravel
behind him. Then he came to Redwoods Natural Reserve,
then to Maillard Redwoods State Natural Reserve even
higher at fifteen hundred feet. It all looked the same: enormous trees on steep mountains. The trees grew so close
and so high, he felt like he was riding through a wood-
paneled tunnel.

The road wrapped itself as tightly as possible to Garcia
River, making every twist and turn, slower going. S-curves
became Z-switchbacks. Mind-numbing changed quickly to
exhilaration ripping around a couple of the sharp corners.
Whipping around a blind corner faster than the posted 15
mph, he came roaring up behind a log truck. What in the
world was it doing way out here on an unimproved road?
The long trailer held three horizontal gigantic redwoods
within the tall metal posts. The truck looked overloaded.
He swore out loud gesturing for the driver to let him by. He
geared down going seven miles per hour and there were no
chances to pass.

After a couple of stressful slow miles, the white-
knuckled truck driver noticed the motorcycle weaving in
and out behind him. The trucker pulled over to the right a
few feet, enough for Harley to pass. Harley, feeling less
than appreciative, signaled a crude hand gesture instead of

a cordial thank you wave. He about jumped off his seat when the truck driver laid on his air horn.

The trucker cussed a blue streak ending in, "I could squash that bug if I wanted to and nobody would probably even miss him. Something mysteriously might happen to his chopper." The trucker's mind wandered hoping he'd catch up with him somewhere along the coast highway.

In one stretch of a steep downward stretch of zigzags it took Harley back to when, as a kid, he ran down the eight hairpin turns of the crookedest one-way street in the world —Lombard Street. He remembered it had been much steeper than it first looked. He did it again one night on his chopper when there were no tourists around. He did not obey the "Speed Limit 5 MPH" sign.

In one portion on Fish Rock Road, several left curves and right turns were so narrow he felt relieved no vehicles of any size were coming towards him. Hundred-foot tall redwoods closely bordered both sides of the road, like a hedgerow. No sunlight seeped through the green canopy. Even on his chopper, it'd be a tight squeeze. His hands, wrists and arms ached. He loosened his tense grip on the straight stretches.

Driving slowly around a bend he saw a coyote ahead trotting along the roadside. He slowed down to six miles per hour until he got even with it. He figured it must be old and deaf as the animal didn't seem fearful of him or the noise his bike generated. But that wasn't it at all. She had two pups keeping up with her. One was ebony and other one creamy. The pups had shorter muzzles, small ears and dainty little feet. Even though their tails weren't bushy like their mothers, their tails were still pointed downwards when they ran.

Harley thought she was a handsome animal with a pointed muzzle, perky ears, all golden-colored legs with gray and gold fur covering her lean body. She looked at Harley with her yellow eyes. Her stare startled him.

He remembered some cock and bull story his grandmother told him. She mentioned that they had some native American Indian blood in their heritage. Some great-great-grandfather was a Navajo, supposedly.

She told him folklore stories about animals. Maybe that's where his fondness for dogs started. He recalled she said that the coyote is an omen of an unfortunate event of things in your past or in your future. Then if a coyote stares at you it generally is a message to take a look within, to not take life too seriously, and to learn to laugh at ourselves and even our mistakes. Coyotes also remind us that anything we do to others will come back to us—good or bad. In a flash, she moved her cubs into the thick trees.

Dropping about one thousand feet, and finally, two and a half hours later, his newly dubbed crookedest road in the world ended at the village of Fish Rock. He pulled into a gas station to stretch. Inside he bought a bag of crunchy orange Cheetos, the largest box of Red Hots they had, and two bottles of Dr Pepper. Now his back hurt. At least he could see the ocean. Surely the rest of the way north would be much easier. About one hundred twenty miles from his departure point, it had taken him half a day.

Now on South Highway 1 he continued north hugging the shoreline. Little villages like Steens Landing were few and far between. At Schooner Gulch State Beach, the road turned inland through Gallaway then back along the coastline. He slowed down through tiny towns.

He saw signs for Mendocino. Before long he crossed Big River into the largest town he'd see since leaving home. He parked in a lookout area. A couple hundred feet above the ocean, the view sprawled northward. He could see the horizon line dozens of miles out to sea.

Glancing left, he saw fishing boats below in the bay. A line of people waiting at a small hole-in-the-wall indicated some type of good food. He meandered that way. It turned out to be his favorite dessert—ice cream. He had a double scoop: rocky road with marshmallow bits and chopped almonds in chocolate and the other, butter pecan. He liked the buttery vanilla base chock-full with toasted pecans. Like a kid, he stood licking the cone watching fisherman pull in nets of something.

Highway 1 or Shoreline Highway from Mendocino took him through Pine Grove and Caspar. He crossed the Noyo River at Fort Bragg with a big bay and ocean on his left. He spotted a Motel 6 and contemplated staying overnight. Even though he'd only travelled two hundred miles, it had been five hours of surprisingly grueling riding through a lot of mountains. Now his butt hurt, too.

He continued on through Cleone, then back along the coast now on North Highway 1 to Union Landing with water on his left. Mountains were on his right. Each village had a tavern, little grocery store and a church or two.

The South Fork of the Eel River provided some diversion from trees. Before long he was at Standish Hickey State Recreation Area with the hamlet of Riverdale sandwiched within Smithe Redwoods State Natural Reserve. Good grief, miles and miles of more redwoods.

Highway 101 N slalomed around the South Fork of the Eel River taking a sharp west turn to Redway. At Scotia the highway crossed over the Eel River a few times. At Humboldt Hill the highway followed Humboldt Bay north then east then due north again. He preferred seeing the ocean. He'd gone about two hundred fifty miles.

Signs indicated sixty-six miles to the next bigger town, Eureka. But first he had to get through Humboldt Bay National Wildlife Refuge. He crept along as he'd seen signs

13

along the road "Beware of Deer." He did not want to hit a deer. What he did see were the largest geese he'd ever seen. Canada Geese flew overhead in flocks creating distinctive V shapes. He just didn't want any of them to let loose their latest meal on him.

He noticed several black-tail deer. One had antlers. One doe had spotted twin fawns close by. Ponds were teeming with ducks and other waterfowl. What they were, he had no idea. He didn't like ducks. Driving over two-hundred-foot tall Humboldt Hill, he continued along the coastline.

More than five hours since his Cheetos, Red Hots and Dr Pepper snack, he arrived in Eureka, population twenty thousand, on Humboldt Bay. He'd driven about ten hours total and only three hundred miles. Warm and sunny at six o'clock didn't matter. He felt exhausted. His butt hurt. His legs ached. He felt a back spasm. His shoulders and neck throbbed from being in one position for so long. He needed a map to see what might be lurking ahead. He couldn't be all that far from the California/Oregon border, right?

He saw a billboard for the Eureka Inn. Taking the next exit, he turned onto 7th Street, and into the hotel parking lot. He didn't care what it looked like on the outside, which wasn't much. He didn't care it had been "The Place" to stay in the 30s and 40s. He didn't care the placard proudly boasted that Boris Karloff stayed here on Oct. 31, 1931. Nor the Rockefellers, Lady Bird Johnson, Shirley Temple and others.

It sat in the middle of town with a restaurant nearby. He craved a steak. And a brew or two or three. He paid $32 for one night and after getting the room key, the clerk answered his question, only one hundred miles to the border. On a full stomach and the quietest night probably in his entire life, he slept like a baby.

After a big breakfast in the hotel dining room of the supposedly world-renowned, fresh-caught abalone along with scrambled eggs and three cups of scalding hot coffee, he checked out. He got the impression the clerk might be glad to see him go even though no one said anything derogatory to him. He knew his obsidian leather clothing and jacket emblem immediately tagged him. He doubted anyone would bother him, except a member of another gang. Fortunately, he hadn't seen any.

Back on his bike, he headed north past Arcata where the Trinity Scenic Byway, Highway 299 merged to 101. McKinleyville led to Moonstone. From Moonstone, some eleven miles, he reached Big Lagoon where he crossed the Big Lagoon Marsh picking up some speed to Klamath.

Now in the upper northwest corner of his state, at a Crescent City Texaco station, he stopped to relieve himself of the three cups of coffee. Turning inland for some miles until he crossed Smith River and altered westward once again.

About twenty miles later at the fenceless border he read a large green and white "Welcome to Oregon" sign. Then a roadside billboard read: "Don't Californicate Oregon." He'd seen Oregon's radical governor interviewed on TV. One of the governor's remarks particularly stuck with him: "We want you to visit our State of Excitement often. Come again and again. But for heaven's safe, don't move here to live. Or if you do have to move in to live, don't tell any of your neighbors where you are going."

Evidently there wasn't a strong love for those moving from California. One thing that received national attention, this governor claimed all Oregon beaches open to the public. No hotel could purchase or claim beaches as their own. Called The Beach Bill, he faced an uphill battle with members of his own party. He felt passionately that Oregon beaches should be accessible to the public and not controlled by commercial or private landowners. Republicans disagreed. The Oregon governor had a reputation for bucking the system and pushed it through. Harley thought California should copy this regulation.

Now on the Oregon Coast Highway, ten minutes later he arrived at Harbor, Oregon. He would barely call it a town. At Harbor he crossed the Chetco River and skirted Azalea State Park.

Three miles later in the coastal town of Brookings it felt much hotter than in the shady forests. A sign on a US National Bank read seventy-eight degrees. The highway went right through the middle of Harris Beach State Park. He pulled over at Pistol River State Scenic Viewpoint. Overlooking what seemed like miles of sand dunes, white foamy waves gently rolled onto the flat tan sandy beach. There wasn't a soul on the beach. Tall sand dunes mixed in with the wide-sweeping curve of the beach. There were thousands of shore birds of all kinds, but he couldn't much tell the difference except for sea gulls. Large stumps, seaweed and tree roots littered the beach.

At yet another park, Cape Sebastian State Scenic Corridor, he got off his chopper, seeing a panoramic view at over two hundred feet above the ocean. South he could see nearly fifty miles toward Crescent City. Looking north he saw miles and miles of ocean and beach until it blended in with mountains jutting out into the water. The sign pointed to Humbug Mountain miles to the north. It sloped gently from hills to a moderate peak at one thousand seven hundred feet. He wasn't easily impressed, but this day had already been full of scenic surprises. Tall spruce trees shaded him from the glaring sun.

At Buena Vista Ocean Wayside State Park, some lady volunteer handed him a cup of coffee. About one hundred twenty miles from breakfast, jeez, his butt already smarted. He decided he needed to stop and stretch more often.

He stopped for gas, a toilet break and a Dr Pepper at the Texaco in Gold Beach then rode across an immensely long bridge with not much for side railings. He certainly didn't want anybody to side-swipe or bump him over the side. "Lincoln City 200 miles," the sign read. Glancing left, the rocks in the ocean were framed by sand dunes and long, sweeping grass. At Meyers Beach, peaceful golden sands with huge smoky black boulders jutted dramatically out of the ocean waves.

He crossed the Rogue River and veered west once again. Westerly turned northerly. Enormous trees clung to mountainsides and the spectacular craggy coastline dotted with sandy beaches and sea stacks. He noticed birds swarming around the tall rocks.

Before reaching Port Orford, he saw some gardens advertised on a billboard. "Prehistoric Gardens in Oregon's Rain Forest," the sign promoted. At the roadside attraction a toothy, twenty-foot tall Tyrannosaurus Rex stood not looking very inviting. He could see several life-sized sculptures of dinosaurs set among thick lush greenery. Some of the bushes had leaves the size of a Volkswagen Bug.

He snaked his way through twisty Humbug Mountain State Park hugging the northern base of the mountain. He was in an old-growth rainforest according to signs. Obviously a popular tourist area, Volkswagen camper vans and generic station wagons crammed with families unloaded children, bicycles, and picnic baskets.

Going around a corner ahead he could see a lineup of vehicles. A highway crew was doing some type of road

maintenance. He parked his chopper and stood, appreciating the time to stand instead of sit. A red and white Ford
Ranch Wagon pulling a silver bullet, really an Airstream
trailer house, parked behind him. Mom hopped out and
opened the travel trailer door, coming out with a cooler of
sandwiches. Four kids swarmed her gobbling down the
treat. Then she returned the empty cooler, shut the door
and they were all back in their places once the lineup
started moving ten minutes later. He laughed as it looked
like a comedy movie.

Barreling through Port Orford then Cape Blanco State
Park and Floras Lake State Natural Area, he'd never seen
so many natural areas and state parks. At Langlois he
stayed inland to Bandon. The scenery changed into huge
sand dunes. He couldn't see the ocean anywhere. Then he
spotted a sign for Cranberry Corners and a billboard
advertising Ocean Spray cranberry juice. He'd never given
a thought about where cranberries came from. He recalled
a tart bite at somebody's place for Thanksgiving dinner
one time.

All he could see were gigantic sand dunes. He saw signs
for Coos Bay, North Bend, Coquille. It was pretty enough
scenery with trees but no beach.

He rode across the Coquille River. How to pronounce
this one, he wondered. He stopped trying. At Winchester
Bay, the Umpqua River separated land and an island.
Reedsport looked to be a timber town and he crossed a
bridge to Bolon Island and back across on the mainland
towards Gardiner. With the Umpqua River to his left and
mountains to his right, he drove on.

He saw signs to Florence but kept going. In the distance he saw more mountainous sand dunes. Should he
detour and ride his chopper over the dunes? His butt hurt
more just thinking about the roller-coaster-looking-ride.

Veering back towards the Pacific, about ten miles north of Florence, helmet-less Harley could smell, but not hear the barks of the sea lions over the rumble of his bike. What was that smell? Two employees in the parking lot were wiring an orange cardboard sign to the bumper of each tourist vehicle. The inky bold print read, "Sea Lion Caves, Oregon Coast Highway." Anyone stopping would be driving away with this banner of pride on its rear.

A sign showed a picture of sea lions lounging about on the caves below. He stopped in the parking lot and spotted some large noisy sea lions on rocks sunning themselves. Looking north he saw a lighthouse across a cove. He looked straight down into the aqua green foamy water.

A couple miles later he saw signs for Heceta Head Lighthouse. He parked and walked a short distance to the historic lighthouse. The white lighthouse has a red cap protecting the light. The light atop the fifty-six-foot tower was first illuminated in 1894. Its automated beacon can be seen twenty-one miles from land. It is rated the most powerful light on the Oregon coast according to a volunteer happily and proudly sharing historic and current facts. The lighthouse sits on top of Heceta Head at a stunningly high one thousand feet elevation.

Harley sat on a picnic table looking north mesmerized by the waves and white lacey ribbons left behind on the golden sandy beach.

Down the beach he saw a large dog. There were no people in sight. Turned out to be a coyote minding his own business dashing down the beach swerving around driftwood and logs.

Standing there watching the graceful, solitary animal he determined if there was an afterlife, which he totally didn't believe there was, but just in case, he'd respectfully request coming back as a coyote.

His grandmother said Native Americans thought everyone had a spirit animal. They say coyotes symbolize selfishness and deceit . He is often outwitted by the animals who he tries to trick. Just another cockamamie story.

Harley noticed a few people nervously looking at him. He laughed to himself. Yes, a motorcycle guy could appreciate nature and beauty.

At Yachats, he wasn't sure how to pronounce it, Yaachats or Yah Hauts. In Waldport, a Ford pickup truck towing a turquoise and white Shasta trailer house pulled out from a gas station, slowing him down. The orange cardboard advertisement from the smelly Sea Lion Caves on the bumper stood out as bright as a pumpkin.

Fifteen miles farther, driving under the arch of the massive Yaquina Bay Bridge in Newport, on the north edge of the bridge he swerved down off the highway winding down to the waterfront. The smell of fresh fish and saltwater hung heavy in the air. He heard sea lions barking below a pier. He'd heard about Mo's, supposedly the best clam chowder along the central Oregon coast.

A friendly waitress greeted him wondering to herself, "What hole did he climb out from?" She saw a biker insignia on the back of his jacket. Another had passed through several months earlier. When she told her boyfriend, he said, "Where there's one gang member, there's more. Like rats."

If he could have read her mind, he wouldn't have cared. Because he didn't care what anybody thought. All he cared about at this point was food. Soft flavorful clams and chunky potatoes were in each bite of the steamy chowder. The hint of bacon added a perfect touch. To him, everything tasted better with bacon. With the soup plus a Budweiser, his hunger pangs disappeared. He asked the waitress, "How far to Lincoln City?"

She pointed north and said, "Twenty-three miles," just like she'd told the one a few months ago. She wondered what in the world could be happening in the little town of Lincoln City.

He followed a silver Chevy Impala up the hill back to the highway. It had an orange "Sea Lion Caves" sign on the left side of the bumper with a yellow sign printed in red, "Trees of Mystery, Shrine of the Redwood Highway," on the right side.

Back on 101, most of the road hugged the coastline. This part of the beach looked much different than previous beaches with lots of rocks.

He pulled off Highway 101 toward Otter Rock. Winding down and out to the viewpoint, he could see miles of views in both directions. Not far below him erosion had created a bowl in the rocks. He could see where water came in through two holes on the outer sides of the massive rock. The punchbowl was created from years of ocean crashing up against the rock wall. Waves spouted water through Devils Punchbowl. In this area there were many rock formations. One large flat rock offshore had hundreds of birds flying around.

Crossing an unexciting bridge, into the tiny community of Depoe Bay, he saw storefronts on the righthand side of the highway. The blue ocean glistened on the left. A slight breeze produced a few white caps. A sign proudly proclaimed, "The World's Smallest Navigable Port." Looking to his left, he saw probably the dinkiest bay he'd ever seen.

He pulled over. Standing along the rock seawall, the ebony volcanic rocks below were craggy and jagged. Left-over white lacey foam from the last wave crept in between cracks. Sea water in eroded ponds would remain until the next wave flooded it.

At the middle of the seawall, some people were pointing to something just outside the small bay. He saw a spout, then a second one. A child yelled in pure delight, "Whales!" Harley had never seen one before and thought it pretty neat. He stood for ten minutes just staring at the two gargantuan smoky black bodies as they cruised by, blowing water high in the air and surfacing enough to see their fins. One emerged like a submarine. It swam for a bit then submerged and the only thing showing was its tail. Then it disappeared below.

The town is perched above the ocean on volcanic basalts. Over time seawater eroded a blowhole or waterspout. Vertical shafts develop as the roof of the sea cave erodes or collapses to expose the surface to air, creating a vent. The geometry of the cave and blowhole, along with the tide levels, swell conditions and weather, determine the height and volume of the marine geyser. He read all this information on a brown sign along the sidewalk.

Several waves combined into one that created an exhilarating thundering sound slamming into the rocks generating an explosion of water and upwards mist. He got wet. Soaking wet. Children screamed with glee. He didn't care; it wasn't cold, maybe sixty degrees.

He laughed. A true deep belly laugh. He hadn't done that in years. He took out a red and white checkered handkerchief and wiped his face. His tongue licked the salt off his lips. The sounds of ocean waves crashing against the rocks, movement of water, blaring of ship horns; he wondered if he shouldn't just stay here. The high tides created big waves that shot through the waterspout making a loud hissing sound. It sounded like a giant breathing in and out.

Hesitantly he departed. A half hour later he drove into Lincoln City. Nineteen blocks later he turned left off of

Highway 101. He spotted the house easily. Parked in the front were about fifteen choppers.

After two weeks of sitting around drinking and doing drugs, the house got too small for Harley. Several of the gang were heading east. They'd heard about cheap housing and property in the high desert region of central Oregon.

They left sea level one morning and four hours later arrived at thirty-six hundred feet in Bend. The bikers camped out in the woods. They drove around checking out rural acreages away from curious neighbors. They found two acres with a dilapidated barn and a two-story house that had seen better days. All they cared about was running water and electricity. About a football field away, Harley saw a lone coyote looking towards the house and men. It was the only sign Harley needed. They pooled their funds and bought the two acres and rundown buildings.

Shortly after moving in, one of the guys was firing off his rifle shooting at anything that moved. Harley warned him never to shoot a coyote or a dog. He was deadly serious, and the guy knew it.

CHAPTER TWO

 **Canada**

Somewhere. Anywhere. Stuck on Highway 16A, sixteen hundred miles north of San Francisco on the way to nowhere, an hour east of the largest city he'd ever been to, Edmonton, he wanted out. Arlo checked off another day on the calendar with a big red X.

His town had quickly become known for the congeniality and acceptance of many people from different cultures living and working together. The *Vegreville Observer*, the weekly newspaper for the region printed that by the 1950s there were more than thirty different ethnic groups living in the area with the four largest being English, French, German, and Ukrainian. The town is positioned at one of the southern points of what is known as the largest Ukrainian bloc settlement in Alberta. With the arrival of Ukrainians to Vegreville came a colorful folk culture with its lively dance and other folk traditions, such as egg-decorating. He didn't dance or paint eggs.

Arlo's mother's parents emigrated from Ukraine to Canada in the 1920s. They called their homeland the Old Country. Their three children were all under the age of five when they hurriedly departed. Fortunately, beside the parents, only the oldest son remembered the distressing ordeal, especially the long trip on the big ship with lots of sick people.

Arlo's father's grandparents had come twenty years earlier, around the 1900s. It was tiny village when they arrived. The Canadian Northern Railway came through four and a half miles northeast of what was then a hamlet. Being too far to transfer goods, developers decided to move the tiny town next to the rail line. His great grandpa had worked placing rail around the province.

His grandparents all had heavy accents and were hard to understand. They looked really old and dressed in funny clothing. They spoke the language of their homeland most of the time.

The next generation understood some Ukrainian but had been urged to learn English. Ani spent afternoons when she got home from school, teaching her mother English. Andy's family, arriving a generation earlier, had more time to adapt.

All the Ukrainian children stuck together. They went to the same colorful onion-domed church and sat together in school. Both of his grandfathers had helped build St. Vladimir's Orthodox Church. They were tight knit, yet they mixed in well with others from European countries. They all had been foreigners. Now they were Canadians.

Arlo's parents knew each other from their junior high school days. They dated in high school. In 1935, the oldest child and first generation-born Canadian, a twenty-year-old son from the Bortnick family got engaged. A few months later he married the nineteen-year-old daughter from the Panchenko family.

Arlo's father is Andriy Bortnick. His first name means "warrior." Their last name means "beekeeper." Everyone calls him Andy. He married Anichka Panchenko, her names meaning "grace and fisher." To everyone she is called Ani.

For two years there was no pregnancy. Ani nervously fretted. She did get pregnant and the soon-to-be father hesitantly hinted they should name all the children beginning with the letter A. His amenable wife agreed. They wanted their children's names to sound North American, not eastern European. Andy felt pride in being a first generation Canadian. Andy and Ani's children would be fluent in English. Their first son would be called Adam. It sounded powerful, firm and biblical.

Once the flood gates opened for Ani, children came often, usually a couple of years apart. Abigail called Abby, Aaron, and Annabella or Bella, followed. Then Arlo arrived. Five children in about eight years. He was the cherished baby for three years. His two older brothers and two sisters carried him around with them, coddled him. He felt loved.

His momma had a beautiful smile and gentle, maple syrup-brown eyes. When she dressed up, which wasn't often, she wore the same dress, probably her only dress-up outfit. It had bold paisley prints of gold, peach, and rose that created the border for the sky blue interior. A bouquet of tangerine and starburst yellow flowers sat atop each paisley and a row of multicolored flowers trickled down into the blue. The design reminded him of a curved feather. Or a twisted teardrop or raindrop. Or a large comma. He loved her "going-out" dress which he maybe saw once or twice a year. His schoolteacher wore a scarf with the same paisley design but different colors.

Of course, they had a father, they just didn't see much of him. He worked hard at two jobs. All the undivided attention the baby of the family got ended abruptly when their mother got pregnant again.

He'd heard stories about his momma being sick well after he'd been born. She had been rushed to the hospital when ten-year-old Abby found her in a pool of blood in the bathroom. As a four-year-old, he didn't understand the comment, "She lost it." It meant she had a miscarriage of the one who would have been baby number six.

Fortunately, Arlo's momma recovered almost good as new. She did seem more tired though. A couple of years later she was pregnant again. They received gigantic news that she would be having twins. The doctor told her she must stay in bed the final month. All the older kids helped as much as they could. Adam and Aaron brought in wood and helped more outside. Abby and Bella helped with all the inside tasks. Arlo found himself in the way a lot. He read stories to his bedbound momma. She was proud of his English. His cherished place of being the baby disappeared. All attention went to the twins, numbers six and seven, named Alan and Alvin.

Two years later came more twins. Aleksander called Alex, and Alexandra nicknamed Lexie. Adam was almost fifteen when the last set of twins were born. When the youngest twins were about five years old, Adam married and started a family of his own.

Arlo looked like the rest of his siblings. They all had dark brown hair. Round-shaped head, straight forehead, and dark eyes. Each had a nose that curved up or sort of bulged out. Dad had a bushy dark beard, mustache and

27

chest hair that showed through any shirt. Arlo and his siblings were a Ukrainian and Canadian blend.

Most kids' favorite wintertime sport was ice hockey on the frozen ponds. It wasn't Arlo's favorite thing to do. He didn't like the cold or snow no matter how many layers of clothing his mother piled on him. He'd take rain and warmer temperatures anytime.

He read everything he could. He didn't care for team sports. He didn't want to be in a crowd. He just didn't fit in. His mother called him a loner. She promised him that it was okay. He'd heard his parents discussing how different he seemed from the rest of the kids. She said, "He's his own self. An individualist." Whatever that meant.

He heard his older brother Adam say to his sister Abby one day after Arlo again declined sports outside, "Arlo has a screw loose." His pregnant mother overheard them. She whipped around the corner and replied, "That's not the case. He prefers doing different things and that's okay. Not everyone has to be like everyone else." All because he didn't want to romp through the farmland and play with animals in the barn in below freezing temperatures.

He felt lost, stuck in the middle. And very different. He hadn't found his way. He was smart enough in school and did like to read. Mostly about other places. And transportation: trains, car, motorcycles.

He imagined living somewhere warm and sunny all the time. He read about California, in The States. They called America, The States. A new theme park called Disneyland looked thrilling. He wanted to see palm trees and the Pacific Ocean. Stuck on prairies and on flat land with dust wasn't his idea of paradise. He dreamed nightly about what paradise looked like for him. His mom caught him daydreaming frequently. She tried to encourage him to get outside and play with his brothers. Inside activities for his sisters were mostly learning to cook, sew and be good housewives and mothers.

———

He'd worked up the courage and set a goal. His goal—turning twelve, then a train ride. On the third day of June he turned twelve. The following day he hoisted himself into the open boxcar door of the first Canadian Northern train that stopped at the Vegreville station. He didn't care about the direction. He hopped out about five miles away and walked home. He'd been planning this adventure for several months.

Escaping the dusty, flat suffocating surroundings became his next goal. Months rolled into years. With each train ride he'd go farther away. Riding one hour west to Edmonton had been a thrill but the city was too big. Then he hitchhiked home to his small town of about three thousand.

Another time he jumped on an early morning train going east. The dreary countryside whizzed by as they crossed over the Saskatchewan river at the province's border. He got a thrill from the speed of the train when the conductor opened it up on the flatland. He could barely focus on the sparse scenery as the train sped on.

Four hours later he hopped off in Saskatoon on the South Saskatchewan River and two hundred sixty miles from home. He hitched home with a sympathetic long haul truck driver. He said to Arlo, "Get out of dodge and head for the States."

Arlo snuck in the back door of the family home and cleaned up and made it in time for supper. But this adventure had been a close call. He took dozens of short one-to-two hour rides from home. He wouldn't tempt fate like the Saskatoon trip again.

He'd met some interesting characters on his escapades. One man named Herbie was an artist. Using chalk on the side of a freight car, he drew a man wearing a sombrero resting under a palm tree. The men Arlo met were usually down on their luck and looking for something better. Or they might be looking for temporary work then would return home to their families.

To Arlo there wasn't anything better than hopping a boxcar and speeding through the countryside. He wanted a completely different life. He didn't think too deeply about why. After he graduated from high school, he'd ride it all the way to the United States.

Andy found him out. Arlo's dad rarely raised his voice, but Arlo's foolishness made him very mad. His face turned beet red. He lectured him on the dangers of what could happen.

Arlo had some serious planning to do if he was to travel farther. His next goal—Vancouver, British Columbia, almost at the border of the United States. Then on across to The States.

When he did leave, it would be for good. Maybe somebody would miss him. His older siblings escaped in their own way: Adam married first. Abby got married and had a child on the way. At eighteen, Aaron married into a ready-made job—his wife's father owned a grocery store. Bella was the first sibling to attend university and lived sixty miles away in Edmonton studying to be a teacher. This was not the humdrum lifestyle Arlo wanted to live. As Number Five and now the oldest living at home, both sets of twins looked up to him. They were all young teenagers. He didn't like or want the pressure of being looked up to.

He had saved $275 from working odd jobs through

high school. Arlo developed a variety of skills. Most were manual labor jobs, hauling lumber and building supplies up ladders for contractors. Then the foreman taught him how to frame a house, install a roof and shingle it, too. He saved his money. He didn't spend money on booze, cigs, or girls.

The popular hairstyle for teenage boys got longer. They watched "The Ed Sullivan Show" when America (and Canada) first met the Beatles from England. They were the first to show their over-the-ears-length hair. Arlo's brothers and sisters sat with eyes glued to their little boxy TV that sat on the stereo console. Learning music and studying were more essential to their parents than watching TV. They'd only purchased one because the heavens were opening up due to space exploration.

Arlo let his hair grow. His mom thought he was going through a phase. It wasn't a major issue to her. They all went through phases. She had more important concerns such as the teenage twin boys. They were a handful and "Mischief" seemed to be their middle names. It was an abnormal day if she didn't get a call from the junior high school principal. Arlo continued to slip through the cracks of the family home.

His next major goal—his nineteenth birthday. He'd been planning for a while. He packed some basic clothing items, a toothbrush and razor. He figured out what packaged food would travel okay. He could find water somewhere along the way. He'd found a duffle bag at the Goodwill store that somebody had dropped off before opening hours. It wasn't really stealing since somebody had donated it. He just picked it up and took it home.

He woke on the third of June. His nineteenth birthday. He left a note for his mother. "I'll write once I get settled. I'm heading to sunny California by train." He added "Love, Arlo." He thought that might help his mom to feel a little better. She'd be the only one who cared.

When his fourteen-year-old sister Lexie found the note propped against the black rotary telephone, he was already hundreds of miles away heading to Vancouver. Lexie handed the note to her mom. And their mother cried.

On the two-day train ride, stopping at every podunk hamlet now seven hundred miles from home and almost to Vancouver, he thought about his great escape. He scrutinized this mode of transportation. Huddled in a corner of a boxcar behind bales of hay with straw scattered on the floor, he ate about a third of his favorite brand of salty, crisp potato chips, Old Dutch. He liked the taste of cheddar cheese with the salty chips. He had half a brick of it left. He brought six of his favorite candy bars, Neilson Liquid Four Flavor. He broke apart two rows of dark chocolate, each side enfolding four different square pillows of flavorful heaven. First vanilla, then caramel, next one milk chocolate and the last cube being his favorite, Bordeaux; a box of chocolates in one candy bar. He savored each bite. He tucked away the last half for later in the day.

He composed a strategy. He didn't want to spend all of his money getting to his promised land. He might need to get a job before reaching California.

Getting off the train in Vancouver, he hitched a ride to Seattle, Washington, with a talkative log truck driver whose black lab slept behind the driver's seat. Getting dropped off, he walked from the Interstate 5 freeway to the downtown train station. He didn't buy a ticket. Instead he hopped into an open boxcar heading southbound.

After three days without a shower and a good start on a bushy dark beard, arriving in Portland he decided he was done with train travel for a while. He spotted a tall Trailways bus sign and walked in. He asked the ticket agent where the next bus was headed. The agent replied, "Bend, in twenty minutes."

Arlo asked, "Where's Bend?"

"Sunny Central Oregon. You can be there in five hours. Four seventy-five one way. Plenty of seats available."

Arlo heard "Sunny." He pulled out his wad of cash and handed over a five-dollar bill, saying "I'd like a ticket, please."

"Sorry, we don't take Canadian currency. You can exchange it over there," pointing to a woman sitting behind a counter at a currency exchange office.

Ten minutes later his original 275 Canadian dollars ended up 248 US dollars. Back he walked to the ticket agent and handed him the correct five-dollar bill, getting a quarter back.

The bus headed south on Interstate 5 exiting at Salem, the state capital. Looking west he could actually see the wedding cake-shaped marble building with gold man standing on top.

Heading east on Highway 22 outside of Salem the bus climbed in elevation as they drove through miles of teeny communities and lumber mills. A miles-long reservoir had been created by a huge dam. The blue water seemed about highway level as he gazed from the right side of the bus. The bus wove around mountains opposite Detroit Lake. He felt uncomfortable with the water so close to the roadway with very little separating him and it. He closed his eyes and about a half hour later, they had passed all that water. They followed a river and continued to climb.

33

There were impressive mountains and the sun glinted on the snowcaps.

About the top of the Cascade Pass he looked down, seeing a blue lake. Crossing over the pass they dropped quickly. The scenery changed. The trees were scrubbier and brush scarcer. The road became a brickish red color.

Driving through the little town of Sisters with log store-fronts and wooden sidewalks, he thought it looked a lot like a John Wayne western. Forty-five minutes later, the bus pulled into the Bend Trailways station. Five hours later, bushy faced Arlo needed a shower badly.

He took the first hotel he could find. On Franklin Avenue, The Uptown Motel sign boasted "1 block to city's center, quiet, individually controlled heat, TV, tubs and showers." It would cost him $18 per night. He handed the clerk a twenty dollar bill and with the key for cabin #10 he got two one dollar bills back.

Opening the door, it looked like a flower shop exploded. Orange and gold tones were on the walls and bedspread. The gold curtains matched the wall-to-wall gold carpet. Were those tiny orange paisley shapes in the gold curtains? The wooden paneling morphed into floral wallpaper behind the bed. A small boxy TV sat on the dresser. There were a few western photographs on the walls.

He dropped his duffle bag on the floor and stripped off his days-old smelly clothing leaving them in a heap outside the bathroom door. He stood naked, letting hot water pour down his head, through his new beard, until the water ran cold.

He slept for fifteen hours straight. Looking at himself in the bathroom mirror the next morning, he decided not to shave off his first-time beard. It made him look older and tougher. He looked like a different person. And that's what he wanted—new person, new life.

During his trip with plenty of time to reflect, things that bugged him about his family didn't seem so bad after all. But he was a loner. He had thought so anyway. Even though he yearned for adventure and to get away from his overbearing, noisy, outgoing family, maybe they weren't so bad. But he'd made his decision. He would find a job to earn plenty of cash before proceeding to sundrenched California.

He asked the front desk clerk where he could get a good hamburger. A quick reply came. The Midget Drive-In had pizza and burgers for only 25 cents; Fish & Chips, 70 cents plus it included salad, french fries and toast. They used halibut from the coast. About a ten-minute walk later he saw the tall red, white and blue SEA Food sign. Below printed in bright blue, MIDGET DRIVE-IN.

He about burned his fingers on the hottest, crispest french fries ever. He sprinkled extra salt and doused the batch with malted vinegar from the bottle on the table. He used a spoon to eat the thick chocolate milkshake. The half-inch thick burger was topped with a slice of onion, tomatoes and lettuce with both buns slathered with some kind of special sauce. The Midget became one of his favorite burger joints.

Arlo learned quickly not to stand out. He tried to remember to say words the way the locals did.

He said PROcess but here they said PRAcess.

He said Pass-ta and they said Pah-sta.

People looked at him weird when he said, "Eh?" pronounced "ay." He used it to indicate that he didn't understand something. Instead, he heard "Huh?" used frequently.

One thing he learned the difference of quickly was buying beer. In Canada it would be referred to as two-four, a case of brew. Here it was a six-pack.

He would have called a nerd a "keener." He'd been called a keener throughout his school years. He never liked the word.

When he went to a movie, he went to the back of the queue. Here it is called a "line."

A waitress at D&D Bar & Grill on Bond Street gave him a napkin that he almost called a "serviette" when requesting an extra one while eating a messy sloppy joe.

Business and residential construction in the area was booming. On Friday, six days after he left home, he found a construction job. He'd been in Bend three days.

After a full week of manual labor and pretty good wages, he paid for cabin #10 ahead for an entire month. They gave him a deal at $15 per night instead of $18. There were several keeners on his construction crew. He picked up a free motel postcard at the front desk. In the upper left-hand corner in small print was the address.

He got paid on Friday afternoons. He socked his money away. He'd heard that saying before, but he really was. He tucked away his wages in a sock hidden under some jeans in the third drawer of the dresser.

Thinking of his mother, he knew she'd be concerned for him. One evening he wrote her a note and mailed the motel postcard the next morning. It read, "I am fine and working a new job in Central Oregon. Restaurant food is okay but not as good as yours. Your son, Arlo."

In the evenings if he wasn't exhausted from twelve-to-fourteen-hour workdays, he wandered through Drake Park along the Deschutes River. It flowed right through the middle of town. Families were picnicking. He felt a little twang in his heart.

He tried different restaurants. He was now considered a regular at the popular diner, the D&D. He ate there most evenings. He liked the quirky owner, John Daly, who always dressed in a suit and tie.

John wove a yarn about how he and another guy with the last name of Doody opened the bar in 1941, naming it "Double D." Several years later, John took over the sole proprietorship and kept the original name but shortened it to D&D. Thirteen years earlier John replaced the original wood structure using pumice blocks and brick adding a kitchen and counter seating.

Daly was known to help those new to the country. He helped with small loans. He helped them navigate a path to citizenship. He played big brother, making sure patrons didn't spend their entire paychecks at the bar. Many Irish who came to Central Oregon found each other at Daly's bar. John even had a barber located in the back of the bar. Arlo chuckled when John suggested he visit the barber one day soon.

Arlo had even gone to the Tower to see a movie. He bought a ticket for fifty cents. He took a seat in the middle of the sixth row to view "The Dirty Dozen." He sat enthralled by a real-life WWII unit of behind-the-lines demolition specialists from the 101st Airborne Division named the "Filthy Thirteen." The actions of these heroes and measures they went to for their country confounded him. Military wasn't in his blood. If either of his grandfathers had ever served in a war, he sure hadn't heard anything about it. No one spoke much about why they left the Old Country.

The following week he bought a ticket for "You Only Live Twice." Sitting on the edge of the cushy theater seat, he first watched a two-minute movie clip for "The Mummy's Shroud." It looked ridiculous. A second clip showed "The Shuttered Room." Nope, the story about a couple discovering they lived in a haunted mill didn't interested him. He had no interest in cartoons like "Snow White and the Seven Dwarfs." Or the mushy "To Sir, With Love." However, the criminal escapades of the notorious couple named Bonnie & Clyde, coming next month, did grab his attention.

When the flick began, he hardly blinked during the entire film. The capers of the fictional MI6 agent, 007 James Bond, were dizzying and dazzling. Arlo stared at the scenery of Japan. Then there were all the gorgeous women. He'd never met anyone who looked like these beauties. He sat back and finally took a deep breath. His pulse raced and his heart beat faster than usual.

Another night Arlo contemplated his dinner choices. Which one? The historic Pine Tavern for a steak or his standby, the D&D? The Pine Tavern was really cool. There were two gigantic ponderosa pines growing through the wooden patio. Even though called a tavern, it really was a family restaurant. He'd had a few bouts of homesickness lately. He thought seeing families enjoying dinner might be depressing for him. And the cost would be more.

He sauntered into the D&D bar for a brew and dinner. While eating swiss steak with mashed potatoes and dark gravy, he thought about saving money to buy some wheels. Maybe not a car. Something cheaper, maybe a motorcycle. He was getting tired of walking everywhere. Or relying on a ride from other guys on the job site.

About a month later, Arlo figured he had socked away almost enough cash for a well-used motorcycle. His foreman really liked him and kept offering him more work. The overtime provided much needed cash.

One night at the D&D for dinner, he asked the owner, John, if he knew of anyone who had any bikes for sale.

"See that guy over there? He's got lots of bikes. Name is Harley."

Harley told Arlo where he hung out and worked on his chopper. After payday on Friday afternoon, when Arlo arrived, he saw maybe a half dozen long-haired guys working on their unique bikes. All were smoking and drinking beer.

Harley showed Arlo several for sale. Arlo kept his cool exterior but inwardly his heart pounded as hard as when he watched the James Bond movie. He could hardly breathe knowing he'd soon enough have cash to get one of these. Whichever one he would decide to get would need some work done. He could figure it out or find somebody who knew bikes. He heard them call the bikes choppers.

When he got home one evening, the front desk clerk, Suzanne, ran up to him presenting him with a bulging cream envelope. He recognized his mother's handwriting. He sat outside at a picnic table eating fish and chips that he had picked up at the Midget Drive-In, staring at the envelope.

It felt sort of like a gift he'd get at Christmas. On the other hand, it felt kind of like a heavy weight. He couldn't really tell how he was feeling. He ripped it open pulling out seven separate sheets. The first pages were from different siblings. His sister Abby had her first child and she'd sent a picture of his new nephew, named Abraham. She laughed that she was continuing the "A" lineage. The second was from his sister Bella going to university. Another one was from this oldest brother, Adam. He was surprised to find one from his youngest sister Lexie. Each letter filled him in on what was happening in their small world and life in general. He chuckled after reading Lexie's letter because she signed it, "Love, Lexie, your youngest and nicest sister."

He read his mother's last. She wrote how relieved and elated she was to receive the postcard and that he had been doing fine. She apologized for why he felt he needed to leave so abruptly. She filled him in on the entire family, including how the twin boys, Alan and Alvin, continued to get in a lot of trouble at school. His parents were at a loss what to do with them. Both sets of grandparents were fine, and they had just celebrated his great grandmother's ninetieth birthday with a big party. Many from the community came. The only one missing was Arlo.

As she described everyday happenings, he felt like he was right there experiencing it with her. She always had been a wonderful storyteller. He recalled the stories she made up or sometimes read to him at night. Where did that memory pop out of?

She closed her portion with much love, great hopes for him and asked him to please, please write again soon. The big shock was the second half of the last page of her letter that contained a message from his father. He hardly recognized his dad's handwriting as he'd really never seen it before.

His father wrote that they appreciated hearing from him, especially his mother. She had been very worried and lost weight wondering about him. He wrote he had no doubt Arlo would succeed at whatever he wanted. He'd heard very good reports from men who Arlo had done work for. He had a good reputation for hard work and honesty. "Son, you are welcome home anytime you feel like returning. Your Father."

Arlo was blown away. He'd never heard those words from his father before.

That night he dreamed his entire family was sitting on overstuffed paisley printed chairs, eating fish and chips in a boxcar. A bottle of malt vinegar fell onto the straw. They all laughed. Arlo wrote a message, put it in the bottle and tossed it out the open door.

Two weeks later Arlo bought his first bike, a cool black and silver 1965 Harley Scat. Harley filled him in on some stats like the V-Twin engine mated to a three-speed manual transition. It had a scrambler-style, high-mounted exhaust pipe, a high-mounted front fender, a single, spring-mounted seat with passenger grab rails, high handlebars and laced wheels. All Arlo saw were the high handlebars and mostly all-black motorcycle.

Though not that old, it had been dumped a few times, but it was in okay condition. At least it ran. Harley made it clear he'd just done Arlo a big favor. He got him a really great deal. Harley never told him how he had gotten the chopper from a guy who hadn't paid him for drugs. The idiot, now minus a chopper, had gotten a beating to boot. He'd limp forever from a broken leg.

Arlo talked to Harley about the work needed on his bike when he saw him again at the D&D. Harley told him to come out for some help anytime. Harley could read people pretty well. This loner kid would be a perfect addition to their gang. He would adjust fast. And he had a good paying job that could help all of them.

On Arlo's second visit to the biker hangout, he felt a familiar tug he'd been missing—family, commonality, camaraderie.

Evidently Arlo did want to be part of something. He just didn't know it would be a gang. An outlaw motorcycle gang.

Arlo went on Saturday and sometimes Sunday to the biker camp to work on his pride and joy. Most of the men were older than him. Arlo had a life of working long hours. So, when he went on weekends, he stayed to himself working on his bike. He did hear some conversations but didn't focus on them. Harley saw Arlo as young, impressionable, naïve and gullible. Easily manageable. Harley never called Arlo by his name. He was Kid.

Getting ready to head back into town, Harley asked Arlo innocently enough, "Hey Kid, can you drop off this package at a friend's place?" Arlo owed Harley a lot for getting him such a deal on his motorcycle and the expertise in repairs.

Arlo said, "Sure thing." Harley handed him a small three-by-three-inch package all wrapped in duct tape.

When Arlo dropped it off, the weasely looking guy looked quizzically at him and asked, "What do you want?"

Arlo replied, "Harley asked me to give this to you." He never gave it a second thought. Unknowingly, this was Arlo's first drug involvement.

When Arlo paid the next two months in advance for his cabin, Suzanne at the front desk jokingly commented on his fast-growing hair.

———

Harley knew the naïve Arlo would work out well passing along drugs without him even realizing what it was. He wasn't sure how Arlo would react to things so if Arlo didn't ask, Harley didn't tell. He didn't think The Kid had it in him to be a member of their outlaw gang.

CHAPTER THREE

*J*t's **Summertime Summertime Sum Sum Summertime**

Leaning back in a wooden chair swiveling right then left and rocking back and forth, he wondered why it had been a quiet Thursday. Standing six foot, two inches, he was almost too tall for the medium size chair. The twenty-nine-year-old just got his walnut-colored hair chopped off into an easy crewcut. He did not like the long hair styles young men had nowadays. Blue-eyed Deputy Clayton Malloy sat at his desk during the lunch hour. Everyone called him Clay, except his mother. She always used his full name. The Sheriff called him Malloy. He had been answering telephone calls, plus catching up on nearly past due paper-work. Neither were his favorite tasks of his job. He heard a door open somewhere on the second floor in the brick building that held the Jefferson County Sheriff's Office.

Even though time consuming, he still preferred hand-writing the reports. He'd rather write than try to line up the one-page form perfectly in the manual typewriter. He tried tediously to find the perfect center point on the line for the typed consonants and vowels. Using the two-finger method, his chunky fingers always hit two keys at a time. If there were too many errors, he would have to begin again. Typing was his nemesis.

He rested his chin in his left palm as he scribbled the first case. A male from Texas had been arrested for auto theft. He sat in one of the two jail cells until the judge decided how long he'd be a guest of the county. The second report was the arrest of a man for drunk and disorderly behavior. He had escaped from a city hospital by jumping out of a window before being moved to the state mental hospital in Salem. The next case was spotlighting and killing a deer. The fourth crime, becoming more prevalent, was driving under the influence of alcohol. This particular person had been arrested for going fifty-five miles per hour in a marked school zone. At noon no less. Deputy Malloy had escorted him directly to cell number two. The judge would decide how long he'd be a temporary resident of the county jail.

Malloy appreciated his department's mission: Safeguard all people and their property, serving all equally, with empathy, dignity, and respect. He lived by these words.

After seven years on the job, he felt comfortable. His job had plenty of challenges though. Maybe one day he'd think about an upward move to detective. Or if the department ever hired more personnel, maybe to sergeant or lieutenant. He knew himself well enough that he wouldn't want the headaches of the politics or having to run an election to be sheriff.

Central Oregon would be his forever home. He flourished in the outdoors and all that it had to offer his lifestyle. He'd never be able to live and work in a big city like Portland, Salem or Eugene. They had their different societal issues and more problems with drug trafficking along the Interstate 5 corridor. The freeway is almost fourteen hundred miles all the way from the south end beginning at the Mexico-southern California border to the northern Washington border ending at Canada. Unfortunately, it made for fairly easy access for criminal activity. The law enforcement prognostications were not positive. He hoped it would take years for serious drug issues to migrate their way. Realistically, he knew that would not be the case.

Malloy looked at Jefferson County, the entire county, as his home. It is wide open farm and ranch land with miles of flat to hilly into mountainous terrain. It is named after President Jefferson and the mountain.

He thrived on being in the great outdoors. He felt his best fly-fishing on the Metolius and Deschutes rivers in the summer. Then skiing and snowshoeing in the winter on Mount Bachelor and HooDoo. He found it exhilarating flying down a snowy mountain on two wood planks, skis, on a wintry February day. He might even try mountain climbing in the future.

His county is surrounded by Linn County to the west, a sliver of Marion County to the northwest, Wasco County to the north, Wheeler County to the east, Crook County to the south and east, and Deschutes County to the south.

It had been his childhood dream of working in a rural area in law enforcement. His grandpa had been sheriff in a county in southeastern Nebraska. Grandpa Lorimer and his parents had instilled the desire to help others. He had memorized his grandpa's sheriffs' department motto: "Keeping the peace, with dignity, honesty, and compassion."

If anything was lacking it would have to be his social life. His happily-ever-after married buddies and younger sister Heather, would remind him often of it. He'd had a couple of semi-serious relationships while attending Oregon State University in Corvallis. Unfortunately, neither lasted.

But wide-open outdoor space and lifestyle wasn't everyone's dream. Especially his former lady friends. He'd found that both had desired to stay in bigger towns for more job opportunities using their hard-earned four-year degrees. At least they were upfront about it.

Starving, his co-worker, Detective Grant Walker, went out for a lunch break. Walker was always hungry. He promised to bring something back for him. Malloy figured it would be a burger, Walker's favorite food. He requested a BLT with a side of extra-crispy onion rings and tartar sauce instead of ketchup.

Sheriff Perkins had been called out for some emergency with the Jefferson Board of County Commissioners. The conversation would probably be about the upcoming budget cycle. Again.

Sheriff Halim Preston Perkins had been elected five months earlier in January 1969. He moved to Oregon in 1955 working as a rancher.

Perkins wore a western style hat at all times. And a solid-colored tie, with or without a jacket. He wouldn't be caught dead without his shiny star badge. He'd never been called handsome. His facial strong points were his sincere hazel eyes and square chin that seemed to reassure people immediately. But noticeable creases on his face where dimples would be on some people, and deepening crow's feet around the corners of his eyes depicted responsibility, maturity and stress.

Deputy Malloy had worked under several sheriffs. First was Spencer Summerfield elected in 1953 and resigned in January 1968. Sheriff Summerfield had hired him. Ronald Toms had been appointed to take Summerfield's place, serving as sheriff one year. He had also been county coroner from 1958 to 1962. Three sheriffs in seven years was enough transition for him. He'd respected each of them. He hoped Sheriff Perkins would be a long timer.

The Jefferson County Sheriff's Office had earned an excellent reputation and was highly regarded by locals. Being a newbie to local politics with only five months on the job, the straight-shooting Sheriff Perkins would be having his first go-round before the commissioners getting a budget approved for the next two years.

He'd been duly warned by the prior sheriff of personality conflicts, high opinions of themselves, plus blatantly looking out for their personal best interests. Staying positive and open-minded, he decided to make his own opinions before passing judgment on these yahoos, as someone had called them.

Five months had passed with bi-weekly meetings about this and that. He concluded that the previous sheriff had correctly assessed this group of so-called "public servants," he thought sarcastically to himself.

He would request two more full-time officers and a full-time secretarial position for their understaffed department. Their department was solely responsible for covering almost eighteen hundred square miles and protecting and serving eight thousand five hundred people. And growing by the month. Only one deputy working nights covering the territory was ridiculous in his book.

The fourth member of their department was Deputy Jensen Foster. He was what they called a resident deputy, because he lived at Camp Sherman on the Metolius River about an hour west. He was out-of-state on a much-deserved vacation for a few more days. Several counties in the state used resident deputies who live among a community that could be quite a distance from the county seat and sheriff's main headquarters.

The final deputy in the team was Williams, who worked the night shift. Malloy didn't see him much except during shift changes. Working five nights a week, that left Monday and Tuesday nights in their county unattended by any law enforcement.

Perkins wasn't putting up with this nonsense any longer and was going to demand more help. Malloy wondered if the budget process would become easier if one of the commissioners had a crisis and needed help in the middle of the night and it was Williams' night off. The corners of his mouth curved up when he speculated what a few of those emergencies might look like.

Malloy felt contentment when he walked down the main drag of Madras. It stretched along Highway 97 and looking right he spotted the Town House Restaurant he frequented for a fancy meal out, the Dodge Chrysler, Plymouth dealership, the Madras Market, then his favorite V Café. Across the street stood Erickson's Dept. Store, Thrifty Drug, the Nugget Café, the Texaco station, United States National Bank, and the new Shell station. More businesses were being added monthly.

He lived on D Street two miles away from his parents and just a couple of blocks from Madras High School. He'd helped build his home along with a contractor friend three years earlier. He enjoyed putting his own sweat and hard work into his two-bedroom home. It was the perfect size for him with a lawn that wasn't too big to maintain. Yard work wasn't his favorite pastime. When he had free time, he'd rather be doing outdoor sports. One day he'd have a dog. Maybe a golden retriever or a yellow lab—he'd enjoy the companionship. His sister and her family had a golden. Their dog was amazingly smart and loving. But his schedule was still too irregular for that responsibility.

He dropped in on his parents as often as possible. He'd promised to help his dad paint their home, just not this weekend. He'd grown up in this house. He wanted to help his parents stay there as long as possible. Malloy's sister Heather, her husband and six-year-old twin boys, lived three hours away in Salem, the state capital. She was two years younger than him. They all made sure to visit each other five or six times a year.

Deputy Malloy was concentrating and writing a report about an arrest he'd made for disorderly conduct by a man providing beer to a minor. The phone rang. It startled him enough that he almost tipped far enough backwards in the old chair to tumble over. With his arms flailing he laughed out loud as he steadied himself reaching for the phone.

If someone had witnessed this awkward spectacle it might have looked like some scene right out of "The Andy Griffith Show," him being Deputy Barney Fife. The new comedy television program was about small-town life in Mayberry, North Carolina, population two thousand. It was close in population to their own small town of Madras, with seventeen hundred residents.

He chuckled along with his parents once a week on Monday night at the shenanigans of the affable cast of characters. Weekly, his mother fixed him a pot roast dinner with all the trimmings and expounded on how proud she was of her son much like Aunt Bea did for her nephew, Sheriff Andy, on the show.

"Jefferson County Sheriff's Office," he answered after the third ring. The voice on the line spoke loudly, "Howdy." Malloy moved the receiver away from his ear, "There's some idiot letting his dadgum cows wander through my property. Those blasted animals are all over my newly planted yard and in my wife's garden." The deputy assured the caller he'd be out soon.

The upcoming Memorial Day Weekend would begin on Friday for many, making it a four-day weekend. He knew from past experience the department would be extra busy.

A late-spring snowstorm certainly could happen. Their town sat at over two thousand feet in elevation. Fortunately, it wasn't in the forecast. He guessed campers from the Willamette Valley would be showing up in droves brushing off their dusty gear from last time they'd used it in the fall. He hoped that the wandering cow incident would be the biggest issue of the weekend. He seriously doubted it.

One hundred fifty miles to the west, school was almost out for the summer. It's a nippy morning, so I wore my gold sweatshirt with Calapooya Vikings imprinted in royal purple. My name is Anne.

By ten o'clock I removed my bulky sweatshirt and stuffed it into my locker. I'd returned all my schoolbooks to the office in exchange for our new yearbook. I looked at the bright gold cover with Calapooya Vikings printed in royal purple, proud that I'd worked to put it together as part of the yearbook staff. I looked forward to getting many autographs from favorite friends and teachers. We pronounced our school, Kal-uh-POOH-yuh, named for Native Americans who lived in the area.

At my locker, I took down the picture I'd cut out of *Teen Life* magazine of my favorite singing group, Davey, Mickey, Mike and Peter of The Monkees. It had been taped to the inside of my combination locker door for the past nine months. I threw away green Doublemint gum wrappers and a few used tissues that got crammed in the back. I rolled up my gold and royal purple Calapooya Vikings pennant that hung below the Monkees. It would be moved to my bedroom wall at home. Other than that, I didn't have a thing to carry home except my bag.

We celebrated completing another year at our junior high farewell picnic. Our salty-colored hair principal, Mr. Gibbs, about the same height as my dad, praised us all for being such good students. Most of us, that is. To the freshman going off to high school, he wished them well. I guessed he was glad to get rid of a few troublemaker boys in particular.

Our school secretary, Mrs. Johnston, was my favorite person in junior high. She gave the appearance of easily running the office. Really the entire school. She had short dark hair and wore pointy-rimmed sable eyeglasses with little shiny diamonds on each side. When the light hit the tiny stones just right, they sparkled, radiating different colors. She smiled a lot. Unless she caught a troublesome boy doing something he knew he shouldn't. Then she would contact Mr. Gibbs.

She had a pleasant yet firm voice that came through loud and clear on the intercom into the classrooms at 8:10 a.m., giving announcements and updates. When she said, "Mr. Gibbs to the office, please," we all knew somebody was in for it.

During study hall, I had been allowed to help Mrs. Johnston in the office. I'd do tasks like sorting mail into the teacher's boxes or delivering messages to their classrooms. Sometimes I'd pick up student absentee slips.

I enjoyed operating the ditto machine. I watched as Mrs. Johnston put two sheets together that she or a teacher had handwritten or typed on. The second sheet inked the markings on the back of the front sheet. The front sheet was then torn off and wrapped around the drum of the machine, with the back side out. Once she had it set up, I got to run the machine that pulled blank paper into the press, coating it with the pretty purple color. I copied dozens and dozens of purple printed handouts or sometimes tests.

The unusual purple color on the slightly shiny paper had a distinct odor. I sort of liked the fresh-off-the-press sharp chemical smell. I could tell when a class assignment was hot-out-of-the-machine by the strength of the odor on the pages and darkness of purple.

Many purple-inked flyers went home with the reminder from Mrs. Johnston who would say, "Now, girls and boys, don't forget to give this to your parents so that they will know about our field trip," while handing out the purple forms. I knew there had been several times when, the night before a school party, Mom found crumpled purple announcements in the trash from one of my brothers in which she was asked to make cupcakes or cookies.

Mrs. Johnston complimented and appreciated my help. She mentioned that if I wanted to help again in the office the next school year, she'd be delighted to have me. Now finishing the eighth grade, next year I'd be top dog, a ninth grader and a freshman. When she offered to help work it out on my class schedule, I told her yes on the spot.

I did think several times that year that when I grew up maybe I'd be in charge of a school, too. She'd even told the principal what do to and where he should be. I really liked that. I knew I'd be really good at telling people what to do. I'd had practice as class president several times in elementary school along with bossing my younger brothers around.

Mr. Halstead taught and brought alive World History and Geography. He was one of my two favorite teachers. His parting remark at the picnic was to be sure to watch our television sets on July 20. We wouldn't want to miss the first manned moon landing. Astronauts Neil Armstrong and Edwin Aldrin, Jr. were to become the first humans to walk on the moon.

School was officially dismissed at one o'clock. After saying farewell to my school chums Donna, Carol, Sheri, Pam and Ilynn, I walked one and a half miles toward home with my friends Debby and Jackie.

Debby reminded me of a delicate doll. She was petite with fly-away shoulder length teaky hair that she secured with a ponytail band. Some thought she was stuck-up since she was quiet and shy. She wasn't, and we talked a lot. We were in Bluebirds, then Campfire Girls together. She always took first in every category.

The only thing I took first in was selling boxes of Campfire Girls chocolate mints. I'd get the okay from several banks and sit outside the door and nab everyone either coming or going. In each box of delectable delights were two layers of round mint patties cradled in an inky plastic sheet pressed into individual compartments. The top layer held fourteen milk chocolate, two on each side, with a creamy mint in the center. The bottom layer hid scrumptious, luscious, mouthwatering dark chocolate coating surrounding the creamy white mint.

This would be my first memory of the aroma and taste of the semi-sweet dark goodness. This began my addiction. There was nothing else that compared to the mixed aromas of spicy vanilla, sharp-smelling flavors and maybe even some citrus. The semi-sweetness left a pleasant after-taste long after it melted away. And I always wanted more.

I knew all it would take was one small nibble of the divine chocolatey heaven, and people would buy it. I purchased a box myself, cut the candy into quarters and offered samples. My sales skyrocketed.

Even though I refer to Jackie as a "friend," really, she was a pill. With her chin-level uncontrollable spidery-black hair, she looked wild, like a witch. Her laughter reminded me of the cackle from the Wicked Witch of the West from one of my favorite movies, "The Wizard of Oz." She had a temper to match. We had some past pushing and shoving history from our elementary school days. Her childish behavior caused us to be suspended for an entire day in second grade. It wouldn't surprise me if she had pet flying monkeys.

At five foot six, I am the tallest in the trio. Thick wavy honey blonde hair drops just below my shoulders. I have crystal clear blue eyes, like my dad. Deep dimples magically appear when I smile. I am what they refer to as "Big Boned," definitely not petite. This combination along with my fair complexion reveals I am a mix of Scottish, Norwegian and Irish ancestry. I am not shy nor am I a witch.

As we passed the A-frame Hansel & Gretel Ginger-bread House, something on the sidewalk caught my attention. I bent down and picked up a shiny penny. Finding a penny was good luck. I'd add it to other coins in my yellow ceramic piggy bank that sat on top of my white dresser in my pink bedroom. It felt as exciting as finding nature's treasurers at the beach—colorful agates.

We were about halfway between school and our homes. We contemplated stopping for a Coke. One year earlier I had been introduced to this dark brown, sweet fizzy drink. I liked it a lot especially straight from a glass bottle. It took on a slightly different flavor coming from a machine into a paper cup when half full of crushed ice. When opening an ice-cold bottle of Coke, sometimes I could pick up a hint of vanilla. When slowly prying off the crown cap, I loved the phzzzzzz sound. Then the final pop, releasing small bubbles rocketing out of the narrow bottleneck.

I wasn't comfortable with spending my hard-earned allowance or babysitting money on pop and candy, but it was totally fine if a boy wanted to buy those things for me. But I'd spend my money on nylons and makeup.

Because of lack of funds, we passed up the Cokes. Instead we crossed the street stopping at the Bob's Superette. This small family-run market on the corner of Hill and Queen Streets had been there forever. Bob, the owner, worked at the meat counter in the back. Mom bought most of her meat from him and some groceries. Whenever he saw me, he'd wave and tell me to say hello to my mother.

Pooling our one dime and three nickels, we stood there deciding between a Nestle Crunch Bar or a Hershey Bar with or without almonds. Three girls and three choices to be split in three ways. I let the chocolate melt on my tongue then crunched the crispy bits. The midday temperatures caused the chocolate to soften quickly. I licked each finger not to miss any, then noticed Debby and Jackie doing the same thing.

We linked arms reminding me of Dorothy, the Scarecrow and Tin Man in "The Wizard of Oz." Debby burst out in a fun song, "Well no more studying history, And no more reading geography, And no more dull geometry," and Jackie and I joined in at, "Because it's summertime. It's summertime, summertime sum sum summertime," which we repeated about ten times.

Our first stop was at Debby's house on Tudor Drive. We waved farewell for three months. Her older brother was far away as a soldier in the Vietnam war. I talked to her about it because a favorite older cousin of mine, Jeff, was there too. She told me her parents were very nervous and fretting about him all the time. It made her fidgety. They'd been told he'd get to come home during the summer for a two-week visit.

About ten minutes later we reached Jackie's house on Old Oak Place. I politely said, "See you in a few months." I hurriedly cut down the side of their golf-course-like back-yard glancing skyward partially expecting the crows in the trees to transform into her dive-bombing flying monkeys. I carefully walked sideways down an embankment across unused railroad tracks. Then back up on a path we'd walked on so many times, it was now bare of weeds.

Walking down Sherman Street I waved at our oldish neighbor, rockhound, and homebuilder. He leaned himself into a large cloth-covered wheel. Dirty water droplets were spinning off in all directions. He was carefully polishing a thunderegg the size of a baseball he'd found in eastern Oregon. Fred, we all called him, because he never wanted us to call him Mister. He could run and jump like a deer with his licorice-colored hair flopping around his ears.

Over the years, each of us amateur geologists prospected with him. We traipsed around the local countryside rock hunting for valuable gemstones and minerals. Depending on the size of the rock, he taught us how to use his lapidary wheel for polishing large pieces like petrified wood. Then he taught us the patience of polishing smaller agates and rocks in the tumbler with its barrel going around and around for what seemed weeks at a time.

On our family trips to the Oregon coast, I'd hunt for agates then bring them home to put into Fred's tumbler. I also liked the mossy green or sometimes red agates called Jasper. I kept all my special mementos in a jar covered in earthy-smelling mineral oil. He even gave me two raw opals.

Across the street, Mrs. Slack wore a bright floral print dress that she made herself. She was a master seamstress and had created many garments for her two daughters and the neighborhood kids. Her dark walnut hair looked like two-inch pink foam curlers had been pulled out from the side leaving her hair perfectly in place.

She had just planted my favorite summer vegetable, lemon cucumbers. They would be ripe in July and be light yellow and about the size of a small apple. We just brushed off the pokey things on the skin and ate them right off the bush. When I grew up, I'd have a garden just to plant lemon cucumbers. Gardening wasn't my favorite thing to do and certainly not raking leaves from a dozen oak trees in the fall. But for these special cucumbers, I would absolutely learn some basic gardening skills

As I waved to Mrs. Slack, I heard a very loud achoo. Dad must have come home early from work as county clerk at the courthouse. The only time he took time off would be for a vacation. He was a strict seven a.m. to five p.m. county employee. He took his elected job extremely seriously. He was the official keeper of public records for the county. He ensured that all records were retained, archived, and made accessible to the public. Couples would go to him for marriage applications and licenses. His office kept vital records of births, deaths, divorces, business and professional licenses, permits and registration, and much more. He also was extra busy during any elections.

He oversaw the local elections, voter registration and poll locations.

When I got home about five minutes later and after a hug, I asked him if he'd sneezed a few minutes earlier. "Yes, come to think of it, I did." Dad seemed astonished he'd been so loud. I'd heard it plenty of times before, so I wasn't surprised at all.

I had a sinking suspicion that he might be "helping" Mom by fixing one of his favorite dinners that we had twice a year. This happened two times too many in my book. Oh, please no, not the dreaded liver dinner. And that wasn't all of it. I only hoped this wouldn't be case but didn't dare ask. I really wanted takeout from my favorite restaurant, Hasty Freez, which made the best deluxe cheeseburger, salty crunchy fries and handmade milk shakes with their homemade ice cream.

My afternoon tasks were to help Mom get ready for leaving early the next morning. We were going on a one-week camping trip at our favorite place in the world, the Metolius River (Muh-TOLL-ee-us) in Central Oregon.

I'm the only daughter. My full name is Annette, but I go by Anne. Age: one week short of fourteen and oldest child. I have two younger brothers, ages ten and seven.

As the family-lore goes, at the dinner table one evening, me being around age seven, I announced that I wanted to be called Kate. My first brother is Max, really Maxwell, then age three, spit out the mouthful of tuna noodle casserole he had just inhaled. My parents looked at each other and Dad said, "I think we'll stick with your given name of Annette."

Even with my whining and thought-provoking reasoning, "But Daaaddddd, your favorite Aunt Katie from Montana and my favorite actress Katherine Hepburn have the same first name—it's a sign, I should be Kate," not taking a breath in my run-on sentence. He suggested we compromise and could use Ann, a shortened version of Annette. I gave in as long as it could be unusual like adding the "e" on the end. We all agreed on Anne, with an "e." Then three-year-old Max asked if he could change his name to Sam. My father calmly stated the discussion of name changes had concluded. I became Anne during the dinner hour.

My baby brother William, Will or Willy, slouched barely sitting upright in a highchair. He alternated between popping dry Cheerios and raisins in his mouth, drinking a bottle of milk and jabbering gibberish. He was far too young to know what was going on.

Our miniature wiener dog, really a dachshund, has short brickish-red hair and we call him Duke, short for Little Red Duke, his registered AKC name.

Now seven years later, my two brothers in elementary school were having their own end-of-year parties. I knew they were as eager as I was about going camping. We'd been talking about it all week at the dinner table along with the places and things we wanted to do. This had become our family tradition—camping on Memorial Day weekend.

Even though each outing would be a repeat from past annual camping trips, it didn't matter. We'd venture to the headwaters of the river and walk to the Camp Sherman historic store numerous times for treats. We'd probably cross the bridge to the Metolius River Resort where the little restaurant had an outside window where we could order a soft ice cream cone. We'd drive to Wizard Falls Fish Hatchery so we could feed the two-foot long trout. Hopefully we'd even have a lunch at the Sno Cap or The Gallery in the western village of Sisters, fifteen miles away. I really, really, really hoped I could go horseback riding as I had done a couple times in the past. I had saved my winter babysitting money for this expensive treat.

Mom did all the cooking ahead of time for the week. She made a large pan of lasagna that would feed us for two nights, a pot of chili using pinto beans and homemade canned tomatoes plus her secret ingredients, a meat loaf, potato salad and a macaroni salad with mayonnaise not Miracle Whip, two yummy pies and two sheet cakes, before leaving home. It didn't seem like much of a vacation for her since she still made three meals a day. She had all the meals planned by night and once or twice we'd share a potluck with other campers. She had already made one cake. We called it Camping Cake and was made with a can of fruit cocktail. This was Max's favorite. For some reason he didn't like coconut.

She let me help her make one of my favorite desserts, Carrot Cake. I smeared Crisco into a sheet cake pan, carefully dusting white flour into the four corners.

I followed the instructions carefully, as I read her recipe.

2 cups sugar

3 eggs

1 cup oil

½ tsp. vanilla

3 cups flour

½ tsp. cinnamon

2 tsp. soda

1 tsp. salt

2 cups grated carrots
¾ cup pineapple juice
1 cup shredded coconut
2 cup chopped nuts, we used walnuts from our tree.

I creamed the sugar, eggs and oil and slowly added the vanilla, after I'd already sifted the flour together with the other dry ingredients, folded it in with the carrots, coconut and nuts that would bake at 350 degrees for one hour.

While I made the cake, upstairs Mom selected clothing for the boys. She packed all of their washed jeans, shorts and shirts, which wouldn't stay clean long once we were there. One duffle bag would be full of a change of underwear for each one of us for every day. She abided by the rule, "Always change your underwear. You never know when you'll be in an accident." I truly hoped that day would never come. If it did, I would never tell her.

Even though I was old enough to pack my own things, she checked on my choices a couple times. I slipped in my new blue S.S. Kresge A.M. transistor radio along with my boxy, silver and black Kodak Instamatic camera.

The cinnamon and vanilla aromas wafted upstairs. I remembered that I needed to be making the special icing to pour over the top of the cake as soon as it came out of the oven. I took three steps at a time with both hands on the railings from upstairs to the main floor in a couple of seconds. I landed in the dining room and rounded the corner to the kitchen.

I whipped into action making the icing by mixing all the ingredients in a pan on the stove, then brought it to a boil and stirred constantly for five minutes.

1 cup sugar
¼ cup butter, real butter not margarine

1 cup buttermilk
½ tsp. soda
½ tsp. vanilla
½ tsp. lemon extract
1 T. white syrup

The timer went off alerting me the cake was ready to have toothpicks poked in a variety of spots to make sure it was done to perfection. I followed the instructions to pour the hot icing on the hot cake. The icing drips and sinks into the cake, keeping it moist for a week or longer. It smelled so delicious.

Mom thanked me for making the cake. I knew when we got home, she had to basically reverse all of this. She'd unpack the trailer, even though we carried some things in. She had to wash machine-loads full of all the grimy clothes. Then she'd still make our meals at home. But I never once heard her complain. She seemed to love it as much as we did.

When my brothers got home, Mom gave them their marching orders. First, she fixed them peanut butter and jelly sandwiches to tide them over until dinner. With their groans and moans you'd think she'd ask them to clean out a barn or wash the truck. Rolling my eyes, I mumbled something about them being wimps. Mom assured me that these little rascals would one day become my best friends. Men I could depend on most. I couldn't even imagine them as men at this point.

Being the first child and only girl had its advantages. But it also came with its own set of inconveniences. I knew full well I was special. But my parents were raising me on a mixture of hope and a prayer. Plus, trial-and-error. They were pretty much by-the-book. To me, they were overly observant and way too strict with the rules. For goodness sakes, I had been a teenager almost a year now.

As their firstborn for three years I had everything my way and was the center of their attention. Then came Max, the thick peppery hair, hazel and sage-colored-eyed first son. Very special in his own right. Growing up, nothing really bothered him. He liked to make people feel good. He paid close attention to details, especially polishing rocks for Fred. He thrived on having lots of friends but a couple of really close buddies. He was way too tenderhearted. He needed to toughen up, I thought. He had this attitude of "let's just go-with-the-flow" which seemed contrary to how I thought. He had such strong hands for a kid. He made polishing rocks look effortless. When I worked on the wheel for any length of time, my hands really hurt the next day.

Then there was William. The second son and the baby of the family. He had his own special place in the sibling lineup. By the time he came along seven years after me, our morphing parents had relaxed and adapted a far more carefree attitude. Compared to all my woes being the first child, I unknowingly forged the way for a much easier life for my younger siblings.

Willy was fun-loving, uncomplicated, and usually wanted to get his own way. He could finagle a situation his way without anybody even realizing it. He was really clever at getting me to do tasks for him. He'd ask me to show him for the millionth time how to use the electric popcorn popper.

He was a real charmer with an outgoing personality that drew people to him. His big blue eyes, long eyelashes and deep dimples in his cheeks helped too. He tended to be a big ham, hogging the spotlight with his adventurousness. In other words, a real hot dog. He got right in there with us older kids playing softball and soccer. I saw him as undisciplined. My folks coddled him when it came to chores and rules. Clearly, they failed to hold him to the same high standards I had. He was spoiled rotten, in my book of life.

As a teenager, I was given responsibility at home. I helped with chores and watched over my younger brothers. I was quick to take charge. And possibly, well probably, a bit bossy when I did. I felt trustworthy, reliable, conscientious, and somewhat of an achiever. I also loved to have lots of fun.

Dad had indeed come home early from work to help out. With the good came the bad. It was undeniably the dreaded, nauseating liver dinner night. He sliced thin pieces of beef liver and onions and seared it fast in bacon grease in a cast iron skillet. Meanwhile the peeled boiling potatoes would become mashed. Then dark, thick liver gravy, made from crispy drippings, would be poured over the top like lava dripping down a volcano.

Then there were the tiny green mystery vegetables, really miniature peas straight from a Del Monte can. These horrible tiny marbles created their own unusual aroma. The army-green color when cooked looked gross. When a scoop somehow appeared on my plate, they rolled into the liver gravy.

To make it even worse, the dinner grand finale was a fish-egg texture pudding for dessert. Tapioca. Yuck. Forcing us three kids to eat a few bites was trying for my parents at best.

This meal was a disaster. I put a small bite into my mouth. Trying not to gag, I gently slipped the bite to the side of my cheek. I counted to sixty. After a minute, which seemed much longer, I faked a cough, moving my napkin to my mouth. Another cough and I gently spit the bite into the napkin nonchalantly returning it to my lap. Without moving my arm and barely my hand, I passed bite after bite down to our anxiously waiting little wiener dog Duke, who patiently sat at my feet.

Then the expected comment, "Clean your plate, children are starving in Africa," would come at some point. This time it was just too much. I suggested we should send it to Africa to those poor starving children. That didn't go over well. I went to bed somewhat hungry. It only happened a couple of times a year though. Duke ate very well those nights.

We all went to bed early that night. We knew the next morning Dad would be standing at the bottom of the staircase to our upstairs three bedrooms belting out and waking us up with his sing-song lighthearted morning mantra, "Ohhhhhh, it's nice to get up in the morning." I'd reply, "But it's nicer to stay in bed." If he didn't hear us stirring in a few minutes, he'd say, "Hey, what's the hold up?"

It was late Thursday night around 12:30. Technically early Friday morning. Normally bikers would never share a ride. But two noisy choppers would bring unwanted attention. One sat uncomfortably behind the other on the '68 Harley Shovelhead. His hand hurt. It throbbed because of the cold. He tried slipping on gloves and it hurt even worse. He'd gotten a tattoo of a train engine drilled into the top of his right hand several days earlier. He hoped it wasn't infected.

It concerned him what they were doing. He was asked, or sort of instructed to come along to help with a task. He didn't dare ask what. He wanted to keep getting help on his bike on the weekends. He would continue to do some favors for Harley as long as he got what he wanted in return.

Parked behind a big ponderosa outside the bar, they had tracked a cockroach here. The rider asked, "What are we doing out here in the cold?"

The driver replied, "You know what I do to a cockroach? I step on it." Then he sneezed three times and complained about allergies this time of year.

A month earlier, the drug dealer discovered something was off. It was on two drops the fourth and fifth time his new recruit Rusty had made deliveries. The first, second and third payments were spot on. Collecting money after the fourth and fifth drop-offs, the two cockroaches were short in their payment. He called anybody who cheated him a cockroach. If the dealer had given the buyers a chance, they would have shown him the numbers from the weight they purchased. Most buyers and sellers kept surprisingly good records. These losers were actually telling the truth. They were paying for what they received.

The dealer began to track the weight of the packages even closer. Yep, the courier was cheating him. Harley assumed the redhead was keeping a tiny portion for himself probably thinking it wouldn't be noticed. Time had come to put a stop to this. He'd teach this punk and others a lesson. "Enough is enough. I'm gonna make an example of him. Word will get around what I've done to him." No one would dare cheat him. Ever. He had to establish his turf. Setting an example using this kid would be a big step in defining his territory. "Stupid cockroach. I will squash him."

―――――――

Coop MacNeill, Vern Christopherson, and Rusty Kavanagh sat drinking their last brew with about fifteen minutes until closing time. They sat side by side on tall stools at the bar in the second tavern in tiny Sisters. The other one closed an hour earlier. The more Vern and Rusty drank the louder they got. This evening's discussion had been like many others―The Vietnam War. Involvement began when North Vietnamese gunboats attacked two U.S. Navy destroyers in some gulf far from home. The boys were in junior high when it all started, none paying any attention.

Now five years later, all three were prime candidates because of their ages. They all agreed on one thing. They would not enlist. Coop said he'd go if drafted. Vern said he'd hightail it to his brother's home in Canada. Rusty said he'd use a hardship deferment, if he could get away with it. Being away would be a financial and physical hardship on his mother. Just let somebody call him a draft dodger.

The entire war was a ridiculous joke to Rusty and Vern. If he did get drafted, he'd burn the draft card like he'd seen hundreds of boys doing on TV. "Hell No, We Won't Go," Rusty chanted regularly. It had been all over the news that in about six months the government would institute the first draft lottery since World War II. Each eligible male would be assigned a rating and just their luck, each one would be drafted.

Rusty had no regard for President Johnson who got the U.S. into a senseless war. What business did we have interfering with other countries? Johnson had announced he wasn't running for a second term.

President Nixon had campaigned and won partially by promising to restore law and order and to end the draft. Maybe he'd actually do what he promised. Around and around they went speculating on their futures.

It was too early to return to the house they shared on the west end of this podunk town. Vern and Rusty were too loud. Coop had three beers in as many hours. Not nearly as much as his two lifelong buddies. After all these years together, he felt responsible for them. Sometimes they called themselves the Three Musketeers. Cooper's mom called them the Three Stooges a few times when they were younger.

People were nosy in this rural community. Everybody knew everything about everyone. The trio made a pact earlier that evening they would move to the Willamette Valley and get jobs. They definitely needed more nightlife with more action.

They had attended school together starting in elementary, junior high and graduated together last June except for Vern. He was one year older. Cooper graduated with the best grades, straight As in Math. But didn't feel particularly smart. His first year out of high school he hadn't decided yet what he wanted to do with his life. But he did know working at the First National Bank as a teller wasn't his idea of a lifetime profession. He felt okay that his mom pulled some strings to get him a job in Sisters with another branch of the bank she worked at in Bend. But just because his mom started this way and had been successful didn't mean it was for him. Plus, Coop didn't like having to dress fancy. He preferred the comfort of jeans and boots.

Basketball had been their sport's passion throughout school. Their mothers were glad their sons had some outlet to keep them busy. And exhausted after practices and games. The press reported that a new professional basketball team called the Portland Trail Blazers would be starting up the next year. It would be very cool to go to some of those games. Yep, the Valley was the place to be.

Rusty lowered his head of bushy red hair motioning for his two chums to scooch in closer. Quietly he whispered that an unnamed acquaintance told him about a shipment of brew coming in later to a certain grocery store. He'd already scoped it out and the delivery area was at the rear of the store. Perfect. There were no streetlights back there. Coop knew that this unnamed buddy was of questionable character and a really bad influence on Rusty. They'd already had several heated talks about his involvement with some sketchy guys. Unfortunately, more and more talks lately had become shouting matches between Coop and Rusty.

After drinking away all of his cash and payday not until the next day at the garage where he worked parttime, Rusty thought they should go "borrow" a few cases of beer. They just needed to figure out a diversion to get the driver away from a delivery truck for a couple of minutes while two of them grabbed a case or two.

Vern blurted out, "Don't think just 'cause I'm biggest, I'm gonna whack him. No way."

Rusty said, "Jeez, Vern, I don't think it'll come to that. Just create some commotion to distract him." The two began scheming and dreaming up different nonsensical scenarios.

Coop sort of blanked out, not listening to the ridiculous conversation. He ran his fingers through his medium-length, thick wavy honey-colored hair. He rubbed his sky-blue eyes. His thoughts drifted away wondering if he should get a crew cut. He'd look more business-like. Snapping back, he was getting tired of this familiar routine. Coop just couldn't grasp Rusty's lack of moral code. Rusty never had any qualms about taking something that wasn't his. He knew Rusty's upbringing hadn't been good. But neither was his.

Yes, Rusty's pop had taken his frustrations out on him as a kid. His mom got the brunt of it. Rusty bragged how one day he hit his pop square in the jaw warning him to never touch his mom or him again.

Wiry is how people described Rusty's build. Slim, rough and not too tall. His steely blue eyes got even steelier when he became outraged. He hated his name. Russell. He hated Russ even more. He hated that he had a sissy complexion. Somebody called it a fair complexion, probably because he was Irish. If he was out in the sun too much, freckles popped out on his arms and sometimes his face. He could get really hacked off easily. He hated his curly unruly hair. Somebody called him Rusty when he was about three and it stuck. He thought it was because of his red hair.

Rusty was about eleven when his pop was never to be heard from again. Dead or alive, didn't matter to Rusty just as long as he never saw him again or that his dad never contacted his mom again. His mom worked hard at the Sisters Hotel cleaning rooms. She just had her thirty-eighth birthday. She looked sixty to her son. He vowed no matter what he had to do, it wouldn't been cleaning rooms after who knows who or what had been in there. He owed her, though. He needed to make some money to take care of her.

One positive thing about Rusty was he could fix just about anything. He was self-taught from all the years helping his mom, who could never afford to hire a professional to fix her car, kitchen sink, or leaky toilet. But Rusty could. He worked off and on at the service station in the garage at the east end of town. Work was sporadic but Rusty liked working with his hands. He felt a sense of accomplishment when somebody drove off in their repaired vehicle. But he didn't like working for somebody else.

If Coop would be worried about a friend, it was Rusty who had a fiery temper that could explode at the littlest things. Rusty talked about his grandparents from Ireland. Coop figured his buddy had inherited an Irish temper. His rage, mixed with alcohol could be bad combo.

His temper flares were happening more and more. Rusty's temper made Coop feel extremely uncomfortable. When they were kids, Coop could calm Rusty down. Not so much anymore.

Rusty was always short of money. He justified his new side job saying it would help him financially. Oh, and help his mom. He could pay his share of a place when the three of them moved to the Valley. It was just a delivery job or two for some dork. Rusty made it sound small-time, not a big deal. Coop guessed it was already going on for some time.

Rusty's money issues didn't jive with what Coop observed. Rusty was sporting a new leather chestnut-colored leather jacket. He had another new pair of Tiger Cortez shoes. Coop knew they weren't cheap. Over the past month, he noticed Rusty had several new pairs of this brand of shoe.

They'd laughed over the years about Rusty's really wide feet. He never could find a comfortable pair of boots. Basketball shoes were always more comfortable for him. These were an instant hit for comfort and sturdiness, but more importantly, for the stylish design.

Rusty told them some far-fetched story about a track and field coach at the University of Oregon who altered some shoes and came up with a new design. The coach made a cushioned innersole, soft spongey rubber in the forefoot and top of the heel, hard spongey rubber in the middle of the heal and firm rubber outsole. He was partners with another guy, and they proposed the shoe to the Tiger Shoe Company.

Now Rusty's favorite shoe, The Tiger Cortez was born. Supposedly, the coach had come up with $500 to finance half of the Japanese inventory. He spent time in his evenings at the kitchen table tinkering with the imported shoes, a stitch here, a little more padding there, anything to help athletes and runners. Once these guys got some shoes back from a Japanese Company who produced them, one of the guys was named Phil, started selling the shoes out of the back of his car trunk in Eugene. Even though they were supposedly for athletes, mostly runners, they felt terrific to Rusty who paid cash for three pairs on the spot. He had driven his mom the three-hour drive to visit the only relative he liked, his mom's sister, Aunt Rebecca. She was a nurse and worked close to the university.

Coop didn't know much but figured Rusty could also be experimenting with some illegal drugs. Or whom Rusty had gotten involved with. Coop didn't approve at all. He didn't want to be the bad guy, acting all judgmental. But Rusty already had several run-ins with law enforcement. He had been tossed in jail for a couple of days last Thanksgiving for providing alcohol to a minor, his fifteen-year-old cousin, Butch. Then there was the deer shooting–a buck– using a bright spotlight at night. The list was growing for Rusty and it wasn't good.

Recently Rusty bragged to Coop and Vern that some biker dude heard that he was a whiz at fixing choppers. Evidently Harley didn't let just anyone touch his bike, but admitted he needed some extra help. He'd just gotten a used 1968 Harley Shovelhead. He found out Rusty worked for a garage in Sisters and called him. Harley asked Rusty to meet him at a bar in Bend.

When Rusty showed up at the D&D Bar & Grill on Bond Street in downtown Bend a couple of weeks later, a second guy was there.

The taller guy was Harley. He motioned Rusty to a booth. Rusty guessed he stood probably six-foot, two inches. He probably weighed two hundred twenty-five pounds easy. Rusty's first impression was the guy should see a dentist. Harley towered over the other guy.

Harley had shoulder length medium brown hair down to his eyebrows with sideburns that morphed into a full beard. Maybe he was one of those hippies, Rusty thought. He was all hair except for all black clothing. He wore a headband. His hair was clean, which surprised Rusty. His didn't smile, he snarled. His teeth were gray, one almost black. He wore several rings on his hands. On the top of both hands were tattoos of different designs of skulls. He wore a black leather jacket over a black shirt with black pants. He even had black boots on. When Harley got up to go to the bathroom, Rusty noticed on the back his jacket was a patch or some squiggly writing that spelled out something.

Rusty was intimidated by both guys. He thought he was meeting with Harley about fixing his bike, but it seemed more like an interview for something else, too.

Harley called the other guy Arlo. The second guy was probably five-foot, nine or ten inches and medium build. He had thick dark hair that fell past his shoulders. He could see his brown eyes through the bushy beard and mustache. He didn't look as old as Harley. His teeth were in okay condition. Arlo noticed when Rusty glanced down at Harley's hands mistakenly assuming Rusty was admiring the tattoos. Acting cool, Arlo showed him a new tat on his hand.

Rusty stayed quiet. Arlo set a ring of different types of keys on the table. Some coins were mixed in. A Canadian nickel rolled off in Rusty's lap. He handed it to him and mentioned Canada. Arlo mumbled he had family in Alberta. Rusty didn't know where Alberta was but didn't say a word. Vern would know since his brother lived in Vancouver, British Columbia. There must have been a dozen, if not fifteen keys. Arlo nervously fingered them constantly.

The dark-haired one didn't have a special jacket. He seemed jumpy, uneasy. Or scared. He didn't smile. When standing to leave, Arlo jangled the keys then stuffed the key ring and coins into his right pocket. His tight jeans bulged. Rusty felt uneasy. Harley and Rusty each picked up a book of matches by the cash register on the way out.

At a rundown shack east of Bend, Rusty did the work on Harley's 1968 Shovelhead. Rusty admired the now, like-new bike, a beautiful piece of work, all silver and black with a red gas tank. It was a V-twin, 60.0 horsepower, 5200 RPM and topped out at 99.4 miles per hour. Harley paid Rusty seventy-five dollars in cash. That was it Rusty told Coop.

Rusty conveniently didn't mention that Harley told him if he wanted to make some easy money, to let him know. Coop was pretty sure they had talked Rusty into doing something illegal involving drugs. To him it sounded like these guys were part of a club. Rusty had mentioned something about them doing pretty well. They both owned Harley-Davidson motorcycles.

Rusty had realized quickly he wanted more and more of the easy cash. He could be making more with each delivery than fixing vehicles. Each time he did one they passed along a crisp fifty dollar bill to him.

Rusty was nonchalantly passing along crystal meth. Most came from the I-5 corridor in the Willamette Valley. Somehow Harley got the drugs but didn't want to be involved in the delivery. Yet, he would be the one to collect the money. Rusty began thinking about his options.

Coop's first concern for his friend started two months earlier. Having a beef stew supper one night, Rusty bragged he'd gotten a side job. He pulled out two bills from his wallet. He slid two crisp fifty dollar bills across the table to Coop. "Here's my share of the rent for next month. Have I ever paid early before?" This impressed Vern. Coop was skeptical.

Vern asked, "Man, where did you get that?" Rusty indifferently answered he just delivered a small package to some guy named Raymond. He laughed and explained that's what he'd heard them say but the guy's name was actually Racoon. That was it. No money exchanged. His job was only to deliver. A week later the same guy had him deliver another package to a different guy named Rowdy.

That's what he told Coop and Vern, anyway. Rusty started collecting fifties on a regular basis.

When Coop and Vern were at work, Rusty had the house to himself. The first time he meticulously opened a packet of the meth, he thought he was having a heart attack. His heart raced. He decided there and then he was overdue for some of this for himself. Preachy Coop didn't know the half of it.

Coop figured if Rusty's recent behavior went on much longer, he'd have to kick him out of their shared house. Coop regretted that the two of them had gotten into a pushing and shoving match almost to fist-a-cuffs. If Vern hadn't jumped in, he wasn't sure what might have happened. Coop really wanted to beat some sense into Rusty.

Should I or shouldn't I? Coop went back and forth trying to decide if he should speak with his only male cousin, Clay, who was a deputy at the Jefferson County Sheriff's Office. But he really didn't have details. No legit names—Racoon and Rowdy, seriously? Then the two bikers. Rusty let slip one name. Harley. But Coop didn't know if that was really his name or a nickname. Maybe it was his motorcycle. He thought he remembered some guy named Arlo. Maybe from Alberta, Canada. He couldn't recall why or when he'd heard it. It stuck with him. Arlo from Alberta. It reminded him of Arlo Guthrie, the singer.

Being a year older, nearly everyone expected Vern to be the responsible one. That didn't hold true in his case. He went along with almost everything. Usually he'd be laughing mostly from nervousness, especially if he was doing something questionable. He loved an adventure, of any kind.

Swiping some beer was right up his alley. The trio would have to keep this escapade between themselves because if his dad ever found out, his folks would disown him for good. He'd been part of a few questionable ventures in the past year. His strict parents warned him, "Vernon," they always called him Vernon, which he hated. He had been named after one of his great grandfathers from Norway, who meant nothing to him. "Vernon, are you listening? This is the last time we will bail you out." His parents went to a conservative Lutheran church. Growing up, he did too. His eyes were the same color as his mom's. Light blue, she said. He corrected her, powder blue.

Each time they'd gotten him off the hook for something, they'd make him help with janitorial work at the church. He hated working and not getting paid. He knew better than to steal but it was sure fun. He could never get enough beer. He loved the buzz.

Vern had no ambition, no plans for the future. This attitude baffled his parents and his friend Coop. Vern's folks both worked hard their entire lives. It also went directly against his family's heritage. They had Viking roots from Norway. Fair-haired, he'd heard way too many stupid blonde jokes, usually aimed at girls. He wondered if they didn't apply to him also.

Coop didn't think Vern had it all that bad. His parents were together, cared about each other, and both sons. They might be stricter than some, but it proved they were interested. His dad had served in World War II. He still wore a military buzz-cut and acted like a drill sergeant. So what? Boy oh boy, could Vern's mom ever cook. She made the best desserts. Especially during any holiday. Every

Christmas she shared boxes of cookies with Coop and his mom that they devoured within hours. Coop's mom felt grateful to Vern's mom for looking out for her son.

Vern's mom pronounced each funny-named cookie with a Norwegian accent. Sirupssniper was Coop's favorite. He loved the gingersnaps shaped like diamonds with an almond on top. Then there were the Krumkaker, a thin, waffle cookie. He enjoyed hearing her describe how she wrapped the dough around a cone-shaped mold as soon as they came off an iron. While they're still hot, they are flexible and held the cone shape as they cooled. After they cooled, she served them either plain or filled with whipped cream. He preferred the ones filled with cream.

Then she'd always make Berlinerkranser, a butter cookie with extra egg yolks in the batter. She'd form the stiff dough into long snake-like shapes before wrapping into a loose bow. They became a little wreath.

Another favorite she made was Kringla. This one had sour cream, heavy cream and lots of butter and sugar in the batter. She had shown him one day after school several years earlier, how she formed the dough into long rolls with her hands. Then she cut off a narrow slice of dough and rolled it on a floured board into a pencil-width strip. Magically she'd create a figure eight and pinch the ends together. She added sparkle by brushing the cookie after it formed with some melted butter. At Christmas she used red and green sprinkles to brighten the cookie.

Coop remembered one gigantic flour fight between Vern, his mom and himself one year. He still laughed out loud when he thought about it.

The only thing Coop couldn't figure out was the flat potato tortilla they called lefse, their flatbread. She mashed potatoes, combined flour, lots of butter and cream. She rolled it thin with a special rolling pin with deep grooves.

Then she grilled one at a time on a flat pan until toasty on each side. He enjoyed watching her use long wooden turning sticks to flip over the thin pancake-like patty.

The family loved them slathered in butter, then sprinkled with brown sugar and cinnamon all over it. Coop couldn't do it. It seemed contrary. Sugar on potatoes? He ate it rolled up and plain.

Coop considered Vern's mom his second mom. She had told him years ago to call her Daphne, her first name. He just couldn't. Respectfully he called her Mrs. Christopherson. He tried Mrs. C, since he called Rusty's mother Mrs. K, but it didn't fit her. Then one winter he figured it out. His mom, along with Vern and his parents drove together to Bend to see a newly released James Bond 007 movie called "Thunderball." The action-packed flick took place in the Bahamas and MI6 was to recover two nuclear warheads stolen by some S.P.E.C.T.R.E. agent. The head of the mission department was the fictional character named James Bond–MI6. He knew on the spot Mrs. C was now his M2, mom #2. Anytime Coop called her M2, she giggled like a little girl.

Coop's mom had worked full-time all through his childhood at First National Bank in Bend. It was a thirty-minute drive from their home in Sisters. She had attended Merritt Davis Business College for a year in Salem, which included bookkeeping, shorthand, and other office skills. She started as a file clerk, then was quickly promoted to teller. She knew most of the people in Bend.

Now twenty years later, she held the position of assistant manager, the first woman ever at the branch. She had to be there before eight o'clock. She always had his lunch packed by 7:15. In elementary school, lunch was tucked away in his Roy Rogers lunchbox. In junior high and high school, he preferred a brown paper bag. When he was young, the night before school days, she'd lay his freshly washed clothes on the extra twin bed in his room. He ate either Cheerios, Raisin Bran or on a special occasion, Frosted Flakes, before leaving Monday through Friday mornings for a three-block walk to school. This left Coop getting ready for school on his own, but he managed fine.

She worked until 5:30 then came home and fixed dinner for the two of them. Over dinner she'd make him fill her in on his day. Secretly he loved dinnertime with his mom. It was just the two of them. He knew she worked very hard to support them.

Vern's mom had been there every afternoon when her son got home from school. Their dog Cappy eagerly greeted Coop anytime he walked in the door. Their pooch was some kind of terrier mix and had night sky black ears with an almost perfect circle of black around his entire right eye. His stout body had short white hair.

Instead of going home to an empty house, the moms had agreed during elementary school Coop should go home with Vern almost every afternoon. They just lived a couple of streets apart. Vern's mom always offered an afternoon snack of some kind. A peanut butter grape jelly sandwich was a treat. Vern didn't have it bad off at all.

Vern's meager funds came from odd jobs. He had been working at a new development called Sunriver Resort, about fifteen miles south of Bend. Construction was underway creating a planned residential and resort community. More people were buying property in the area for their second homes.

Located on the grounds of the former Camp Abbot, the World War II training facility had been designed to train combat engineers in a simulated combat environment in 1942. By 1944, it had been abandoned and most of the settlement was flattened. Vern particularly liked a building that originally housed the Officers' Club. It still stood but was now called the Great Hall. He thrived working at the beginning of projects when excitement and enthusiasm was high. His assignment was landscaping the new post office grounds which would open in July. He didn't particularly care about working on the end of projects. It left him feeling ho-hum. Thirty-eight miles one-way became too far of a drive and not having dependable transportation, he quit.

Currently, he worked reseeding and grooming lawns at a private golf course called Prineville Golf & Country Club. It opened thirteen years earlier and now was the time for some upgrades. Its reputation included 2,525 yards from the longest tees and a slope rating of 112 and a 32.1 USGA rating. Golfers were coming from all over and many were being introduced to Central Oregon for the first time.

Vern had a bulky build and stood a little taller than Coop. They had him lifting and moving wheelbarrows full of soil and dumping it where machinery couldn't reach. Pushing a heavy lawn flattening roller, he pressed the earth smooth and even. It really wasn't a big effort for him. He'd just finished four twelve-hour days. Management gave him Friday off making it a four-day weekend for him. Manual labor worked for him; he didn't have to think much. One day his work would become a lush eighteen-hole golf course. He'd helped an uncle paint his house one time. He did like that. He had a flair for colors. If somebody pointed at a blue house, he'd call it sapphire. Or a barn to him would never be just red; it would be scarlet or cherry.

————

Coop had the gumption to put his foot down and said, "Nope. Conversation over. I'm not going to be a part of it. I never intend to steal anything and not going to start now especially something stupid like beer. Plus, we're in my pickup."

His own flaky father had been in and out of jail for really stupid decisions. Coop would not follow in his footsteps. He also felt responsible for his mom. She'd raised him on her own since he was nine. By then his dad had been in the slammer four or five times. He couldn't even remember how many times his mom got a call at night from his dad asking for bail money. His flakey father knew to call her at night because she wasn't able to take personal calls at the bank. She had sent money too many times.

Then one night she let Coop answer the phone because he had the fortitude to say no better than she did. The pleading calls stopped.

She sat in the second row at his high school graduation last June wearing a smile as big as a crescent moon. College had been her dream for him. He'd heard it repeatedly since junior high. He'd been checking out the catalog from Central Oregon Community College. But he'd rather move to the Valley with the guys and go to Oregon State University in Corvallis. Or maybe a community college in the Portland area.

————

Just because his mom loved this small town of supporting, honest, helpful people, she realized it probably would not be where he would choose to stay. It had taken her years through her challenging life's journey to find this secure feeling place. She was raised in Helena, Montana, where her Scottish family settled decades earlier. It was also the same hometown of a movie star, Gary Cooper. It was obvious where Cooper got his name. It was shortened to Coop when he was a kid. Her lifetime mistake was marrying the jerk, but she got Coop out of it. He was the bright spot of her life.

Since the three guys were in his '63 green Chevy pickup truck and he refused to participate, it was a no go for the beer stealing escapade. To appease his whiny, irritated buddies, Coop suggested they stop at home and pick up the cooler and several six-packs of Rainier beer then drive to Camp Sherman. They could sit on the bridge and enjoy a couple bottles each. Their complaining ceased and they headed home for beer.

CHAPTER FOUR

Oh, What A Beautiful Morning

Marleen belted her neon fuchsia and yellow poppy bathrobe tightly around her waist. She opened the creaking front door that she'd been meaning to oil for months and gently shoved her dark gray cat Smokey out. He'd been yowling, obviously restless, roaming the house. She heard a drinking glass shatter on the floor in the kitchen. Smokey knocked it off of the counter, which he wasn't supposed to be on. That was it. Out he went. The German-made six-foot tall grandfather clock against the wall in her living room ding-donged once. "Only one o'clock?" she said out loud.

About to close the door, she noticed the boys who lived just two houses away. She always called them boys. They were just coming home. The three hopped out and ran into the house. Quickly back out she noticed Rusty had changed into a heavier jacket. Vern had put on a thick fleece shirt. Coop wore his wool Pendleton jacket. One carried a plastic blue cooler as they returned to the truck.

Undoubtedly, they were going to a party somewhere, she thought judgingly. On a Thursday night? She'd known them all of their lives. Rusty had always been the trouble-maker. But he also was a nice boy to her and a real charmer. They were all appreciative when she brought them pie from the restaurant. Rusty fixed her car once when it wouldn't start. He saved her some money. She thought of him as a lost puppy.

Stopping in the bathroom she looked in the mirror hanging over the sink. She admired her handiwork. Her newly colored coal black hair was securely wrapped around the extra-large pink sponge rollers. Was that a little tinge of purple? Or blue? There better not be. She had been overdue in covering up her gray roots. About an inch of the silvery strands had been showing through with more popping up around her forehead. Maybe she should let some show through in her bangs? Or better yet, all black hair with swishy bangs all white, like Cruella de Vil in the movie "101 Dalmatians."

She abided by the Clairol motto: "Hate that gray? Wash it away!" Quarterly she used Loving Care 22d Jet Black to perform its magic. She liked the drama and contrast of the darkness against her pale skin. Her goal was to look delicate, like a china doll she'd seen in a store in Portland. That would be hard to achieve since she was five foot, six inches. Not exactly petite. She wanted porcelain skin and black, black, black hair. She laughed at the promo-tion, "If I've only one life…let me live it as a blonde!" She preferred, "The closer he gets, the better you look."

She came in contact daily with dozens if not hundreds of people. She wanted people to remember her not just for her outgoing personality. Even though almost middle age at forty-four, she didn't have to look it. She'd keep people wondering, "Does She, or Doesn't She?" She laughed at herself. One rancher in particular had been paying a bit more attention to her the past month. If Mort asked her out, she'd say yes.

She carefully read the print on the side of the Lady Clairol box:

Ultra Comfort--no sting, no bite, no burn, perfect for all heads.

Ultra Creamy--always stays in place. Won't run, drip or dry out. Good thing. She didn't want black running down the side of her face or forehead.

Ultra Convenient--mattered since she was doing it to herself. It mixes instantly into a thick, cream consistency that's a pleasure to work with. Perfect for use with the new time-saving plastic applicator, swab or brush.

Ultra Conditioning-- Conditions the protein structure of the hair giving better hair texture than ever before possible.

She spent way too long making sure she followed the instructions perfectly. But she didn't want to do anything wrong. She didn't take the time to read the page in tiny print of all the things that could go wrong, called "special precautions."

1/Prep.

#1. Put on gloves, comb hair gently.

#2. Open bottle 1 & pour contents into bottle

#3. Shake until color mixture is blended."

2/Application.

#1. Apply color to damp hair free of styling product build-up, starting at the roots and where you have the most gray. Next, apply remaining color to the rest of your hair.

#2. Section hair and work color through each section from roots to tips to ensure full saturation. Do not rub into your scalp.

#3. Wait. Leave color mixture on your hair for ten minutes. Tip: for resistant grays, leave on for an additional five minutes.

3/Finish.

#1. When time is up, rinse until water runs clear.

#2. Apply a quarter-size amount of conditioner (tube 3) through your hair.

#3. Leave on for two minutes. Use remaining conditioner once a week after shampooing.

Now she just needed an updated style. She was done with the outdated pouffy Priscilla Presley look. The six-inch beehive perched daily on top of her head had become way too much work.

The French had introduced a new smart-looking pixie cut, not taking much maintenance. Should her bangs be that short on her long forehead? Maybe the swooping bangs with the large curl off to the right? Maybe a modified beehive, just not as high.

She did have plenty of ribbons to tie a bow in the back. It had become her signature statement and flair for style. Over the Fourth of July the ribbon would be flags. Christmas had been ivy. Valentine's Day were red hearts, of course. St. Patrick's Day was obviously green four-leaf clover material. If she wore a headband it always had a bow at the top.

Well, she couldn't decide on a new look now. She needed her sleep. She would be opening The Gallery restaurant in several hours. It was her job at the restaurant to get coffee going before the cook and waitresses arrived. She loved her job as hostess and cashier. She knew who had switched to decaf for health reasons and who drank regular. As regulars filtered through the door needing that first cup of caffeine, Marleen greeted them by name. If anyone came through the door she didn't recognize, they would probably be a tourist. Or maybe somebody's relative visiting the area. She would know their story before leaving. Everyone loved her outgoing friendly personality, and nobody was a stranger to her.

She certainly didn't consider herself a busybody. Everyone just looked after each other. Like last Tuesday after she'd gotten home from work, when she was getting her mail from the box on the street. She overheard Rusty in a yelling match with a big guy on a big motorcycle. He pulled away just as Coop drove in. Then she heard more shouting between the two roommates.

Standing close to the street she got a pretty good look at the biker. His head was mostly covered by shoulder-length brown hair and a bushy brown beard. His leather jacket had some writing and designs on the back. He had a skull tattoo on his right hand. She'd never seen him before.

It was the third time in the past couple of weeks that shouting had been heard from the usually pretty quiet house. And she knew without a doubt she'd heard the words "marijuana" and "drugs" used a few times. She hoped the boys weren't taking those dreadful drugs that she was reading more about it all in the news. She assumed all wasn't well with the boys two houses down.

Marleeen walked down the hallway to her bedroom. She removed her bathrobe and crawled back to bed. Her squishy curler-covered head rested on her pillow. Before she dozed off, she heard the familiar rumble of Cooper's truck. Just as she fell asleep, she heard a second rumble. She fell asleep in three minutes flat.

As they pulled out a safe distance behind the truck, the uptight rider yelled into the left ear of the driver of the chopper, "Why didn't you get the stupid headlight fixed like I told you? I can't see a thing except the truck ahead of us. If we hit a deer, we're goners." The driver ignored his uneasy passenger.

While driving the ten miles west to the Camp Sherman Metolius River exit, glancing in the rearview mirror, Coop noticed a mile or so behind them a vehicle with one randomly blinking headlight. He thought with one head-light not working and the other blinking off and on, it could be dangerous.

They drove several more miles on their way to the Camp Sherman bridge. When driving by the parking lot of the headwaters, Vern mentioned had to take a pee badly. He recalled a forest service outhouse.

Coop turned in, parked, and he and Vern took their turn. Rusty couldn't wait any longer and stepped on the other side of a bush.

Vern mentioned how cool the headwaters would be in the dark. Coop pulled out a boxy Eveready Commander flashlight from the glove compartment and grabbed a six pack from the back. Rusty took the second pack. The moon was almost half full yet very bright on this cloudless night.

Coop handed a flashlight to Vern, who pulled it from a cloth case. Coop prided himself on keeping anything he owned clean and in mint condition. Vern clumsily dropped the bag and it fell slightly under the truck. Dang. He'd get down on his hands and knees to retrieve it when they got back. Beer was more important.

In little towns like theirs, no one was ever concerned about leaving keys in the ignition of their vehicles. No one locked their front door or vehicles. But Coop took the truck keys with him.

The trio walked down the dirt path, two of the three swaggering a bit. Vern pointed the flashlight ahead showing the way. Rusty popped a bottle cap and drank on the way to the headwaters.

———

The chopper with two riders slowly slipped into the dark parking lot. Harley parked it opposite of the truck. Arlo pulled his heavy key ring from his pocket and placed it on the seat. A coin landed in the dirt. Harley removed his driving gloves and slid spiked brass knuckles on his right hand. It was too dark for Arlo to see. Harley flicked on his silver Ray-O-Vac flashlight. He picked up a sturdy broken tree branch and handed it to Arlo. Harley kept his hand on the top of the flashlight providing just a sliver of light.

———

Vern said, "Did you just hear thunder?" Rusty said, "You're hearing things." Coop thought he heard something. But stars twinkled brightly along with a glowing moon. There were no clouds for lightning and thunder. They walked down the dark dirt path, lit by one powerful flashlight, and moon and stars. They returned to the earlier conversation about moving to the Valley. Two of the three were pretty tipsy from drinking too much and were mildly zigzagging down the sloping path.

———

At the river's headwaters, really two clusters of springs coming from the base of Black Butte, Vern set the flashlight down, pointing inward. The grasses and bushes were slick from the powerful stream shooting out of the side of the hill. Tipsy Rusty slipped in ankle-deep water. He let out a blue streak, swearing about how cold it was. Now his feet were freezing and wet. He sat on the soft bushes and removed his favorite gray Tiger sneakers. He pulled off his white athletic cotton socks and rang them out as tightly as he could. Putting the wet socks back on was less than appealing but he did it anyway. He tied one shoelace. He was furious and yelling that his new gray Tiger sneakers could be ruined. Vern offered Rusty a hand up and gave him another beer. Rusty forgot about tying the other shoe.

Rusty pulled out a book of matches from his leather jacket pocket. Striking the match, it illuminated the entire area. Then he lit what Coop assumed was a cigarette. He preferred Rusty didn't smoke. Coop had an uncle who died a lingering death from lung cancer after smoking most of his life. But Rusty didn't think of the future or consequences.

However, it wasn't a cigarette. It was a joint. Coop could tell within a few seconds from the way it burned. And the smell of pot was distinct.

Rusty passed the joint to Vern. He laughed and inhaled a deep breath. When offered to Coop, he flicked Rusty's hand away. The matches went flying somewhere. Rusty swore. Vern took another long drag.

Coop patronizingly said he'd pass and added drinking beer was enough, plus he was driving. Rusty didn't appreciate Coop's condescending tone. Drinking and smoking was a bad combo in Coop's book.

Coop didn't want to sound preachy, but when he said, "Come on, guys, one or the other not both," this set Rusty off. He roared at his friend to shut up and keep his judgmental opinions to himself. Rusty got right in Coop's face. His smelly beer breath irritated Coop ever more. Coop lambasted Rusty with a barrage of pent-up anger lashing out and criticizing him for his poor choices.

The first shove came from Rusty. Coop snapped and pushed back. A wrestling match started. Coop was about to deck Rusty when the larger of the trio, Vern, stepped in.

Coop saw a quick movement and without any notice one or two others jumped into the melee, pounding on Rusty. They didn't say a thing. But Rusty's cussing and yelling made up for it. Coop's kicked flashlight fell over, shining through the grass towards the river. Besides the moon, only the fizzling joint provided a little light. Somebody sneezed.

Coop and Vern hurdled in. Somebody whacked Coop in the face dragging something sharp down his face. Blood spurt out and he tasted it in his mouth. A person grabbed Coop by the shoulders. Coop clawed him with his fingernails deep in the neck. He heard a cry from the attacker. Somebody punched Coop in the gut hard and as he gasped for air, he smelled a sharp odor. It reminded him of paint thinner or cleaner. He bent over in agony and fell on the ground. Maybe he smelled cat pee?

Vern was swearing. Somebody hit him in the right cheek with something spikey. He screamed like a girl. He started hitting somebody. Then he got hit in the knees with something. Then over the head. Maybe a bat or a tree limb. Knocked to the ground, groaning in pain, he didn't know who was hitting who.

Both Coop and Vern were on the ground, useless. These boys were not fighters.

One of them wore a leather jacket. Rusty could feel it. With two hands free, he ripped his fingernails down somebody's face as the person pounded him. One person battered Rusty. His face hurt. He was sure his nose was broken. It hurt to breathe. He assumed some ribs were broken. He knew his lip was bleeding a lot. Spikes from something punctured his face.

He heard a familiar voice whisper, "This is what you get for cheating me, you cockroach." Rusty had hoped the small amounts of drugs wouldn't be noticed. He was so wrong. One whacked Rusty with something hard like a tree limb. He was punched in the head with something metal and Rusty heard a gurgle. He screamed but couldn't hear himself. With one blow to his right temple he heard a loud crack. He realized it was his own head. It would be the last thing he would ever remember.

Vern got back on his feet and hit somebody again and again. He heard someone expel air. Something tumbled down the gently sloped bank. Hearing a splash, Coop uncrumpled himself and chased down the flashlight that had been kicked away during the fight.

He screamed, "Vern? Rusty?" Vern mumbled, "Over here." "Rusty? Rusty!" Coop yelled. They tried to figure out what the splash had come from. It all happened so quickly.

Fleeing footsteps crunched on pine needles, running up the trail. One lit a cigarette about halfway up, indicating the location. A matchbook with D&D on the cover fell to the ground. The other tossed the sturdy tree limb used in the beating off the pathway. The glowing cigarette tip got dimmer and dimmer.

Arlo hissed, "Turn on the flashlight."

Harley, reaching in his jacket pocket said, "I don't have

it. I gave it to you." Wheezing heavily, then he spit out, "Jeez, you are worthless. You don't know how to fight and can't even carry a flashlight."

Of course, it didn't make any sense to Arlo since he hadn't been carrying the flashlight, but he said nothing to Harley, who was clearly unhinged.

Vern asked, "Was there one or two? Who were they? Why didn't we see them coming? What happened?" He talked but hardly knew what he was saying. There was just enough bright moonlight; Coop thought he saw two.

Jumping in the shallow, fairly narrow headwaters, they were instantly drenched from the freezing river's spigot shooting water from the opening. Rusty lay several feet from the gushing waterspout. Temperatures were dropping. With the river's shallow bottom, water did not cover the body. Both bent down. One poked and shook their friend to see if he was okay, not moving him in the water. Maybe he was just stunned. Or temporarily knocked out. The shallow water flowed around him. Vern kept yelling Rusty's name, over and over, until Coop told him to shut up.

"There it is again." Vern said. "Thunder." Coop realized then it was probably a motorcycle or vehicle with a loud muffler.

Harley sneezed. "These allergies are killing me," he said, like nothing had just happened. He reached for his red and white cloth handkerchief and it was missing. They certainly couldn't backtrack now. Harley felt assured nobody could trace him and Arlo to this place and time. It was still dark. They hadn't said a word except to Rusty before the final blow.

As the bikers pulled away, one had done what he set out to do. Eliminate the problem. Harley wanted to make an example of the cockroach. Word would get around fast in their circle of influence. He had no remorse; business was business.

Arlo wasn't exactly sure what had just happened and how in the world he became a part of it. He felt like he was in the television program, "The Twilight Zone." It had all started with him working on his bike with a bunch of long-hair guys.

———

Coop lost it. He blurted out jumbled questions without waiting for answers: "What do we do? Haul him out? Take him where? What if he's dead? Do we drive to Sisters to call the Jefferson County Sheriff's office?"

"I'm not doing that," Vern said, "I've already had a few brushes with the law."

Coop countered, "But you weren't ever arrested."

"True, not yet anyway. We should chase those guys down. Run over them in the truck." Sentences from both weren't making much sense.

"We can't just leave him there."

"Why not?"

"Because he's been our friend since childhood, that's why."

"I know, but I'm not getting blamed for this. We've been drinking for hours. I'm pretty blitzed. Plus, the joint. We don't know how this happened. Who were those other two guys?"

The extinguished smoked joint now was unable to be seen in the dark.

Vern pulled out a navy- and white-checked handkerchief from his pocket. He heard something muffled hit the pine needle-covered ground but couldn't see what it was. He wiped water and blood from his face, arms and hands. Now heavy and wet, he wadded it up and threw it as far as he could into the woods.

Ringing his hands, Coop, normally the mature one, was at a loss as to what to do. He asked again, "What are our options? We drag him to the truck and take him to the Sheriff's office an hour away? We go to Sisters twenty minutes away and call for help?"

Vern said, "Or we leave him for someone else to find. What if those maniacs return? They might kill us, too. Are they the ones who came to our house? They know where we live." He could hardly breathe between words.

Coop replied, "Okay, we'll figure it out on the drive home." Neither could think straight. Both were in shock.

They ran to the truck. Out of breath, Vern remembered empty beer bottles left behind. Coop said, "Leave them, neither of us have records so no fingerprints." He could hardly believe he'd thought or said those words out loud. They didn't feel as mature and old as they were. They were scared little boys, not thinking clearly.

Driving back in silence, the entire incident seemed surreal. They didn't discuss the options at all. Three had come together. They'd spent their lives growing up together, having each other's back. Now only two were returning. Closer to home, they hollered at each other pointing fingers and blaming each other. What could they have done differently?

Coop whispered, "I've got to think about this. I'm going to my stay with my cousin in Salem for a while."

97

The other said, "I'm going to my brother's in Vancouver, Canada. I'm never coming back."

Returning to the camp, Arlo jumped on his bike and headed to the motel. Harley climbed in bed and slept like a baby.

Arlo had a recurring nightmare about his motorcycle mysteriously starting up on its own, chasing him down the sidewalk and pinning him against a pine tree until he stopped breathing. He thought he was in the twilight zone.

The clock alarm jarred Marleen from a sound sleep earlier than normal, at 3:30 a.m. She usually got up around four but today she needed to spend some extra time on her hair. She quickly pulled out the spongy pink rollers and brushed out her totally jet-black hair. Today she'd do a perfect pageboy flip all the way around, not her typical beehive height.

She heard a familiar rumble and peeked out the window to see Coop's shamrock-green pickup pull in. Two of the boys slogged into the house. She didn't notice which two of the usual threesome they were.

After her daily bathroom rituals, she pinned on her silver name badge. She cherished her name tag. Not all employees had them. It was a privilege, the restaurant owners told her. She liked her name. It was a combination name made up by her parents. It came from her favorite uncle Mark, her dad's brother. The "leen" portion had been borrowed from a favorite aunt on her mother's side, Aunt Kathleen, or Katy for short.

She got dressed and breezed out the door. The sun just started to light up the street. She would bring home an apple pie from the restaurant tonight as an excuse to check in on the boys two houses down.

———

After not much sleep dozing between the recurring motorcycle nightmare, Arlo went to work early. He couldn't sleep anyway. Nor could he concentrate and was glad he pounded nails all day into wallboard. He thought over and over about what had happened. How? Why? And his involvement. To cover the scratch marks on his neck he wore a shirt with a high collar to work. With warm temperatures at the end of May, he knew it would look weird.

———

Vern tiptoed into his parent's house. Their dog Cappy didn't even bother to crawl out of his warm bed in the laundry room, but Vern heard his wagging tail thumping on the floor. He scribbled a quick note on the chalkboard with key hooks below. "Going to see Lenny. Back in a few weeks." Hanging where it always was, he grabbed the keys to his mom's car.

When his folks got up and read it, his mom said, "Why is he going back so soon? He was just there last month." He only called his brother Lenny when they were kids. His mother became suspicious when Vern had used the name Lenny. Something was wrong. And her white Buick was missing.

It was way too early to contact his supervisor Mr. Pringle at the bank, so Coop wrote a note and taped the envelope to the door at the employee entrance to the bank.

He wrote there was a family emergency and he would return Tuesday. His supervisor thought this very unusual behavior for Cooper. He'd never called in sick or needed time off in an entire year of working there. Coop headed west in his truck.

Sure enough, my brothers and I were awakened by Dad's lyrics. It was still dark. We jumped up and got dressed in clothing all laid out by Mom. Willy became easily bored and distracted. While waiting for his turn in the bathroom he jetted back to his bedroom and was jumping on his bed. Then we all heard a loud, "Beds are for sleeping not jumping," from Mom. We brushed our teeth and washed our faces. Today Max and I were fine with sharing our one bathroom in our three-story home. We were cleaned up and ready to roll.

Mom carefully loaded the cold food items into the trailer's mini-fridge. Dad rolled in the boys' homemade modified stingray bikes with high-rise handlebars and long, banana-shaped seats. Dad couldn't afford the real Schwinn ones. He wanted our family to pull out of the driveway at 4:30 a.m., O-Dark-Thirty, as Dad called it, one hour before sunup.

Whenever embarking on a family vacation in our two-wheel, thirteen-foot travel trailer we'd leave before sunup. Our family had been fortunate to have taken an outing each summer, camping over the years around the Pacific Northwest, into Alberta, down through Glacier National Park, Yellowstone and the Tetons. My parents instilled a sense of adventure and wanderlust in me. Because of a special world geography teacher in junior high, Mr. Halstead, I wanted to experience the world. He made the world come alive in his classroom. I caught the travel bug at an early age.

We were getting an extra early start to the two-hour drive, or a bit longer in the pitch dark. Dad wanted to get there very early to check out the site options at Riverside Campground. This campground provided wide open spaces in a pine forest that allowed parking right on the riverbank. It was an unimproved area compared to the campgrounds several miles down the river. Those had wooden outhouses with pine-green roofs, spigots of running water and lots more people.

We went camping several times each summer between Memorial Day and Labor Day weekends. Other families, several with kids about the same ages as us, would join us.

This particular morning seven-year-old Will, preferring we not use Willy anymore, sat in our blue Dodge pickup, snuggled safely between Mom and Dad. He got car sick easily just as I did but I'd outgrown it. Darn it. I missed sitting up front. I wasn't supposed to say "darn it" because it was a substitute for some other swear word that we also didn't say. There had been advantages when younger and getting sick. It meant sitting in the front seat with the grownups.

Dad hooked up our compact thirteen-foot Aladdin camper trailer in about three minutes flat. Max and I slid in over the tailgate and scooched on the bed of the truck to the front. Dad had piled lawn chairs between us and the truck tailgate, keeping us secure. The metal canopy had sliding windows down the sides. We sat on tightly rolled sleeping bags and two rolled up one-inch foam sheets about the size of a twin bed mattress as cushions. I'd use these to sleep on when sharing the back with my best friend Peggy. Maybe our younger friend Maleah, too. They would arrive later that day with their families.

Like in the past, we'd make up the back of the truck into our own private quarters. Masking tape would hold newspapers as curtains over the windows. I brought the comics section of the past Sunday's newspaper for some color. Hunching over we climbed in and out of the truck easily. We could sit totally upright, though not stand up. We'd create an area to stack magazines and games as well as snacks like Fritos, Ding Dongs and 7-Up. It would be our own little escape from bothersome numbskull brothers and parents' watchful eyes.

At 4:35, we drove out on U.S. Route 20, we called it Highway 20, southeast toward Lebanon (LEB-uh-nun). Passing the general hospital, Mom reminded everyone of the momentous occasion of me being born there. Just about every year we heard the story before my birthday cake was cut. Dad drove like a maniac. Then the very lengthy, grueling forty-eight hours of labor for my poor mother. "That was almost fourteen years ago," she sighed. "It was just like yesterday. Where does time go?" I always felt a little sorry about the trouble I caused her. Then when I thought about Max's birth at nine-pounds, nine ounces three years later, I felt better about my two-day long entrance.

My favorite thing about my birth town is it's the home of the annual Strawberry Festival. We'd be going in a few weeks. Picking strawberries was a lot of back-breaking work. You either straddled the row as wide as riding a horse, bending at the waist, or on your knees hunched over the row. Or lastly, scooting along on one's bottom on a piece of burlap in the dirt. None were pleasant. There would not be a future in this type of manual labor for me, as I discovered working several summers in the patches making some extra money. I preferred standing picking raspberries or beans. But babysitting was the best and most fun, plus it went year-round. Even though only thirteen-and-a-half that winter, I'd had a couple of jobs taking care of a family friend's twin daughters, Margie and Marie, and son, Casey. Admittedly, the parents were visiting in another part of the house. It was my early training ground, along with using my brothers as guinea pigs.

I had learned all about Highway 20 in seventh grade U.S. History class. My teacher, Mr. Grimes, really enjoyed talking about old cars, road building, trains and railroads. He interestingly tied it in with history and geography. The road started about sixty miles west of us in the central Oregon coastal town of Newport, right on the Pacific Ocean.

My Auntie Patti and Uncle Norman and cousins, Sheri, Bill and Brian lived there with their bulldog named Blitz. Uncle Norm fixed spicy hot chili soup whenever we visited. Aunt Patti always made something with shrimp. I stared for hours at the view from their living room window of the spectacular ocean.

Highway 20 was built through twelve states. It ended in the historical tea-party city of Boston. I thought it would be cool to drive this route one day in my own car. I'd start in Oregon going to Idaho, Montana, Wyoming, Nebraska, Iowa, Illinois, Indiana, Ohio, Pennsylvania, New York, ending in Massachusetts. Even though three thousand, three hundred sixty-five miles sounded like a long trip, I could stop to visit Dad's relatives in Montana and Mom's in Nebraska. Maybe my folks would let me do this when I turned eighteen and bought my first car.

At the same time about seventy miles to the east, a tan-colored Mule Deer unfolded her long legs as she stood up. Her overnight resting place had been several hundred feet from a river. Momma deer checked to make sure her six-week-old, camouflaged speckled fawn was up also. The deer's thin white ropelike tail had a black tip and twitched to shoo away a pesky fly. She had large ears, as her name suggests, like a mule, that stood at an angle, good for hearing danger.

They took graceful steps through dewy grass. Normally they drank easily from the riverbank. The sun peeked through the lodgepole and ponderosa pines. In the lush meadow beyond she knew others of her kind were waking and meandering toward the cool waters of the Metolius River.

It was a typical morning at the river. The springs gushed from the ground as it had done for centuries.

A familiar sound to the deer was the rushing noise at the beginning of the river. With her excellent hearing, she picked up the sounds of the slight crunching of pine needles under the feet of the scampering chipmunks. Directly across from them some birds cheeped and chirped their early morning songs. Dozens of ducks quacked and splashed in the shallow river. The 10,500 foot Mount Jefferson loomed in the background. The sky lightened with a few delicate wispy cirrus clouds turning pink into orange.

They arrived at their normal watering place. The mother noticed something different in the water at the base of the hill. She snorted her unhappiness. Their usual morning tranquility had changed. The baby bleated as they trotted away.

A pair of startled boxy colorful wood ducks jerked their emerald heads back and forth and flew away landing in some marshy grasses downriver. There was an object in the water. The water, too shallow to flow over, instead rushed around it. It was somewhat covered by the early summer brush. The small pecking black-capped chickadees and three vivid cobalt jays pounding on hard seeds didn't seem to care one bit. The white-headed woodpecker continued rat-a-tat nonstop on a ponderosa.

My family of five drove parallel to the South Santiam River. Then to the Narrows, called that because of the twists and turns and narrow curves. If anyone got car sick, it started here. We passed buildings in Sweet Home that were only lit because of the porch or streetlights. Now heading due east, soon we reached the town of Foster that sits on west end of Foster Lake. At the end of the lake we followed a narrower arm of the long lake for about fifteen miles coming to the tiny community of Cascadia with its own state park at one thousand feet elevation. I could tell we were climbing higher because my ears were popping in and out.

Around 5:30, colors in the sky were appearing from the sunrise. Peachy pink wispy clouds now brightened our drive. We drove past one of our favorite stops called the Mountain House, right before Sheep Creek Bridge.

The Mountain House was a two-story building that had changed since my mother's younger years. She and a date used to drive here for a special night out. Decades earlier, walking up the wide stone steps, they would enter the restaurant and to the left was the lounge. To the right sat a big fireplace with sofas and chairs scattered around.

Now this lodge-like building was a more open-style restaurant. The owners lived upstairs. Available for purchase were sundries on several racks. Casual tables were now for families to sit and eat. But the fireplace still served as a gathering spot. At times we'd stand drinking a chocolate milkshake or hot chocolate, depending on the weather.

Sometimes we would be driving by before noon and stop for lunch. With the food came unusual entertainment. We'd listen to the off-color remarks by their coal-black myna bird who also made some interesting noises. The boys always laughed when the bird made a belching or other crude sound. Usually it happened when someone would walk in the front door. The bird would spout something improper. The last time we'd been there, that crazy bird said, "Bang, bang, bang, bang," all in a row, like shooting a gun. But I had misunderstood. He actually said "dang" four times. My parents didn't appreciate that sometimes that unpredictable bizarre bird would say an almost swear word, like dang or shoot. But the owners couldn't control what the crazy bird would squawk out. Dad promised we'd stop on the way home.

No longer pitch dark, I still needed a flashlight to read my book, *My Friend Flicka*, about a son of a rancher and his mustang horse. Max looked through comic books handing *Superboy* through the open window to Will who asked lots of questions about what it took to become a hero or a crimefighter. He thought he'd like to be Spider-Man when he grew up.

For sixteen cents each, Max had bought *Batman* and *Superman*, true American heroes. I wasn't really into comics. But Batman slightly intrigued me. On the cover he stood all dressed in black and some gray. Only his nose and grimacing mouth showed. His body struggled beneath the weight. He held a large round bomb with fuse burning right above his head. He looked like he was ready to toss it somewhere. The yellow oval emblem with the well-recognized black bat with wings stretched out probably indicated he never needed to introduce himself to anyone. I thumbed through, not reading all of the words in floating bubbles above the comic characters. I just looked at the colorful action drawings. It seemed easy to figure out the plot and ending. We all survived the criminals. Thank you, Batman and sidekick Robin.

It wasn't easy reading. We rocked back and forth, over bumps and around the corners. Mom suggested we not look down but out the side windows. It might prevent carsickness. The pass-through window was open to the truck if we needed anything. Will would pop his head through occasionally making faces. Duke lay on his back between Max and me all stretched out with four short feet flopping. One of us would get an occasional nose nudge. This meant we were overdue for a tummy scratch.

Mom watched carefully for deer that might be moving towards water for their morning fill-up. The headlights lit up a sign and Mom announced, "Trout Creek," as we crossed going into the Willamette National Forest.

Many creeks feed into the South Santiam River— Trout Creek and Boulder Creek, then at Sheep Creek the river veers south and out of our sight. Sheep Creek runs to the right and we crossed Crazy Creek then Lamb Creek. The road sort of did a U-shape over Sheep Creek and Ram Creek then Snow Creek and Hackleman Creek.

Hackleman wasn't that common a name like lamb, sheep, ram and snow. We knew about the name because we lived smack dab in the middle of Hackleman's Grove. Growing up, the neighbors all knew the story about a farmer from Iowa named Abner Hackleman. He came west in 1845 by crossing the plains with his team of oxen. He staked his claim but only stayed one year before going home by packhorse to get his family. He died before returning.

A few years later his son, Abram, located his father's claim. He married a local girl and built a two-story house in the oak grove—now our oak grove. Over one hundred years later that old house sat empty down the street and around the corner. It was surrounded and hidden by giant creaky old oaks. It was haunted. All of the kids knew it. Never once did I go up to that house. Nor did I ever think about trying to break in. A really nifty thing was that Abram's great-great granddaughter Kathy attended the same church we did.

———

I loved the local names such as Shotpooch Butte, Menagerie Wilderness, and Tombstone Pass. Two hours after leaving home, we were coming up to the Santiam Junction, which locals called "The Y." Daylight squeezed between giant pine trees. Tops of the mountain had a rosy glow. This is the intersection where drivers coming from Salem and Portland on Highway 22 met those coming from Albany and Eugene on Highway 20. The pavement and rocks on the shoulders of the highway turn from gray to red. The lava rock used in paving the roads was another indication we were getting closer to the Metolius.

A mountain called Three Fingered Jack was dead ahead. Sunbeams ricocheted off its snowy jagged top. It is over 7,800 feet in elevation. Now we were really climbing. The truck slowed down a bit from the load it towed, our efficient thirteen-foot, one-room home on wheels.

We passed Potato Hill Snow Park on the right and to the left of the road is Lost Lake. We were creeping upwards to the Santiam Pass. Much of the area around the lake is a lava bed created by volcanic activity. It was full of blue water from snow melt. Grasses and reeds were already thick and tall. We'd seen it many times in late summer, almost empty. The lake drains through a large lava tube, really a big hole in the middle of the lake. When it's almost empty it turns marshy surrounded by willows. There are plenty of warning signs about not getting too close to the hole because it is unstable and could break under the weight. By Labor Day weekend the normal eighty-five-acre lake would look more like a pond if any water was even visible. This lake is close to a famous hike called the Pacific Crest Trailhead.

We reached HooDoo Bowl, tip top elevation 5,596 feet. That meant we would be coming up on the Santiam Pass summit soon at 4,817. HooDoo is a volcanic cinder cone, with slopes mostly facing northeast.

I knew the history from my Oregon geography class. I explained knowledgeably to Max that in 1938 a group funded by some men in Bend wanted to build on Three Fingered Jack but could not secure funding for a road. I could see how this wouldn't be allowed because my view showed crags and cliffs and no easy way to get there. Following WWII, the HooDoo ski area was built including lodging and chairlifts.

The three-story main lodge at the base was built in the late 1940s, from WWII surplus structures. It included sleeping quarters for one hundred guests. I remembered that it was threatened by a forest fire in the summer of 1967. It was saved by firefighters using a process of lighting backfires. But an old chairlift with wooden towers burned down.

109

Then a year later the big news was that fire destroyed the two-story lodge one month before our annual first camping trip of the season. Driving by that Memorial Day weekend, we could see the burned pile of the lodge. I'd spent many Saturdays in past winters coming here with my friends Diane, Nancy, Dawn, Barbie and the guys, Jay, John, Norm, Dale, Matt, Jan and Nick, from my youth group at church. HooDoo is perfect for inner tubing down slopes. We'd tie several tubes together in a line. Then fly down the hill, hopefully staying onboard and not falling off or breaking anything. There were many bruised bones and twisted ankles over the years.

To warm up we'd head to the lodge to drink hot cocoa heaped with mini-marshmallows. The fireplace was grand and comforting. A new two-story day lodge was constructed later in the year. It just didn't have same comfy, cozy feeling.

If you drew an imaginary line along the mountain range, the first mountain is Jefferson. Then Three Finger Jack, with HooDoo Butte just slightly east. Then Mount Washington, which is in a pretty straight line with the North, Middle and South Sisters in the distance.

Seeing the closest mountain, Mount Washington at 7,794 feet, the glaciers in the deep crevasses glowed pastel pink in the morning sunlight. Blue Lake was so far below we could barely see it.

The biggest and most popular recreational area is Suttle Lake, named after pioneer John Settle. Bouncing sunbeams looked like shimmery diamonds on the smooth water. John Settle was one of the organizers of the Willamette Valley and Cascade Mountain Military Road project in 1866. While on a hunting trip, Mr. Settle found the lake. It bears his name even though misspelled. Dad and his fishing buddies enjoyed catching kokanee, brown trout, whitefish and crayfish at this deep lake.

After a mile or two, the roadway veered south. We started downhill as Dad picked up speed, having about seven miles to go until the cut-off on The Metolius River/Camp Sherman road.

Dad decided since we'd left so early, our first stop would be the Metolius River headwaters. Then onward to select the best location to park our travel trailer for the week. What is so neat about the headwaters is that the river doesn't just trickle out of the ground; it surges from two springs as if it were shot from a fire hose.

As soon as we turned off Highway 20, Duke jumped up, looking out the side window with his nose sticking out. He ran across both Max and me, bouncing from one window to the other. He knew exactly where we were.

Finally reaching the parking lot, we grabbed our jackets, clambered over the safety barrier Dad had created and crawled out of the truck. It felt good to stretch our legs. We all stopped as Mom read the panel at the trailhead, just as she did each time we visited: "Down this path a full-sized river, the Metolius, flows ice cold from huge springs. The springs appear to originate beneath Black Butte. However, geologists say this is misleading and believe the springs have their origin in the Cascade Mountains to the west. The unusual fault that created Green Ridge is thought to have brought the springs to the surface, thus releasing the beautiful Metolius River." She added her own theory that really no one knows for sure where it starts.

I love the smell of the fragrant pines. Walking along the trail was easy even though the air is thinner and drier.

We were now at 3,000 elevation. The fresh clean smell reminded me of Pine Sol Mom used at home for cleaning. Sometimes the area smelled like butterscotch. It reminded me of the round butterscotch candies Dad ate when he quit smoking. I stood really close and stuck my nose close to a ponderosa pine. This time of year, it smelled a bit like a vanilla candle.

The familiar path took a gentle turn. Mom added that the Metolius is a spring-dominated arm of the Deschutes River. The river is a sacred place for the Wasco, Warm Springs and Northern Paiute of the Confederated Tribes of the Warm Springs. They have hunted, gathered, and fished from the river for thousands of years.

Will asked if we'd see any Indians. Mom answered, "Not this trip." She continued by explaining that the turquoise water of the twenty-nine-mile-long river flows north from the base of Black Butte, passing tiny Camp Sherman and through eleven Forest Service campgrounds. After it passes Candle Creek, the river hooks around Castle Rock, a nine-million-year-old volcanic plug, on the south and the Warm Springs Reservation to the north. We'd stayed at Warm Springs several times and they had teepees for rent. The Metolius then flows southeast into Lake Billy Chinook, a reservoir. Then it joins the Deschutes and Crooked Rivers.

The Metolius River gushed noisily, full-grown from the spectacular springs as its headwaters. "Most rivers begin from mountaintops that have gathered snow that melts into little gullies that form streams. Then those streams join to feed bigger streams that then flow into a river, but not the Metolius," Mom said, almost like she stood in awe of this special place. Enough of the geology and history lessons.

We were almost there. Sloping down and rounding the gentle turn there was the familiar sight I never got tired of seeing. Crystal clear blue water, lush green meadow, tall trees and a mountain all in one snapshot.

The five of us walked the dirt path. Mom and Dad side by side, about as wide as the path. This almost secret area wasn't as well known as the Camp Sherman store or campgrounds. Max and Will led the way as Mom said, rounding the corner with the river and Mt. Jefferson in the distance, "Don't get too close to the water. It's too early to get wet." Will turned and scowled at Mom, clearly indicating he had every intention of going in the river. Then she said one of her many momisms, "Your face is going to freeze like that."

I was right behind him with the parents lagging, holding hands. My parents did this often, held hands, I mean. The only sounds were our feet crunching the pine needles. We'd been here many times in the past. Each visit was special in its own way.

Max and Will raced and arrived first. I was seconds behind. The boys slowed down, running onto the gentle bank, through low bushes. Both abruptly stopped at the shallow water's edge. I saw Max grab Will, still facing forward. They backed up the hill, with Max yelling, "DAAAAAAAAD."

I arrived next with my parents close behind and didn't need to go any closer. I saw one foot with a white sock like jocks wear. The other foot still had on a gray sneaker. The feet were among the green shrubbery and poking out of the shallow water. Without even realizing it, my left hand grasped the gold cross hanging around my neck, a gift from my parents on my thirteenth birthday.

Making a straight line from my chin to waist and across from shoulder to shoulder in the air, my mother observed and said, "Were not Catholic, Anne."

"I know, Mom, but it looks cool when the nuns do it in "The Sound of Music."

By now both boys were back up the bank standing behind Dad. I saw something shiny on the ground. Bending over, I plucked a quarter nestled in some pine needles. I stuck it in my pocket. I always picked up a coin if I saw it.

Glancing around I saw several beer bottles scattered around in the dirt. A few were in the grass. There were one or two in the river, but I wasn't looking in that direction again.

Our good moods and humor deteriorated. I felt a little panicky and whispered, "What if whoever did this is still around?" Dad lowered his voice, "We didn't see any other vehicles in the parking lot." He was right, no one else had been in the lot. I had a sensation overcome me, a feeling of helplessness. What could we do? What should we do? My brothers were silent, the quietest ever.

Dad calmly and softly said to Mom, "Drive to the Camp Sherman store. There probably won't be anybody around this early. There's a telephone booth there. Call the Jefferson County Sheriff's Office. Tell them to come to the headwaters."

Now, Mom grew up with eight brothers and sisters in the Dust Bowl and Depression in Nebraska before immigrating to Oregon. She pretty much rolled with anything that came her way. She never really freaked out or yelled. Perturbed but not angry.

She replied quietly almost like in her church voice, "I will take Annette and William with me. You and Maxwell stay here and wait for help. After I make the call, we'll be back." She only used our formal names when she was agitated or trying to get our attention. She said my brothers formal names more often. I'd only heard her use

114

"Annette" three times in seven years since I'd announced years ago that I wanted to be called Kate but settled on Anne.

Max whispered, "Why are we whispering?"

Will blurted out his normal voice, "Ya, it's not like a dead body can hear us." Anne could see that their dad almost laughed. It did slightly lighten the seriousness of the moment.

The three of us, plus doxie Duke, walked silently as fast as we could up the gentle slope. It was about a quarter of a mile to the truck, still the only vehicle in the lot. I knew Will was about to pop with questions.

We all jumped in the cab, Duke, too. Mom drove as fast as she dared on the dirt road for several miles. It seemed to take forever. I asked her if she felt scared. She replied, "No, not really but more like nervous or uneasy." I thought she was brave.

When the rustic Camp Sherman store came into sight, parked in front was a black car with a cool red stripe down the side. "I hope that's the store owner's car," she mumbled. She pounded on the white door. Then pounded again, harder this time. No one answered. She hurried to the phone booth leaving the accordion door open. She flipped through the one-inch thick telephone book, page after page. She found the number for the Sheriff's office. Her shaking fingers seemed to take forever as she dialed the numbers, round and round on the silvery wall-mounted rotary phone.

Deputy Malloy unlocked the door to the Sheriff's office. He smelled the welcoming aroma of coffee. He knew Sheriff Perkins had been in early and already departed for another round of budget meetings. Poor guy, he thought.

The Sheriff had left a hand-written note that Detective Walker called in sick. He guessed probably food poisoning from a bad burger the day before. Malloy was glad he'd opted for a BLT from the same questionable drive-in joint. He picked up the stack of reports that he'd completed the previous day. He double-checked them. He felt relieved he'd finished. Who knew what today might bring their way.

The phone on his desk rang. "Jefferson County Sherriff's Office, Deputy Malloy speaking."

Since the car window was down, I heard my mother say, "I am calling from the phone booth at Camp Sherman store. There is something in the river at the headwaters of the Metolius. Could you please send someone to help?"

Malloy said, "Ma'am, do you mean a deer or coyote?"

I heard Mom reply, "No. One foot is wearing a sock and the other a shoe. It is not moving."

The deputy thought to himself, "Great, just great, maybe a drunken college student too close to the edge, slipped in and hit his head on a rock" but instead evenly replied, "I am leaving Madras now, but it will take about an hour, Ma'am. Our Camp Sherman resident deputy is on vacation."

Resident Deputy Jensen Foster would be returning Sunday and not a day earlier. He normally would have been the first one to respond since he lived in the area.

Even though nothing was confirmed, Deputy Malloy called the commissioner's office. He asked that a message be delivered immediately to Sheriff Perkins explaining the situation. Perkins might appreciate having an excuse to leave the budget meeting. A body in a river wasn't an everyday occurrence in their county.

He locked the office door, sprang into his white Plymouth Belvedere, and sped southwest with red and blue lights flashing. He didn't need the siren blaring this early in the morning.

Twenty-six miles and only fifteen minutes later, he was making excellent time. He turned from Highway 97 at Redmond onto Highway 20 heading west to Sisters. His mind wandered, speculating about the situation ahead and "what iffing" a lot of scenarios. He'd run off the checklist in his mind: Confirm body. Secure the area. Interview witnesses. Take photos. Detective Walker would call for assistance. They would all be involved in the crime scene investigation.

Speeding through the small western village of Sisters at this time of the morning was a breeze. But he slowed anyway, mostly watching for deer instead of people. He picked up speed on the flat terrain where ten miles farther west he turned off the highway onto the Metolius River/Camp Sherman Road. From here he knew he had just three and a half miles to go. He'd made good time, only forty minutes.

———

In the meantime, Sheriff Perkins notified Sheriff Sholes of Deschutes County. With the counties next to each other and both short of staff, they often shared deputies. Interestingly, the Deschutes County Sheriff's Office in Bend was closer than Jefferson County's headquarters in Madras. But neither men were responsible for setting the county lines in 1914.

Sheriff Sholes was commonly called "Poe" and had been elected in 1953. He was born in Bend and lived in the area his whole life. He knew a lot about everything and everyone. After graduating from high school, he spent time in the Marines then returned to the area. He was hired as a patrolman with the Bend Police Department, then he went to work as deputy. He stepped into the sheriff position when Sheriff McCauley decided not to run for another term.

For the first few years, Poe and his wife, who was the jail cook, lived in a little room above the jail. He was infamous. These two sheriffs were friends and fortunately for Perkins, Poe had years of valuable experience.

Sheriff Perkins contacted the lousy-feeling Detective Walker apprising him of the situation. Puny or not, they would be needing him ASAP. Walker slowly got up, took a hot shower and got dressed. He headed west as fast as he dared.

I asked Mom, "Sooooo, when's the Fuzz coming?" Trying to lighten the situation totally backfired. She replied firmly that the word fuzz wasn't an appropriate word to be used about hard-working law enforcement officers. She didn't care if it was a popular slang word. She was probably a little overly sensitive about it since her dad been a sheriff in a county in Nebraska. She wasn't really keen on popular words and phrases, and certainly didn't like the word "Jeez." She also didn't like it when the brothers used the word "cooties," a kind of an unseen force that only uncool people had. Or the word "fink," a taleteller. Mom wasn't cool; nice but not cool.

Mom told Will and me that the deputy was on his way. He would take care of everything. Knowing we were nervous and that I was about ready to burst into tears for a variety of reasons—the overall "body in the river" episode, along with teenage girl hormones, plus being justifiably scolded, she said for us each to take a nice deep breath of the clear fresh air. We all did it together. In and out, in and out and once more, in and out. It was like Will and I were in gym class.

She walked us down a slight hill to the wooden plank bridge. In the turquoise river she pointed out dozens of large trout hanging around waiting for somebody to toss them some bread chunks or popcorn. Even though the sign plainly read, "DO NOT FEED THE FISH OR ANY WILDLIFE," it was clear these fish expected some treats.

I noticed lots of tall dark green bushes on both sides of the bridge, with hot pink starting to peek through wild rosebuds. Being late spring only two roses were blooming. It was the same pink that was used in my bedroom painted with pastel pink walls, white bedspread with matching white furniture and hot pink wild rose-colored pillows.

I asked why we weren't returning to Dad and Max. She replied that there really wasn't any hurry. It would take the deputy a while driving as fast as he could. Obviously, she didn't want us around a body in the river—alive, unconscious, or otherwise.

Will pointed to a movement in the blue sky. An osprey flew overhead. It dropped quickly then for a second or two hovered like a helicopter then splashed feet first into the water. It rose up with a medium size fish in its talons.

Mom announced it was 7:20 a.m., like we needed to remember this for some reason. Somebody inside the store turned the Closed sign in the window to Open. Will said, "This is a pretty neat way to start a vacation." Mom and I looked at each other. I noticed the black car disappeared. I hadn't heard it leave.

―――――

At the headwaters, Dad and Max were just standing like statues guarding an entrance to a castle. They both glanced down several times, not really staring, just checking, and then wide-eyed at each other. They waited patiently for some movement or the body to get up. That didn't happen.

Max asked, "Dad, what's happening? Would officers Malloy and Reed from Adam 12 be coming?" We all enjoyed the action police show but especially Max and Will. "How long would it take for the police to get there?" He was full of questions that Dad answered, "I don't know; No, this wasn't like Adam 12; and I don't know how long it will take them to arrive, son."

Max was getting restless. He paced a while looking around. He yelled, "There's a silver flashlight over here, Dad!"

"Don't touch it, Max!"

―――――

The four of us, counting Duke, drove away from the store and returned to the headwater's parking lot. As we got out of the truck a white sheriff's car pulled in. It came to an abrupt stop next to our rig. A tall, dark, and very handsome deputy said to Mom, "Ma'am, I am Deputy Malloy. I'll be right back and please stay put." He pulled out a black notebook and pen. He logged in 7:45 a.m.

He stated that before they spoke further, he needed to do one thing. He returned to the car. He pulled out heavy roll of barricade tape. The yellow tape was printed in bold with the wording, "CRIME SCENE DO NOT CROSS." He stretched it out then tied it to the two posts opposite each other at the entrance to the parking lot. There was only one way in and one way out. We were locked in.

Will looked Deputy Malloy up and down. We both noticed the totally cool hat, gleaming star-shaped badge, holstered gun, shiny black boots and khaki uniform. Will whispered to me, "Did he say his name is Deputy Malloy?" I hadn't caught his name, being quite taken with his good looks and reassuring smile. Deputy Tall, Dark and Handsome removed his sunglasses. I could see his dreamy blue eyes.

The deputy returned and he and Mom stepped away from us. They spoke quietly between themselves. "Ma'am, can you tell me when you arrived did you see any other vehicles in the parking lot? Did you see anyone walking on the trail? When you reached the headwaters what time was it? What did you see? Did you notice any evidence on the ground? What size shoe do you wear?"

He told her before we were released to go that he needed to ask each one of us these questions. She understood. She answered, "Around 6:45. No, we hadn't seen any other cars or people. We saw beer bottles, that's all. No one touched a thing. And we only saw one white sock and one gray shoe, nothing else."

Malloy took each of us aside and went through the same list of questions. The only thing that wasn't consistent was us answering the exact time of day. We didn't notice. Mom told him all of our shoe sizes.

Will turned to me and announced he wanted to be a deputy when he grew up. And drive a fast car with flashing lights. Maybe I should also become a police officer or at the least, the wife of one.

Driving in, Malloy observed tire tracks in the soft dirt. It had been below thirty-two degrees creating dew on the ground. That was a plus and helpful. There was a set of tracks from the family's truck and trailer. Now two sets from the same vehicle and tag-along trailer. Then a third set. Typically, the detective would measure, but he'd do it for Walker. He knew Detective Walker would be very interested in this. Also, there was a lone tire track. This indicated a motorcycle. He'd note these observations in his black notebook eventually.

He'd take the yellow roll with him to the headwaters. Returning to the trunk, he pulled out his new Orvis hip waders. He figured they would come in handy for more than fly-fishing.

In his parting remarks, he thanked each of us for our cooperation. And that he'd soon return with my dad and brother. There would be one more thing he must do before removing the yellow tape allowing us to leave. We were to stay right where we were and not disturb any of the tire tracks or other footprints.

He could already tell that this family had unfortunately stumbled across a traumatic event. But he still needed to follow protocol, getting as many answers as possible.

As Deputy Malloy walked away out of hearing distance, Will asked Mom if she noticed his name—Malloy? Was he related to Officer Malloy on Adam 12? She thought not.

On the path Malloy spotted a book of matches. He left them there for Detective Walker but snapped a few photos. In the dirt along the path was a tree limb that looked out of place. He took a few more photos. He noticed blood and maybe some hair embedded in the upper section of the branch. It looked sturdy like a base-ball bat.

Evidently Max's eyes bugged out when Deputy Malloy introduced himself. Then looked at Dad with a "I thought so" look. Dad would laugh, later telling us Max's reaction when Deputy Malloy explained to Max that no, he wasn't a brother of Officer Malloy on Adam 12. I am not sure Max or Will believed him.

Malloy asked Dad and Max the same questions he asked us. Max excitedly pointed out the almost hidden flashlight adding quickly that he hadn't touched it. Malloy would leave it there until Walker arrived. He got the same answers, which he wasn't surprised about.

Again, the deputy visually scoured around the area noticing mashed down grasses, broken branches on bushes. He cordoned off the area in yellow tape. The deputy could see from the bank that one foot only wore a sock and the other still had on a gray sneaker. He didn't enter the river.

He left his waders and walked back with Dad and Max. He radioed the Sheriff and confirmed that a body was indeed in the Metolius River headwaters. Perkins indicated he was fifteen minutes out and the detective would arrive within the hour.

Malloy explained to Dad that it was standard procedure to search any vehicles at a crime scene. A crime scene. We stood there in a crime scene. Dad and Mom understood. The brothers were intrigued. I felt helpless and heartbroken.

We moved away from the truck as Deputy Malloy looked all through the cab. He opened the glovebox and looked under the front seat. Then he opened the tailgate seeing all the camping gear. He spent quite a bit of time looking through our stuff. Or so it seemed. He even had Dad unlock the trailer house door. Malloy stepped in. He didn't make Dad unload the bikes. He did see something on the floor but didn't mention it, since it had nothing to do with his case.

Instinctively, he knew this unlucky family had been at the wrong place at the wrong time. He spoke to Dad asking our whereabout if needed. He reminded Dad that if any of us thought of anything to contact him directly at the Sheriff's office. It was unlikely we'd hear from them again.

With our family reunited and back in proper seating order in the truck, Dad told us comfortingly, "Now, we are not going to let this ruin our vacation. The sheriff will take care of it. We are going to have a good time. Maybe we'll hear more about it later but maybe not." It sounded like Dad was trying to convince himself and us. Max and Will were full of questions. Dad and Mom explained they didn't have the answers. This would be the end of this discussion. Or so I hoped. I shivered as I thought about the sneaker and felt queasy.

———

One hundred miles west, Coop pulled into the driveway of his cousin's home in south Salem. He sat in the driveway for a while. He couldn't remember how he'd gotten there. He hurt all over. His twenty-seven-year-old cousin, Heather, spotted him from the living room window. As he walked to the door, she opened it. She gasped when she saw his puffy black and blue eye and blood on his chin which she suspected came from a bloody nose. He had small puncture wounds in his face. Was there a patch of his hair missing?

She threw her arms around him. All she could say was, "Oh Coop" over and over again. He nestled his head on her soft shoulder. Now he didn't feel so alone. Then he thought about Rusty's mom. He felt even worse. Safely in Heather's secure embrace, he sobbed. Heartbroken, so did she.

She led him into their cozy family room. Coop felt at home in this room. He'd known his cousin and her brother Clay longer than any friends. The safe, comforting room had been added on from the dining room a few years earlier by her husband and his father. The project took them an entire year. She admitted that it had been worth the bothersome dust all over the house. The wood stove wasn't needed this time of year. The cedar tongue-and-groove ceiling looked outdoorsy.

He sat on the gold-flecked sofa, silent. His elbows were on his knees and face in his hands. For some reason he thought about his only two cousins. He remembered his mom always said that cousins are the first friends in your life. He had no siblings, so they were more than cousins.

She filled an icepack, warmed a washcloth, and got him a glass of water and four aspirin in about two minutes flat. She cleaned his face. He croaked out, "Thank you." She wrapped him in a cozy afghan her sister-in-law had made. She sat beside him, holding his hand, totally quiet. She was a great listener and the most caring, nurturing woman he knew, except for his mom and M2.

She mentioned he should have the wounds on his face looked at. What if they got infected from the filthy object that caused the damage? He declined to see a doctor. Heather asked if she could contact her neighbor Marian, who was a nurse. Coop agreed to that.

She told him when he was ready to talk to let her know. She made him drink cup after cup of hot tea. Even though cousins, she seemed more like a friend. Her six-year-old twin first graders wouldn't be home until mid-afternoon. It was their last day of school. They'd have several hours to themselves. The fifth member of the family, golden retriever Jasper, hopped up on the sofa. Jasper placed her soft head on his lap. Petting her, he cried even harder. Heather let him be.

Deputy Malloy removed the tape as the family drove out of the crime scene. He wrote in his logbook he released the vehicle at 8:50 a.m. according to his watch. Dad could see in the rearview mirror another car arriving.

Sheriff Perkins parked outside the tape and got out of his vehicle. Standing together, Malloy filled him in. Perkins wished Sheriff Tom, who had also been the county coroner for years before becoming sheriff for one year, still lived locally to help out. Perkins changed into his water-proof boots. Detective Walker parked beside the Sheriff's rig and slipped his waterproof knee-highs over his shoes. The three walked toward the headwaters.

Only being elected in January, Perkins was aware he was lacking in terms of actual crime scene expertise. When it came to examining the site, he was glad to take his clues from people who, although theoretically his subordinates, were far more experienced at the tasks at hand. He was glad they were on the job.

They passed several NO HUNTING signs. A covey of mountain quail shot into the air flying towards the open meadow in the distance. There was physical evidence that would be processed.

Reaching the flat dirt area slightly above the headwa-ters, Malloy put on his waders. Before entering the river,

Detective Walker stood intently studying the scene. He observed broken grasses running along the top edge of bank and continuing down, indicating something heavy, presumably the corpse, had been shoved to the edge or left to roll down the bank. Multiple grasses and low-lying brush had been mashed down. He saw the broken limbs from bushes.

Walker snapped photos of the body from the upper vantage point. He did a quick sketch of the scene in his notebook. He entered the water to view the body with Malloy trailing behind. The male was not unconscious; he was dead. Walker took dozens of photos of the fully clothed body. The water flowed around, but not over the body. Walker reached inside the jacket and jean's pockets searching for ID but finding none.

Whoever smashed his face didn't want him recognized. They'd need a forensic artist to help identify the poor cuss unless they found some identification.

Sheriff Perkins offered to walk back to the car to call the county's medical examiner, Dr. Sellers. He lived in Redmond, almost on the county-shared border. They were fortunate that he could divvy his time between two counties. Only a medical examiner could perform an autopsy and Perkins guessed this would be needed. A medical examiner was almost always required to be a physician and Dr. Sellers had been for decades.

Finishing with the body and exiting the river, Malloy pointed to the silver flashlight and stated that it hadn't been touched. Walker replied, "Hopefully there are some useful prints on it."

Always meticulous with details, Walker used a separate notebook for every investigation. When he arrived, he logged in his time at 9:37 a.m. and entitled it, "Metolius Headwaters." He'd put each notation in chronological order.

Walker and Malloy put numbered evidence markers where they found beer bottles. Walker took photos of each bottle then documented each in his notebook. He walked into the grass, retrieved a bottle and left a marker. He pulled one from the river and noted its whereabouts in his book. He used a marker on a tall thin rod and poked it into the river bottom. He took more photos.

Next he found the butt of a cigarette. Another marker and photos were taken. With gloves on, he picked it up. The minuscule remains looked peculiar so he lifted it to his nose. It was a joint of marijuana. Walker opened a plastic baggie and dropped it in.

While Walker was doing his job of putting down evidence markers, taking crime scene photos, and collecting evidence, Malloy was finding and measuring footprints.

There were obvious signs of a struggle and some blood. Walker marked red droplets found in the dirt and pine needles. They found no identification in the area.

Keeping his head down, Walker searched the wider area for evidence. Walking into the forest he rambled around trees, through brush, limbs, stepping on pinecones, and needles. He noticed a red-and-white-checked handkerchief all wadded up. Before he collected it, he placed a marker and took plenty of photos. It felt heavy. It was still wet. He dropped it into a plastic bag then secured the top. He wrote the description in his black notebook along with where and the time he found it. Both he and Malloy paced out the area searching carefully for anything out of the ordinary.

Sheriff Perkins returned reporting that Dr. Sellers would be there within the hour.

They finished around the river for the time being. Heading back to the parking lot to wait for Dr. Sellers, on the path Perkins pointed out the book of matches with "D&D" printed on the top. Walker placed a marker and took photos. Then he picked up the matches in his gloved hand and placed it in a small plastic bag. He marked the location and time on the outside of the bag. Maybe they'd get some useful fingerprints from the matchbook.

They all knew the reputation of the D&D. It was a classic diner-style watering hole and the oldest bar in Bend. Originally it had been named "Double D." They were known for making powerful drinks, and food to kill a hangover. Apparently now it was being frequented by questionable characters.

Not far from the matches they'd just found, Malloy pointed out the branch he'd seen earlier. It was clearly out of place. It had hair and blood on it. Another marker and lots of photos were taken before it was carefully removed. It would be delivered to Walker's vehicle. Each step on the pathway the three looked for clues. They found more footprints. He took dozens of pictures.

At the parking lot Perkins said, "Let's walk it in three-foot intervals. That's the most organized grid search." There were multiple sets of footprints by the truck tire tracks. The family's footprints were the easiest to determine.

Walker took snaps of footprints in the parking lot. They walked the entire parking lot looking for anything. Beside one set of tire tracks was a black cloth bag. There were two sets of footprints by the single tire tracks, clearly a motorcycle. Malloy discovered a dull coin partially lodged under a rock. He pulled out his Swiss Army knife and used the tip to carefully pry it away from its resting place. It was a Canadian nickel.

"Hey, I've got something over here. I need an evidence marker," Malloy announced. Walker entered the coin information in his black notebook. He measured each set of tire tracks in the parking lot with his ruler tape. This would help them determine the tire tread, size and brand.

We were quiet as Dad drove over the lumpy bumpy dirt road to Riverside Campground. The only people in the area was a group who had pitched two large green tents back in the trees. Dad found us the perfect spot along the river. There was no running water, but there was a wooden forest-service brown outhouse. We didn't really like to stay at the opposite end of the river. The forest service had official campgrounds and constructed campsites. We wanted to rough it and be as close as possible to the river.

We had a certain process and tasks that we all followed. Dad had created a list probably left over from him being in the army in WWII. Dad would pull out leveling jacks. He'd do his routine setting up the outside. Mom worked on the inside. We'd help by setting up chairs and folding tables. Simple. Follow this list each time and we'd be fine.

In this instance Will jumped in the river, wading in the forty-eight-degree water up to his knees. Max and I were helping out with our tasks and anxious to get in the river, too.

Mom unlocked the trailer door and we heard "Oh fiddlesticks" from inside. The fridge door had somehow come open. Two luscious homemade pies lay upside down on the floor. One cherry, my favorite, and one blueberry, Dad and Will's favorite. Mom, exasperated about the loss, was about to throw them away. Both boys insisted they would clean up. They sat on the floor and ate both pies. Gulping down the upside-down blueberry pie, Will's pacing slowed. When Max called him a pantywaist, Will socked him pretty good.

Mom told us not to wander too far from camp. She was understandably concerned about a possible murderer hiding behind any tree. When Max said, "Don't sweat it, Mom." She told him to sit down and read a comic book. I paced, waiting for Peggy to arrive. Then I'd have my best friend to hang around with. I could hardly wait to tell her about what had happened earlier that morning.

After the trailer was set up, Mom and I set lawn chairs in the shallow river. We dangled our feet to cool off. Then switching to lounge chairs, our bottoms touched the freezing water. I glanced at her closed eyes. Her soft, wavy black hair moved ever-so-slightly in the breeze. She looked so pretty. I hoped she could tune out what happened earlier, but I knew she couldn't. Her soft creamy skin glowed with just a touch of red lipstick still on her smile. I wished I had her head of black hair instead of my blonde. Max was lucky. His hair was the same color as Mom's.

I got bored and walked back and forth waiting as patiently as possible. Chipmunks chased each other round and round the base of a tree. Then up one side and down the other side. They were so cute with the black and white stripes, tails standing straight up. I thought about the body in the water and wondered what was going on.

They weren't completely finished in the parking lot when Dr. Sellers' two-vehicle entourage arrived like a speeding funeral procession.

Sheriff Perkins shook hands and greeted him by name, plus the deputy from Deschutes county. Sheriff Sholes assigned Deputy Bruce Fountain to assist as needed. He looked like a six-foot four inch, two hundred thirty-five-pound teddy bear. His only fault they could find was that he was color-blind. When the Sheriff told him to stop at the only blue house on a particular street to pick something up for him, the story goes that he drove up and down the street for quite some time because all the houses looked brown. The yarn had been exaggerated over the years and still made for a good chuckle at Fountain's expense. He just shrugged his shoulders and laughed it off.

Dr. Seller's vehicle was distinctive. Three years earlier he purchased his first new vehicle ever in his life. It had a snazzy turquoise body. The entire top portion including around the windows was stark white. His 1966 Chevy Suburban Carryall worked well for his needs like transporting bodies when the funeral home wasn't able to assist. Working for two counties with hundreds of miles of territory, the population was low and help not always available. The right-hand door at the rear made for easy access to the back. He kept it immaculate inside and out. The chrome wheels gleamed. He had off-road tires mounted for four-wheel drive, if needed. It had a four-speed manual transmission.

He covered the floor carpet with plastic mats. He'd left the clear plastic coating on the passenger front seat and the entire bench seat in the back. He'd ordered a heavy-duty black plastic mat to cover the entire back area. He liked the square, boxy look—utilitarian. The only problem was how recognizable it had become. When people spotted it, they associated it with sorrow and tragedy. But that was his job.

———

Since it had been determined that Walker would be lead investigator at the scene, he added in his notebook the time of the medical examiner and additional deputy's arrival at the headwaters at 11:17 a.m.

Dr. Victor Sellers, Medical Examiner, took his responsibilities seriously. His function was to search for a truthful, logical, and scientifically unbiased statement of the cause and manner of death of an individual. Would it be homicide, suicide, or occurring under suspicious or unknown circumstances? Was it resulting from an unlawful use of a controlled substances, or the use or abuse of chemicals or toxic agents? Was it accidental or following an injury? He would be the one to answer these questions eventually.

He was a well-respected veteran. In his early fifties he looked like he just stepped out of the television program, "The High Chaparral." A partially obscured leather buckle on his belt probably held up his Levi's. Maybe he'd drunk a few too many beers over the years. He had seven pairs of bootcut jeans, a different one for each day of the week. Today he wore a leather mahogany-colored vest over a tan button-down long sleeve-shirt. One would only see his silver gray, comb-over receding hairline when he removed his Stetson, which wasn't often. Some called him a curmudgeon and somewhat aloof. He was professional and really didn't care what the general public thought; he had a serious job to do.

After slipping on his knee-high boots, all five walked to the headwaters. He pulled on rubberized gloves that touched the rolled-up sleeves at his elbows.

"Doc V" waded into the river. Most called him that instead of his actual name, Dr. Sellers. It started years ago when he proved some shoddy police office's findings erroneous with his detailed results and conclusions. Even though it might take him longer than some others to announce the outcome, he prided himself on his thoroughness. He knew it could mean life or death to someone. They nicknamed him Doc V for valiant or victory or some crazy nonsense. But it had stuck.

Once he got a good look by walking around the body, he asked Walker for his black bag that sat on the riverbank. Stepping into the water, Walker held the bag as Doc V pulled out instruments, poking and prodding the body submerged in shallow water.

Doc V asked Deputy Fountain to retrieve and bring down the gurney from the back of his Carryall. He dismissed Walker and motioned for him to return to the river's edge. Doc V removed the sock from the left foot. Then the shoe and sock on the other foot. He noted that the feet and toes weren't blue from the pooling of blood, so hadn't been in the water for a long time.

While Doc V conducted his preliminary examination, Walker and Malloy tenaciously canvassed opposite sides of the river, walking about a half mile searching for the missing gray sneaker. Fountain offered to walk the main path again.

There was no need for the doctor to stay in the freezing water any longer. Walker and Malloy returned with no further evidence. Doc V told Walker, with Malloy and Fountain standing beside him, that unofficially he saw obvious signs of head trauma. Broken nose. Probably broken bones. He suspected massive internal injuries. He couldn't determine the exact time of death but guessed between 1 and 5:30 a.m. He would drive the body to the mortuary and would need to perform an autopsy to determine the exact cause of death. In his estimation, it could be several things. With all the beer bottles, obviously alcohol was a factor. Walker interjected, "Possible drugs, too." They'd already bagged the remains of a joint.

Walker asked if Sheriff Perkins could contact a forensic artist, Detective Menetz, who he knew worked in the Valley. Since they found no ID, this man could really help to identify the victim by creating a drawing of the face.

Doc V and two deputies carefully removed the victim from the water to a plastic tarp on the riverbank. They respectfully, almost reverently, loaded the body into a body bag, zipping it up. Doc V, always mindful that even though now remains of a person, it still had been someone's loved one. Then the same three carried the body and lifted it onto the gurney. They had some distance to go with him. And they'd be pushing uphill.

With everyone back at the parking lot, the body was loaded in the back of the Doc's Carryall. He stripped off his gloves. Perkins and Walker stood nearby while Malloy and Fountain searched the parking lot one more time.

"What can you tell us?" Perkins asked.

"My visual exam concludes: Male. Caucasian. Probably between sixteen and twenty-three years of age. Dead several hours. Broken nose. Probably broken bones. Can't determine the exact time of death but maybe between 1 and 5 or 6 a.m. Appears he was killed there and rolled down. He does have severe head injuries and several smaller puncture wounds around his right temple. That's it for now fellas. I can start the autopsy tomorrow."

They needed to identify the victim as soon as possible and needed help to do it.

A car came barreling down the road generating its own mini-dust storm. It slowed and the driver pulled onto the soft shoulder. Walker recognized the vehicle and thought to himself, "Crap, what did I do to deserve this? How did word get out so quickly?"

A man stepped out of the car, waving enthusiastically in their direction. It was a reporter from the *Bend Bulletin*. And not Walker's favorite person. But he would need the newspaper's cooperation to get the victim's photo out to the public.

The Sheriff muttered, "Play nice. We have a short window to get the photo into the newspaper for Sunday's edition." Then he said words Walker loved to hear, "I'll do you a favor, I'll handle him for now."

Perkins heard Shelton Pugh's southern nasally tenor plea, "Hey Sheriff Perkins, do you have a moment? Can you tell me what's going on?"

Perkins got juvenile devilish delight saying the reporter's last name. Pugh, like a pew in the church or pee-u. This guy's reputation was in the toilet. Most had heard through the grapevine that Pugh had been fired from several jobs in bigger towns for overpromising and underdelivering. And he had a sneaky weaselly look. He reminded him of a short President Nixon but with a narrower jawline. The new president had taken office the same month as he had—January.

The reporter appeared to be in his mid-to-late-forties. He probably dyed his greasy hair because it was just way too black, obsidian black, solid black. Then it was slicked back and always looked perfect. Perkins had never seen it move, even during a press conference on a very windy morning. It was probably a toupée. In Perkins' book, Pugh held the same ranking as the county commissioners—at the very bottom.

In an attempt to head off the pesky reporter, Perkins sauntered toward him, meeting him in the middle of the road.

"This is a crime scene, Pugh. You shouldn't be here." Perkins said, insincerely courteous. The conversation ping-ponged back and forth.

"Is that a body bag they loaded?"

"You know I can't comment on an active investigation."

"Is the victim male or female?"

"You can dream up whatever you want, but I can't officially comment right now."

"Who found the body?"

"No comment."

"Did a local person discover the body?"

"Privileged information."

"Is there any indication how the person died?" Pugh pushed harder.

"Mr. PEEUUU, my deputies are conducting an investigation and you are close to interfering with it. We have serious work to do. But I promise you this. When we have some news, I will let the *Bulletin* know first before calling a press conference."

If all worked according to plan, Walker would deliver a photo to be shared with the public asking for their help in identifying the deceased. No other news would be provided at that time. But Pugh didn't need all these details now. Perkins just wanted Pugh off his back. "Now, GET OUT OF HERE."

Pugh, halfway sarcastically apologetic, said, "Jeeeeez, thanks a lot Sheriff Perkins. I'm only trying to do my job. Freedom of the press, and all that, you know." His irritating accent, maybe Texan or farther east, transported

Perkins back to his elementary school days when some ditz scraped fingernails down a chalkboard.

"And I don't have a problem with you or freedom of the press, as long as you stay out of our way and it doesn't interfere with our work. Now are you going to leave well enough alone for a few days or sit in the back of my vehicle for the next half hour or so, PEEEEUUU?" Perkins childishly drew out his last name again.

"Okay, fine, I'm going. I will call you Sunday if I don't hear from you before then."

Perkins ended the conversation saying, "You will definitely hear from us by Sunday." He turned and walked back to the parking lot crime scene.

Chuckling to himself, Perkins speculated that if the forensic artist were to draw a caricature of Pugh, he might end up like the cartoon character Snidely Whiplash. His children used to watch Rocky & Bullwinkle cartoons on Saturday mornings. Whiplash was the villain and arch enemy of well-meaning, but somewhat dim-witted Canadian Mountie, Dudley Do-Right. Pugh just needed a handlebar moustache and a black top hat and he and Snidely would be identical twins.

Perkins received a call. The answer was yes. The forensic artist Walker knew currently was in another part of the state but would be there tomorrow afternoon. They badly needed him to compose a photo for them to use to help ID the victim.

Sheriff Perkins fully expected Walker would be able to deliver the photo to the *Bulletin* and Madras *Pioneer* in time for the Sunday afternoon weekly edition. They'd hoodwink Pugh once again. If Menetz could get there in time. There were several 'ifs' that needed to work, the stars needed to align in their favor.

A caravan of vehicles left with one more soul than had arrived with them.

Another family arrived that afternoon. Our camping village expanded. The youngest of their four sons, Jeff, was a little younger than Max. As they set up camp, Jeff pulled out his mint condition Schwinn Stingray bike.

Finally, Peggy and her family arrived around three o-clock. I heard a kachunk, kachunk, noise coming from the back of their walnut brown station wagon, which was crammed full including their olive-green, well-used army tent that easily slept two families or a platoon, stove, ice chests, bags full of clothing, sleeping bags, pillows and whatever else they could shove in.

I could only see the top of her younger brothers' Dave and Bill, heads. They were surrounded by items packed in around them. Peggy got to sit up front between her parents. Even though we didn't attend the same school, we were best friends. We went to the same church. One year older than me she also had two knucklehead younger brothers full of tomfoolery. Her dad stood tall and lanky. Her mom had an infectious laugh, and was always a terrific sport, willing to do about anything, at least once.

Sometimes we'd get to roll out our sleeping bags and sleep in the back of the station wagon. I loved riding in their nifty car. The third seat faced the rear window. We'd sit back there and sing, wave at passing vehicles, and whisper plans that her brothers couldn't hear.

I blurted out the entire morning's story. She stood silent shaking her head, her sandy ponytail swishing back and forth. Her mouth opened but nothing came out. The word spread quickly, with others wanting the full scoop. Each of us had a slightly different version with highlights or lowlights.

———

Marleen got off her shift at 4:30 that afternoon. Now home, she dropped off her purse on the floral-patterned sofa and let the cat in. She'd been thinking about the boys all day. She went to the house and rapped hard on the door. Nobody answered. She'd try to deliver the pie again tomorrow.

———

Unlike Coop, who couldn't even recall the three-hour drive from Sisters to Salem, Vern was painfully aware of each minute, hour and every very long mile. The entire trip his whole body hurt. He probably had a broken rib or two. His nose hurt. His knees hurt. His left ankle was killing him. His head pounded. He kept asking himself if he'd killed Rusty.

Seven hours of agony later and idling in the vehicle lineup on Interstate 5 at the Blaine-Surrey border crossing, he looked at the white Peace Arch. He pulled out his Oregon driver's license. The border agent quizzed him with questions: "Do you have any fruits or vegetables?" Uptight, Vern said "No." "Have you been on a farm within the past month?" "No." "Have you been in a foreign country in the past six months?" "No." "Are you carrying a firearm?" "No." "Are you transporting illegal drugs?" "No." Really? Who'd ever answer that truthfully,

Vern questioned silently. "Welcome to Canada," as the agent motioned him to continue on.

———

Now on British Columbia Highway 99, he continued to Vancouver. Forty-five minutes later, he sat as comfortably as he could be, in a rocking chair on his brother's front porch. Even his butt hurt which he hadn't noticed until now. He rocked back and forth on the porch of his brother's historic three-story home in the west end of Vancouver. Each time he visited, one of his favorite things was sitting on the porch watching the neighborhood hustle and bustle. It was a hub of activity with more and more University of British Columbia students renting rooms in many older homes like this one.

When the family's ginger tabby named Apollo jumped on his lap, Vern's tense shoulders started to relax. Apollo's green eyes seemed to question Vern's appearance. Vern looked at the distinctive M-shaped marking on Apollo's forehead, stripes by his eyes and across his cheeks. Vern stroked Apollo's soft head and down his back as the cat purred contentedly.

Vern lay his head back against the sapphire and chartreuse Scottish tartan-cushioned fabric. Now his shoulders hurt, even more it seemed. And both arms and right hand ached. He sat there for a half hour before anyone in the house looked out noticing someone sitting on their porch. Len went out when he saw his brother. Troubled since Vern had just visited recently, turned to sympathy when he got a closer look, revealing his brother's beat-up face.

Before Len could say anything, Vern raised his hand in a stopping motion, and said, "Don't even ask, Bro. It's best you don't know."

Len did ask him if it had happened in British Columbia and Vern said, "No, at home." Len spotted their mother's Buick out front and raised his eyebrows. He thought to himself, this must be serious with Vern driving her old-lady car.

Len grabbed the duffel bag from the car's backseat and told Vern to go upstairs to Nathan's room. Whenever Vern visited, his nephew gave up his room and slept in the basement. Looking at his exhausted brother, Len told him to go bed. Vern could hardly climb the staircase holding on to the antique wooden railing. He collapsed onto his nephew's twin bed. Normally his feet hung over the end of the bed. He curled up in a tight ball and fell asleep in thirty seconds. Len told his wife Joyce all he knew and added, "Let's give him twenty-four hours then we need to know the entire story."

———

That night for dinner we had meat loaf and potato salad, and a piece of carrot cake that I made. We got a larger piece than normal. My guess Mom was thinking about how our trip started out. She probably figured we all deserved a sweet ending to an unreal day.

Another family arrived after dinner. They always came later than everyone else and would only stay the weekend as they had plenty of farm work to be done. They had a trailer and outside camping gear for the boys to use.

One more family with only one girl and two more boys. The daughter, Debby, was two years older than me, tall, and could have been a model. One son, the same age as me. We were in junior high together. The youngest brother fell between Max and Will's ages. We were seriously outnumbered now with all these boys.

Peggy and I were glad that our younger friend Maleah and her parents had arrived. She helped our overall female odds slightly. The first night around the campfire wasn't a typical story night of tall tales and hunting in the dark for the notorious snipes. This evening Dad explained to the latecomers what we had discovered that morning. It was pretty somber around the campfire.

With a possible murderer on the loose, the topic of conversation was whether Peggy and I would be allowed to sleep in the back of the truck. I interjected the words "canopy" and "locked door" and the fact we were only a few feet from our trailer. We would be fine. Peggy pulled out a whistle she'd brought along for whatever reason.

I asked where I would fit in the small overcrowded trailer. Dad already had to climb to the top bunk. We laughed hysterically watching him with his left foot on the edge of the sofa, right foot onto the edge of the miniature kitchen's only countertop, hoisting himself up then sliding into the bunk and squeezing all six foot, two inches of himself into a sleeping bag. Only wearing his white skivvies, as we called them. Mom slept on the pull-out sofa with Willy. Max slept on the fold-out dining area. All were assigned a sleeping space depending on their size and length. They decided not to move me inside since the only space available would have moved Willy on the floor with Duke.

Around 9:40, almost dark, Peggy and I crawled over the tailgate of our blue pickup. We climbed into our sleeping bags, all snug. Not too far away we could hear the howls and yaps of coyotes. Peggy said she was glad to be sleeping in the truck and not in the tent with her family. She never liked sleeping on the ground, especially when the air mattress lost the air. I tried not to think about what I'd seen at the headwaters. We locked the canopy door.

Peggy rechecked it. Also, learning from past experience, if we didn't lock ourselves in, a prankster brother or two might intrude. Or worse yet, they might toss in an unwanted object like a smelly fish or dead rodent. Useless boys. Now we had the added possibility of a crazed murderer running around the area.

Max seemed to be outgrowing this prankster nonsense. Will was just ramping up. One day last year we forgot to lock the canopy door. That night we found fake gooey spiders in the bottom of our sleeping bags. We knew not to react. The boys were lurking outside waiting for screams. We just covered our mouths stifling the awaited reaction. Daggers were shooting from our eyes. We'd get them back sometime, somehow. Peggy and I adopted a motto: We don't get mad, we get even. We decided to wait until the end of our vacation for our justified retaliation.

We talked about the future. What we wanted to be when we grew up. Teachers, nurses, secretaries and moms seemed to be the main choices. Peggy said she wanted to be a teacher but only for elementary school-age children. I didn't know what I preferred. I did like to organize things. Or creating to-do lists. And I enjoyed telling my brothers what to do on a regular basis. I especially liked checking off the boxes when I had finished a task from my lists. Dad said one time I'd make a good administrator. I wasn't sure what that meant.

Where's the rumbling coming from? Marleen thought to herself. Climbing into bed around eleven o'clock, it sounded like thunder. There were no storms in the forecast, so what in the world? It sounded a little familiar. The loudness faded away.

As quietly as he could be on his chopper, Harley drove to Rusty's place and deposited a present on the front porch for his roommates. If this didn't scare them into keeping their mouths shut, he would have to take more drastic measures.

CHAPTER FIVE

*B*eautiful Day In The Neighborhood

Saturday morning Detective Walker had hunger pangs. He felt much better after getting the bad burger out of his system. He and Deputy Malloy sat across from each other in their well-used corner booth at the V Café next to the Dodge dealership on the main drag. The booth was considered hallowed ground. The café kept it reserved for the Sheriff's office to use anytime they wished. Until ten o'clock anyway, then anyone could sit there.

They'd each drunk the first cup of coffee served by a favorite waitress, Twila. She returned with their usual donuts. One glazed for Malloy. One filled with creamy vanilla custard with chocolate frosting on the top for Walker. Three minutes later, Sheriff Perkins sauntered in. He never seemed to be in a big hurry. He carried himself straight and confident. He wore his hat that he rarely removed except in church, eating and a few other activities.

He conveyed self-assurance. This gave those around him a feeling of security.

Malloy scooted over as his boss slid in on the smooth walnut naugahyde fabric bench. He took off his hat placing it between him and his deputy and said, "Well boys, give me an update," just as Twila arrived with a cup of java, as he called it. "Morning, Twila," as he winked at her and added, "Thanks." "Morning, Unc... ummmmm Sheriff," his niece replied. Out of respect to the office he held, she only called him Uncle Ham only at family events.

The closer he looked at his twenty-two-year-old niece, the more she reminded him of his sister. She had passed three years earlier from breast cancer. His brother-in-law was doing the best he could raising three kids on his own. Uncle Ham had been watching out for the oldest child, his favorite niece Twila. For several years he helped as much as possible without interfering. During those ambiguous high school years, he'd helped her figure out what her future might look like. She had been thinking about college in the Valley, over one hundred miles from her family.

In spite of a seven year age difference, he secretly hoped Malloy would wake up and smell the coffee. How could he miss the twinkle in her eyes whenever she saw the deputy? Dense kid. He hoped to keep her in Madras. He knew she wouldn't stay here forever. Unless there was a good enough reason, like Malloy. He might have to speak with his deputy about his personal life sometime. Though it would be against his better judgment, maybe just once.

———

Perkins said, "Fill me in boys." Walker reported that Doc V didn't have anything conclusive yet. There were no stab or bullet wounds. He suspected some puncture wounds were caused by fists with at least one set of brass knuckles. Also, something like a bat or tree limb from obvious gash marks on the right side of the victim's head. Doc V was performing the autopsy this very minute.

The trio knew it was a tree limb that they found along the path. They'd found blood and hair on the branch off the pathway where they'd found the matchbook.

Doc V speculated that the victim had a skull fracture following a hit to the temple. The broken bone tore the middle meningeal artery, which caused blood to accumulate while the heart continued to pump more blood in the area. The epidural hematoma placed excess pressure on the brain, leading to oxygen deprivation.

Another question would be, "Was he dead before he hit the water?" Doc V would be checking for water in the lungs. He sent blood samples to the crime lab to confirm or rule out drugs. And how much alcohol was in his system.

Walker reported that fingerprints would be viable from the flashlight and beer bottles. Once photos were made, all he needed would be hours and hours to sit and go through hundreds of pages to find any matches. If the victim had a record, that would help to identify him faster.

Walker said, "Hopefully the forensic artist could help move the identification process along much faster. That's all for now." They switched topics to minor crimes. Somebody had broken into the post office the night before and made a mess in the lobby.

Starting early at 7:15 at the funeral home, Doc V and his assistant, Walter Olson, rubbed spirits of camphor on the insides of their mask to block the smell. The body of Rusty Kavanagh had been placed on a spotlessly clean, stainless steel table. The assistant flipped on the bright overhead lights and rolled the table of instruments to Doc V.

When finished he would: determine the time of death, the cause of death, any damage to the body, and the type of death (suicide, murder or natural causes). He could already rule out natural causes and suicide.

Photos had been taken when the body arrived the day before while the victim was fully clothed. Doc V checked all the clothing for droplets of blood, organic materials, and residues.

Now he examined the nude body starting externally. He stopped and wrote copious notes. Height, weight, age and sex of the body were noted.

Also noted were a mole on the outside right thigh and a three-centimeter birthmark behind the left ear. No tattoos. One scar on the right side of his scalp four inches above the ear. Doc V took fingerprints. He started a list of the marks that looked out of the ordinary—bruises, wounds and marks on the skin. There were dozens of round gouges all the same size. He noted this with a comment that he speculated brass knuckles had been used.

Assistant Olson took photographs and documented the appearance of the body. He noted any significant findings.

Doc V took X-rays to help find any broken or fractured bones. He took blood samples for drug use, alcohol amounts or whether there might be poisons in his system. He'd have to wait a couple of weeks for the blood test results.

He was known for being meticulous; he took a urine sample from the bladder using a syringe. The urine, like the blood, could be used in tests to detect drugs or poisons.

With his initial examination completed, he picked up the surgical saw, opening the chest cavity, spreading open the skin to see if any ribs were broken. Six were. A broken clavicle, his collarbone, was actually fractured in several places. He split the ribcage using rib shears, examining lungs and heart. The left lung had some damage, as did the spleen. But curiously, these were not recent. He suspected the victim had been punched and beaten as a child.

He removed and weighed each organ. He removed partially digested food to be used to determine the time of death.

He observed the eyes carefully. He discovered several tiny broken blood vessels that could be from choking. Then looking at the victim's head for trauma to the skull, including fractures or bruises, he removed the top of the skull and the brain, which he weighed and cut out a sample.

Doc V noted an epidural hematoma had occurred with bleeding between the dura mater, a tough fibrous layer of tissue between the brain and skull, and the skull bone. He told Olson these occur when arteries are torn as a result of a blow to the head, and injury in the temple area is a common cause. The right side of the victim's head had received a lot of damage. Olson took photos from every angle possible knowing what Doc V had concluded.

At 8:37 a.m. Doc V finished. He would write his report of findings indicating the exact cause of death and how he thought it happened. This was homicide, simple as that. No accident, natural causes, or suicide. His report would show that blunt force trauma to the right temple by a round flat object was the cause of death. The puncture wounds indicated brass knuckles had been used.

Doc V instructed Olson to sew him back up. He put the skull back into place, skin stapled together to prevent leaking. He wiped the body of major blood and fluids.

Doc V would notify Detective Walker immediately, knowing blood and fluid results, plus dental records, would take a few weeks. But they certainly had enough to go on and could proceed with a formal investigation.

Saturday Arlo didn't go to the motorcycle camp. For the first time, he hung the "Do Not Disturb" sign on the outside door that Suzanne saw when she tried to deliver mail to him. She got concerned. She watched for him and didn't see him come out.

He stayed in bed until noon. He paced around his small home, ate some soda crackers and slept more.

His body ached not from working hard but certain muscles hurt, especially his arms. He had a difficult time falling asleep. When he finally did, he had a weird dream. He'd gone to some wild party at the motorcycle camp, then woke up in a totally unfamiliar place and couldn't get home.

He thought over and over about what had transpired early Friday morning. He'd hit at least one guy with a big tree limb. He heard him go down. He prayed he didn't kill the kid; cockroach, as Harley called him. He never wanted to see Harley again. Arlo had no appetite and didn't eat for two days.

Sunbeams poked through our newspaper curtains. It was way too early. My foldable travel alarm clock with glow-in-the-dark numbers read 5:34. I slid farther down into my sleeping bag completely covering my head hoping for a few more hours of sleep. Peggy didn't even stir. It worked until around seven o'clock. Familiar voices outside were talking and starting breakfast.

Peggy's mom cooked bacon, eggs and pancakes on their camp stove perched on a little folding table. A pot of coffee perked on the second burner. It smelled so yummy. Mom fixed sausage patties and scrambled eggs in our trailer. We were off to a great start for the day.

Our family had decided initially we didn't want to think about the "episode" at the headwaters. We wouldn't talk about it. But after one full day, internally we were each wondering what was happening. Had the body been asleep? Unconscious? Or? Like a mind reader, Dad said he'd try to find out something to put our minds at ease but reminded us that Malloy said it could take a long time.

A golden-mantled ground squirrel family found their way to us probably because the boys were shooting pancake spit wads earlier. Yellow-pine chipmunks were everywhere. The cute streaks on a chipmunk's body went all the way to the nose. The stripes stop at the shoulders of the squirrels.

Duke went berserk. He took off like a shot chasing a chipmunk down a hole. Dirt flew everywhere. Soon his head and neck had completely disappeared. He came up with nothing but a snout full of dirt. This would become regular entertainment for us. Pure frustration for Duke, but he never gave up.

The weather warmed up quickly. Three of us girls sat on the log that jutted out into the river. It became one of my favorite places. The plush moss made a natural cushion. We couldn't dangle our feet too long because forty-eight degrees felt even colder than the Pacific Ocean. It was shallow enough that we could walk across to the other side. Our worry-wort mothers never wanted us to try it. Our pleading never helped.

Our camping days would exist mostly of a daily walk to the store, playing in the water, and maybe an official outing somewhere. Maybe not. I'd heard the adults say they liked having no agenda.

After lunch, I organized my entourage of ten: us girls, our four pesky younger brothers, along with three boys from the other families. We were given permission to walk the one mile to the store, each taking with us some coins for treats.

One of the boys spotted four deer wading across the river. A mother deer walked on the left of her little fawn, breaking the swifter current, which was more powerful in this section of the river. We watched some teenage boys climb into inner tubes. One yelled to their parents to pick them up at the bridge. Knee-high, purplish-blue lupines were blooming. The slight breeze caused the tall flowers to sway gently back and forth. It looked like an ocean blue magic carpet that I wanted to ride. The boys found the right length of limbs and played dueling pirates. I mimicked Mom and one of her all-time favorite momisms, "Be careful, you'll poke your eye out."

Peggy educated us that Camp Sherman is an unincorporated hamlet. The year-round population is around ninety-five. That number more than triples in the summer months. The community includes an elementary school, Black Butte School, a general store and a post office. The community also has a volunteer fire department. We sort of knew all of this, but I liked listening to her. She was smart.

Then I heard her say something I didn't know. Some wheat farmers from Sherman County established Camp Sherman in 1918. They wanted to escape the dry summer heat by migrating to the riverbanks of the Metolius River to fish and camp in the cooler river environment. To help guide their friends to the secret spot, farmers nailed a shoebox top with the name "Camp Sherman" to a tree at a fork in the road.

She remembered all this from a report she had written in ninth grade U.S. history class that had to be about something in Oregon's history. I thought she'd told a terrific story. She would be a wonderful teacher when she grew up.

Out front of the store stand two Shell gasoline pumps. One is white with an orange "SHELL GASOLINE" sign in the shape of a shell on the front. Then a big white plastic shell on the top of the pump that appropriately reads "SHELL" in red. The other pump matched the same orange with the "SHELL" sign in orange. The colors were too close and didn't stand out like the other one. It has the same matching plastic white shell on top with "SHELL" in red. Dad would not get gasoline here. It was fifteen cents more a gallon than at home where it was thirty-five cents.

A sign in the window read: "Serving Oregon since 1915, Camp Sherman Live Bait & Tackle Shop." A colorful trout floated in the middle of the poster with the words: "Rods Reels Lures Live Bait Canoe & Rowboat Rentals. Open 7:30 am-7 pm 7 Days a Week."

The store was a place where locals came to share the day's news, get fishing reports, hear local gossip and enjoy the beauty around them. Three elderly men were sitting on a long bench on the store's porch drinking coffee. Each mug had a different name printed: Del, Hank and Clyde.

In the store were wooden bins of penny candies. A freezer case held rows of ice cream bars. A wall-to-wall refrigerated section had milk, cheeses, butter, beer, and soda pop. Tall rows of wooden shelves were covered with food items, magazines and beverages. I went in and purchased a postcard for a nickel. Eyeing the candy selection, I'd be back after writing the card to my other best friend Diane.

Next door, I pushed on the heavy wooden door of the Post Office. I walked into the all-wood reception area where on the wall it read:

STAMPS
PARCEL POST
GENERAL DELIVERY

Lined against one wall were rows and rows of post office boxes with small brass plaques with engraved numbers. Locals picked up their mail daily except on Sundays and major holidays.

Standing at the counter and using a blue pen, I carefully printed, "Wish You Were Here. The weather is warm, and the water is cold. And boy, do I have a story to tell you. XOXO" I addressed it to Diane on Maple Street in Albany. Then bought a four-cent stamp from the white-headed and bearded postman. He had a warm smile and twinkling blue eyes. He could have been the twin of Santa Claus, who I knew didn't really exist though secretly, I hoped he did.

Mr. Postman told me that the post office used to be housed in the store. Mail was delivered from April to September when the weather was good. Mr. Ross Omduff was named the first postmaster. By 1928 the post office became a year-round operation. This postman was not the first postmaster though he looked like he could be. I handed him my postcard. He promised to mail it that day.

Returning to the store, I'd just spent four cents of my winter babysitting funds for the stamp. After the postcard purchase of a nickel, I had a penny left to buy two Pixy

Sticks, lemon being my favorite. Standing at the candy bins there were so many choices. I decided two Pixy Sticks wouldn't be enough.

I pulled out a quarter and dime from my pocket. When paying, the clerk said, "Sorry dear, we don't take Canadian coins." Putting it back in my pocket, I wondered how I'd gotten it by mistake or where it came from. I'd put it in my piggy bank when we got home.

Retrieving the correct quarter, I bought three lemon Pixy Sticks, one Sweet Tart packet, six lemon drops for Dad, and a Snickers bar for Mom, her favorite candy bar. And nothing for my brothers. They had their own money to spend. Max had accumulated his limited wealth from polishing rocks for our neighbor, Fred.

Before we left home, Will discovered a small round gray Kodak film canister hidden under socks tucked in a corner of the second drawer on his dresser. It had four quarters in it. He'd lost four baby teeth a couple of years earlier. He'd placed each tooth under his pillow at night. The next morning, magically he received a shiny quarter. The tooth fairy had increased her dispersal of coins greatly in the seven-year gap in our ages. I'd gotten a nickel.

I would save my fifty-cent piece for later in the week to buy a Big Hunk bar, a slab of chewy sticky white taffy with chunks of almonds. And probably a 100 Grand bar. It was filled with creamy caramel and crunchy crisped rice smothered in milk chocolate. No matter how hard I searched, I found no dark chocolate anything. I'd have to settle for milk chocolate. A display of individually wrapped Ding Dongs and Twinkies caught my eye. The creamy white marshmallow filling smooshed between two layers of cake had a thin coating of chocolate glaze covering the hockey puck-size cakes. The shiny silver foil guarded a round chocolatey cake. This was another serious option.

As we were getting ready to leave with our stash, the cashier informed us that bobcats had been sighted in the area. He warned us to keep the little dogs close by. Seeing a bobcat would sure be exciting. One of the brothers dropped a piece of black licorice on the ground. I parroted Mom, "Don't put that in your mouth; you don't know where it's been." He blew off the dust replying, "Three-second rule." He plopped it in his mouth with a grin on his face. These boys were hopeless.

Walking back to camp, I noticed thin branches of columbine. Their orange trumpets dangled down with yellow petals shooting yellow spurs from its middle. Mom and I really loved flowers. Around Riverside Campground were native wildflowers. Some small islands were created from branches on trees that fell into the river. That gave wildflower seeds a place to land and grow. Many islands of all sizes were covered in wildflowers of mostly yellow, some periwinkle and soft blue.

Mom knew all about trees, too, and had pointed out a tall Western Larch that is a deciduous conifer. In other words, a pine tree that loses its needles each year. The needles are bright green in the spring. We'd seen them a soft golden yellow in the fall. We never called it a Western Larch, but a Tamarack. It sounded like it could be an Indian word. Indian words were so much nicer and prettier sounding. The soft needles kind of looked like a brush to clean the bottom of a bottle. The bark is flat and cinnamon-colored, and scaly like a big fish, with deep ruts that I could stick my finger in between.

At the same time in Madras, the eagerly anticipated and highly skilled forensic artist, John Menetz, arrived at the Sheriff's office. Malloy had conjured up a look for this infamous person. He didn't look at all like a boxer or wrestler. First, he was bald as a cue ball with an olive complexion. His facial hair was dark like his bushy eyebrows. Maybe he had family roots in Italy, Portugal or Spain? Second, he had a medium build and about five foot, nine inches tall.

They sat him in a dinky conference room used to interview witnesses or criminals.

Menetz had created hundreds of drawings over the decades. He'd met with victims who described the attacker from memory. He'd end up with a likeness that would be pretty close to identical to the person being sought. Dozens and dozens, if not hundreds, of cases throughout Oregon and the northwest had been solved because of his illustrations. He had even flown to the east coast to help with a case.

Entering, he saw photos scattered around the table. A white- and maroon-printed bottle of Dr Pepper sat in the middle of the table. He picked it up and placed it on the floor in a corner of the room. Then he heard laughter outside the door. Malloy brought in his favorite soda—a bottle of Coke, and lightheartedly said, "Here's the real thing." They heard he hated Dr Pepper, something to do with his childhood and tasting like carbonated prune juice. Malloy got a sideways glance from Menetz, and a slight smile emerged between the dark mustache and beard. He looked like he could be undercover for any number of cases.

This guy's face had been beaten up something awful. Somebody had it in for him. The face shape, hair and ears were fairly easy. The eyes, nose, mouth, not so much. He would do the best he could. He always did.

Malloy observed through the window. Very curious, he wanted to watch the process. He kept his fingers crossed he wouldn't be called out on a case.

Menetz sat staring at the photos laid out on the table. He drank half of the bottle of Coke without taking a breath. He got up and walked around the entire table looking at the photos from different angles.

He sat down and opened his fold-over, natural-tanned leather case. He pulled out and in a straight line laid out three pencils, one eraser, a sharpener, and several sheets of thick paper. Sometimes he would use different forms of drawing techniques, such as hatching, scribbling, or stippling, when needed. Line drawing and blending were his most used techniques and he suspected these would be adequate for this project.

He picked out a yellow pencil and drew an oval outline of the face. It wasn't perfectly egg-shaped because the chin narrowed. He erased the marks and tapered the lower half of the face a bit more. The victim didn't have a pointed chin, but it definitely wasn't round either, more of a square chin.

Next he started on the hair. He'd been told the dead man had red hair. He could have guessed that just from the texture and curls. His drawing and the replicas in the newspaper wouldn't be in color. Menetz drew unruly curls and waves of bushy hair. The hair fell below the ears almost to the chin. He added darker pencil shadowing in the curves of the curls to create and give dimension to the hair. This kid wouldn't have needed to pay for a perm to get an afro.

He finished off the bottle of fizzy Coke. He held it up indicating a second one would be required. Malloy rushed to the fridge and returned with another bottle placing it on the table in the inner sanctum.

Malloy had heard plenty of stories about Menetz's abilities and uncanny ways. He felt like he was in the presence of someone very special. He didn't want to get all weird about it, but he probably had a bit of hero worship going on. Malloy retreated to his vantage point at the window watching the process continue.

Through his open office door, Perkins asked, "How he is doing?" pushing back his chair. Walker, who had been pacing around the room, now joined Malloy, both mesmerized watching a face being produced before them.

The eyebrows were hidden by hair. Menetz didn't take much time drawing them. Nor the ears. He drew two cavities about an inch apart. Then he sketched in eyes and even top and bottom light lashes. Starting between the eyes, he outlined a thin bridge of the nose down to about the middle of the face. He broadened the nostrils. With his drawing skills, the flat nose on paper appeared in 2-D. With this talent, he crafted a reasonable likeness even though the body's face was smashed. The mouth was always the trickiest. This victim's normally thin lips were ballooned and split. This victim's face had been bashed and slashed, resulting in a lot of swelling. He couldn't draw exactly what he saw. His final version would have no puffiness or gashes.

Tilting a second pencil sideways, he added thicker marks creating shadowing effects under the cheek. Now the victim had noticeably higher cheekbones. He added a crease under the mouth above the chin.

After about two hours, he completed his task. He held up the likeness. With his help and the media, they should be able to find out the name of their victim. A redhead should be easy to ID, since about only two percent of the population have some hue of red hair.

He handed it to Walker simply saying, "This is your guy on a better day. Good luck."

Detective Walker hand-delivered the drawing to the *Madras Pioneer*. The editor agreed to hold space for the photo, but he made it clear it would be a big imposition because of the late notice. Perkins would owe him a favor. A weekly delivery, it would make the Sunday edition the next afternoon.

He drove to Bend. Pulling in on Hill Street he walked in the front door. He'd done as the Sheriff reminded him. Ask for Pugh first. Walker made a point of letting the newspaper staff know it was important that Pugh know the information had been dropped off and that Sheriff Perkins always kept his promises.

He handed the picture to the *Bulletin* staff. Again, just a weekly, he'd made it before the deadline for the next day's weekly edition. Small towns like Sisters and Redmond didn't have their own newspapers but relied on the *Pioneer* or *Bulletin*. Both editors promised the front page. He sent photos to television stations in the Valley. Hopefully somebody would recognize the victim.

One young man staying with his cousin in Salem, and another with his brother in Vancouver B.C., woke Saturday, one man in the morning, the other in midafternoon. Regardless of their location, both had the same thoughts. What actually happened Friday morning in those early hours? Both were stiff and very sore. Both were still shell-shocked. One's face looked like medium rare hamburger. Both slept through the pain and memories.

The three of us girls sat in lawn chairs in the shallow, gentle, rippling water. We passed magazines between us. Occasionally we looked up when interrupted by laughter of younger brothers. They certainly had a language of their own with immature grunts and groans or hoots and hollers.

A little chestnut-colored critter with a blunt nose popped its head from a hole. Its whiskers twitched. It had round hazel eyes and short tail. Its small rounded ears were covered in fur. It looked like a mouse playing a part in a Disney movie, like "Cinderella." We named her Perla after a girl mouse in the movie.

Then a cute little round brownish-gray mouse-like creature with a long nose scampered from a log under a bush close by. It let out a quiet squeak. Maleah had recently studied rodents and assured us it wasn't actually a rodent at all but a shrew. Its relatives were hedgehogs and moles. Its sharp spike-like-teeth gnawed right through a little twig. Its eyes were tiny. It jumped when I turned the page in my magazine. It had excellent hearing because it went into a hole by a log, not to be seen again. Yep, Disney characters for sure.

Late Saturday afternoon Marleen finished work. It had been crazy busy, mostly because of the long weekend. Before she changed clothes and removed her shoes (because once she did, she knew she'd be on the sofa the rest of the night,) she pulled the apple pie from the fridge and walked it over to the boys' house. Coop's pickup truck still wasn't there.

She walked up four well-worn white wooden front steps. On the porch sat a bag. Maybe a pillowcase. She knocked on the door. No answer. Her curiosity got the best of her. She untied the knotted rope and opened the pillowcase. There lay a dead duck. These boys sure had odd friends, she thought to herself. She probably should tell somebody about it, but really wasn't sure who.

Once the sun set, it quickly cooled down the air. Somebody had already gotten the campfire going. Our campfire exploits included a round of songs, "Down by the Riverside" and "Home on the Range." The half moon lit up the area as stars twinkled brightly. They seemed so close, like we could pluck them by the handfuls out of the night sky. With no nearby houses and towns, only the embers of the campfire brightened the ground.

One of the boys pointed out a falling star. It disappeared so quickly only a few of us spotted it. Jeff's mom said it is sometimes called a falling or shooting star, but actually it is a meteor. It could be as small as a grain of sand, or a large rocky softball. It gets heated up, turning shiny by collisions with air molecules in the upper atmosphere. She said she'd seen a meteor shower one time where many fell or appeared to shoot across the sky.

Somebody started humming a song. Dad whistled and others chimed in singing, "Catch a falling star and put it in your pocket, never let it fade away. Catch a falling star and put it in your pocket, save it for a rainy day. For love may come and tap you on your shoulder some starless night, just in case you feel you want to hold her, you'll have a pocketful of starlight." Then we repeated the "catch a falling star" part again.

Jeff's mom drew our attention to the streaks across the night sky called the Milky Way. Not the yummy candy bar, but a disc of stars that makes up our galaxy. Each of the two hundred billion stars in the Milky Way is really a sun, many of them with orbiting plants. We all started asking her questions. She said she'd share more the next night with us.

Mom said the stars reminded her of fireflies. They flickered off and on in the night sky. She'd see them often in the summers growing up in Nebraska. I definitely wanted to see these lightning bugs one day, as she also called them.

Peggy and I scooched into our private bedroom in back of the truck. The brothers banged on the windows expecting to scare the bejeebers of out of us. Peggy yelled for the little dorks to flake off or she'd come out and bust their heads. She would have, too. She didn't tolerate their shenanigans. These were the same knuckleheads who seemed keen on giving each other daily wedgies.

I turned on my transistor radio and couldn't find reception, except from some station in Bend thirty miles away. Country western music wasn't my favorite. I preferred the Monkees and Dave Clark Five, my favorite singing groups. I turned it off, saving the batteries for hopefully when we could find a better station. During the stillness, we could hear the peaceful sounds of the crickets chirping in the distance. We borrowed an extra flashlight to read our magazines before bed. We felt cozy in our truck-bedroom, our very cool pad.

CHAPTER SIX

*B*ack In The Saddle Again

Wide awake early Sunday morning, Coop wondered if he would ever be the same and he didn't mean physically. The neighbor lady checked on him yesterday and undoubtedly would again today. Everyone was treading lightly around his cousin's house not wanting to disturb him. Jasper stretched out beside him on one of twin single beds. She put her back against his. At some point in the night, she moved to the floor maybe sensing he was asleep. He felt unconditional love from this dog. He needed a dog.

Twenty minutes later slowly he eased out of bed. Pulling on jeans and a borrowed sweatshirt from Heather's husband Tim, everything hurt. He discovered muscles he never knew he had. He leashed Jasper and took her for a walk. Birds chirped. Flowers were opening from the bright-ness of the sunbeams. But everything seemed different. To him, the colors looked blah. He wandered aimlessly for two hours. Moving felt better than sitting.

A cup of hot tea was waiting for him when he returned. His sore lips curled up as much as he could and said, "Ok, enough with the tea." His sense of humor was returning, Heather thought to herself. He added, "Can you get Tim? It's time I figure some things out."

Five hundred miles north, the clock on the wall bonged ten times. Len's wife Joyce said, "Enough is enough. Thunder-ation! Get him up, we need some answers." Over a mug of piping hot, strong dark coffee, Vern began the saga. Joyce cried. Len teared up. Vern sobbed. Finally catching his breath to speak, tears flowed as he relived early Friday morning.

Len put a leash on their family dog, a sable Scottish Terrier named Robbie, and off the three of them walked to Nelson Park. Vern needed to talk, so on they walked. Down Thurlow Street past historic homes being trans-formed into apartments and flats for university students. They reached Beach Avenue, strolled through English Bay into Stanley Park. They walked and talked for hours. Both brothers were exhausted when they returned home in time for dinner. A sympathetic Joyce fixed her brother-in-law his favorite Canadian dessert, layered Nanaimo Bars. She snickered to herself knowing he'd want a beer along with several of the delectable delights. The combination sent shivers down her spine, but she'd give him anything he wanted.

Peggy and I had already made arrangements at the stables for this morning. About a dozen horses were available to rent. If you were old enough and experienced, they would let you take the horses out on your own. We'd gone twice before with guides. Dad took us to the stables and said somebody would be back for us at noon. We were off on another lark.

My horse was a pretty chestnut named Buttercup. Peggy rode a dark horse with white socks named Babe who neighed when Peggy got on her. Three much older people, maybe in their twenties, joined us.

Our guide, Buck, reminded me of the very handsome Little Joe Cartwright. He had a full head of wavy auburn hair, copper eyes and nice smile. Buck's television twin, Little Joe, was the youngest and to me, the bravest brother on "Bonanza." It was a wild west adventure television program with his white-headed father Ben and his two brothers, Adam and Hoss. They ran their timber and livestock ranch near Virginia City, Nevada, bordering Lake Tahoe. They were heroes, always helping somebody in the surrounding community.

Even though in the lead, Buck would turn his coffee-colored horse named Cheyenne around and walk back to talk with us. He told us that the name of the river comes from the Warm Springs or Sahaptin word "mitula," meaning "white salmon," referring to the light-colored Chinook salmon.

We followed in single file with the older people up front, and Peggy ahead of me. I brought up the rear of the pack. She turned around often to check on me and wave. It was an easy pace through the forest. I took a deep whiff of the fragrant pine trees. We saw several deer, and our expert guide and nature spotter stopped to show us a porcupine up a tree.

Trotting from the dusty trail down along the refreshing river, Buck pointed out several small trees. They had recently been downed by beavers who had stacked them up and made a round house. This re-routed the river around their home. Buck said this was a fairly small house. Inside would be large enough for the beaver family to hide in away from coyotes and even a bear. He told us that sometimes the house becomes more like a dam. This can change the total direction of a creek or stream.

He showed us a small Quaking Aspen tree with its slender trunk. He said these trees get their name from their leaves, which tremble and rustle next to one another in the soft breeze. The leaves are heart-shaped with short points on the ends and about two to three inches long. The coloring reminded me of celery. He said they would turn deeper green through the summer. In the fall, they turn a stunning gold or orange.

The greenish-white bark looked smooth and had funny spots that looked like eyes peeking out from the tree. Buck told us that a cool fact is that aspens are the widest ranging American tree, growing from Alaska to New England and down the Rockies and Sierra Madres into Mexico. Almost two hundred species of birds and mammals use aspens. They are also fire-adapted. While all the trunks may die in a fire, the roots survive all but the most intense fires, sending up shoots, with entire groves having interconnecting root systems. The oldest is estimated to be eighty thousand years old, possibly the oldest living thing on earth. I wondered what type of college education it would take to become a tree expert like him.

Buck pointed out all kinds of unusual things including badger holes that we wouldn't have even noticed. He said coyotes have a habit of digging holes as they chase after ground squirrels and gophers. It sounded just like Duke.

Buck said he could tell the difference in the holes. He said badgers were pretty nasty creatures so never get close to one. He'd only seen a few over the years. Bobcats were around but you were lucky to see one. I enjoyed the information on the trees and animals. Now I wondered if I should work for the forest service being a park ranger.

Popping up between some rocks along the river were small yellow bells with long, tall green leaves almost like grass. Buck called them a Yellow Bell.

We rode through an area that we had walked through many times. Today would be our official education on fir trees. Buck grabbed a small limb of a tree and told us it was a grand fir or a true fir. They are called that to distinguish them from Douglas firs and a number of other pretenders. Grand firs are medium tall and tend to have a narrow shape and rigid upright or horizontal branching. Buck handed me two needles and I smelled citrus, maybe an orange or lemon blend.

We saw some small flowers he called Phlox growing around stones and fallen trees. They had five pink petals. When walking in the future, we'd need to be careful not to step on them because some were so tiny.

Buck then told us about the enormous ponderosa pines. Its needles are four to ten inches long and in bunches of three. Cones are three to six inches long with hard curvy barbs. He passed one down the line for each of us to touch. It felt sharp and spiky.

One of the older people in the group pointed out how the cinnamon-colored bark had unusual shaped scales, reminding her of gigantic pieces of a jigsaw puzzle. I noticed wide gaps in the bark that started at the base working their way upwards. It looked like dozens of wavy roadways or paths. I guessed my brother's Hot Wheel cars could have easily fit in the tracks.

Then Buck turned our attention to the Douglas fir.
They are an evergreen whose common name is misleading
—they are not true firs at all, he explained. They are the
most abundant tree species in Oregon and also the conifer
with the greatest north-south range all the way to Mexico.
Needles are single, about one inch long and with a white
stripe on the underside. The needles are blunt-tipped and
not sharp to touch. Needles encircle the whole branch,
making it look like a pipe cleaner with three-inch long
cones. It looked like our Christmas tree.

In a clearing were some grasses where scattered
bunches of white sand lilies stood. They looked like tissue
paper moving in the breeze. The flowers have six petals,
flat and straight, and looked almost fake they were so
perfectly shaped.

I found it fascinating learning about trees and flowers. I
wondered more about whether I should work in the forest
when I grew up. None of the typical jobs for girls seemed
particularly appealing to me. But maybe I'd become a
secretary like Mrs. Johnston and run a school. Maybe even
the school where Peggy would be a teacher.

Our two-hour ride had come to an end. Peggy and I
slipped off the saddles. We patted our horses a thank you
and farewell until next year.

After lunch several of us meandered along the river.
Max saw something popping its head up and down. If we
had been at the beach it could be have been a seal. This
was a party of river otters playing with one another. We
watched and laughed for some time as they rolled, dipped,
jumped and climbed all over each other. Will tossed out a
stick hoping one might catch it and play with him, maybe

like the neighbor's yellow lab named Callie. I never knew how he came up with these farfetched ideas.

––––––

The afternoon newspapers were delivered in Jefferson and Deschutes counties. Exhausted, Marleen had gotten off her shift arriving home at 4:45, only fifteen minutes later than usual. She picked up the folded newspaper from her porch. The Memorial Day weekend tourist crowd was killing her. Her feet hurt. Her back hurt. Her knees hurt. She dropped the newspaper on the coffee table. She fell asleep on the couch without any dinner.

––––––

Walker and Malloy were hoping the phone would start ringing off the hook with people ID'ing the photo. They got a few calls but not as many as they thought. Nothing really conclusive. Malloy commiserated many were probably gone for the long weekend.

Harley and Arlo didn't read newspapers. But Raccoon did. He phoned Harley telling him what had shown up on the front page of the *Bend Bulletin*. Obviously, Harley thought, the cops didn't find any ID and were on a wild goose chase.

––––––

That evening around the campfire, Peggy's dad told us a scary story. He lowered his voice, sounding creepy and said, "A teenage couple went to the movies on a Friday night. Afterwards they went to lover's lane to spend some time necking. The boy turned on the radio for some mood music and put his arm around his girlfriend. A news bulletin interrupted the music saying that a convicted murderer had just escaped from a hospital for the criminally insane. During the murder, he had lost his hand, so now he used a hook instead of a right hand."

Peggy's mom interrupted saying, "I'm cold, go put your sweaters on." My mother agreed. These women were part of a clan all parroting the same instructions to their children.

Peggy's dad resumed the story. "The boy wasn't particularly mature for his age. He teased his girlfriend telling her he bet the murderer would find lover's lane a perfect place to hide. She dismissed this teasing at first, but he kept doing it. Before long, she got creeped out and demanded they leave immediately.

The stupid boy figured out quickly his words just lost himself some kissing time with his girlfriend. They drove to the girlfriend's home. As she got out of the car, she gave a scream and fainted. The boy got out of the car and there on the car door handle hung a bloody hook."

Mom thought we should lighten up and end the evening on a happier note. She suggested all of us doing the Hokey Pokey. "In the dark?" someone asked. "All ten verses?" She replied, "Let's see how far we get."

"You put your right foot in, you put your right foot out, your put your right foot in and shake it all about, you do the hokey pokey and turn yourself around, that's what it's all about." We did the left foot, right arm, left arm, right elbow, and for some reason there is no left elbow verse. At the head verse some of us were petering out. We skipped the right hip, left hip, whole self and backside. We laughed so hard. It felt good. One of the kids stepped in a hole and let out a painful yell. That ended the Hokey Pokey nighttime silliness.

Each night the moon grew brighter towards becoming full. We could even see some shadows that Dad explained were craters. He said to imagine a rocket delivering two men that would land and walk on it in July.

Someone pointed out something moving across the sky in a straight line. Mom called it Sputnik, an object the Russians had launched to view Earth from outer space. From then on, each night we scanned for Sputnik. The new word was fun to say.

One of the boys asked Jeff's mom if she'd share more about stars and galaxies. She explained that long before books were printed, people told stories about the same stars we see today. She pointed upward and said, "There's Draco the dragon, just above Hercules the warrior and Pegasus the magical winged horse. Cygnus the swan flies overhead. Each August, in a few months, meteors will shoot from the Perseus constellation, named for the Greek god who took off Medusa's head."

She pointed out Cassiopeia in the dark sky. I could see the Big and Little Dippers, which were easy, but when she drew a huge W shape in the sky, I just couldn't see it. Even using the Big Dipper's pointer stars, the part of the bowl farthest from the handle, to locate Polaris in the sky's W, I just couldn't make it. A surprise "OH" or "AH" came one at a time when someone discovered the starry pattern. Try as I might, I just couldn't see the dragon, winged horse or the W in the sky. Dad leaned over to me and said he couldn't either. We decided to be satisfied just to see the Dippers.

Max asked how we can tell a star from a planet and Jeff's mom replied, "Planets don't twinkle. They reflect the sun's steady light. That makes them easy to spot." She pointed out Jupiter and Saturn, and sure enough, they didn't twinkle. A couple of dads pulled out binoculars. I zoomed in on Jupiter, still a dinky dot.

I asked Jeff's mom how she knew so much about the heavens. She replied she had always been interested in astronomy. She loved space and the heavens. Sitting beside her I leaned over and quietly asked her if she thought I could grow up to be an astrologer and she replied, "Well, dear, it would be an astronomer and yes, you certainly could be. Knowing you, you can be whatever you set your mind to." Now I'd be an astronomer.

Maleah was several years younger than Peggy and me. Her mother was a fussbucket, to us down-right persnickety. "Just you wait until you have kids of your own—then you'll understand," she often said. Peggy and I hadn't been kidnapped or worse. Dad showed her mother how we locked the door from the inside. Maleah's parents agreed to let her stay the night with us.

With Maleah came her cool teen magazines, even though she wasn't a teen yet. Her older sister, age sixteen, had given her the leftovers. We thumbed through *16 Magazine* March edition that cost twenty-five cents. She also had an August 1968 issue of *FaVE!* with the Monkees' Davey Jones on the cover. We survived just fine.

———

Sunday hadn't been a good day for Arlo. He dozed off and on. He hadn't walked any farther than Cabin #10's front door. Finally, he went out for supper. He saw the front page of the *Bulletin* on the table at the Midget. A photo of Rusty, the kid he'd met once at the D&D with Harley, stared at him, accusing him of murder. It was like he was sitting right across from him in the booth. He grabbed his burger and left.

Suzanne saw him return and ran out to hand him an envelope. He looked horrible and she asked if he was okay. He shrugged his shoulders and mumbled, "I'm okay." She knew he was certainly not okay. She ended by saying, "If you need anything Arlo, and I mean anything, just let me know." He just nodded his head.

In the letter written on pale blue paper, his mother wrote that he'd be turning twenty soon. He lifted it to his nose. It smelled like her favorite perfume, White Shoulders. "Happy Birthday, Sonshine." He tried to recall when she'd started calling him Sonshine. She wrote she wished they could spend it together as a family. They hadn't seen him in almost one year. She asked him to call her collect; she just wanted to hear his voice. She promised to make him his favorite pie, Saskatoon Berry. His mouth watered thinking of his favorite berry, sort of a blueberry with an apple flavor. He had a piece of blueberry pie with vanilla ice cream at D&D and it was fine but nothing like the flavor of the not-too-sweet fruity Saskatoon berries. Nobody baked and cooked like his mother.

That night he dreamed about a guy who loved loud noises, like motorcycle sounds, gunshots and fireworks. But went crazy with trivial trills and peeps of birds that became deafening to him. Arlo woke up in a cold sweat.

CHAPTER SEVEN

I Scream, You Scream, We All Scream For Ice Cream

Monday morning of Memorial Day Weekend, Marleen got up earlier than usual. One more day, she thought. Those tourists! She'd get a cup of coffee at The Gallery. On the coffee table lay yesterday afternoon's newspaper. She opened it up. On the front page was a picture of Rusty. She read the caption underneath: *If you know this person, contact Detective Walker at the Jefferson County Sheriff's Office.* "Now what has he done?" she said out loud. She'd have to do it later. She had a restaurant to open.

Detective Walker picked up the medical examiner's report. He filled in Perkins, Foster and Malloy at their booth waiting for Twila to deliver breakfast. A blow to the right temple by a circular blunt object had been the cause of

176

death. There was no water in the lungs. There were a number of puncture wounds, speculated from spiked brass knuckles. And many blows to his torso with six broken ribs. A broken clavicle was actually fractured in several places indicating serious force against the shoulder. It could have broken when he fell. The victim was beaten badly. Death occurred between 1:45 and 4 a.m.

They had a silver flashlight in their possession. Fingerprints had been pulled from it finding two fairly clear sets. But they didn't have anything to compare them with just yet.

Since they had two books of D&D matches, hopefully with viable prints, Walker decided to start at the popular restaurant. During the lunch crowd, he showed Rusty's photo around. The bartender told him he'd seen the kid in the photo with a couple of rough guys from the East Side outlaw motorcycle gang. He knew one guy called Harley wore a dark leather jacket. He couldn't remember exactly when, but it had been within the past couple of months. The owner of the D&D verified he'd seen the kid in the photo a couple of times with the one biker for sure. He couldn't recall if there was a second biker or not.

The detective realized right then that their small department needed some help. They needed to get photos and fingerprints from this Harley guy.

Memorial Day, a legal holiday, Coop had the day off from the bank. He knew he had to return home and go to the Sheriff's office. His brain felt clearer now. A few days with Heather and her family had helped brush away the cobwebs. Heather had always been a terrific listener. As she let him talk, occasionally she'd ask a question. Each

answer led him on a path of realization. He told her everything he could recall.

She reminded him who he was as a person, with his
high moral code and values. He believed in the Golden
Rule and Ten Commandments, well at least the ones he
could remember: You shall not murder. You shall not steal.
Honor your parents.

Most of the fear about confronting the people who'd
done this melted away. He had to help find who killed his
friend. He went from fear, to the pain of losing his friend.
He felt fury. He wanted to help avenge his childhood pal.

He still couldn't call his mom, but he agreed that
Heather should. His mother had been worried sick. And
she'd seen the newspaper and photo of Rusty the night
before; Heather passed that information along to him. His
eye was still black and blue, but other gouges weren't as red
and swollen. His cousin insisted aloe vera would help him
heal faster. It seemed to be doing the job. But he was far
from looking good or normal.

He'd drunk enough hot tea in a couple of days to last
him a lifetime. He admitted he did like it almost better
than coffee. Heather suggested using some of her makeup
to help cover up the black eye before returning to work.
"Don't push it," he said affectionately and he pulled her
into his arms.

It wasn't a holiday in Canada and Len needed to get to
work as a city bus driver. His love was crafting and creating
pieces of furniture and art from wood. Maybe someday
he'd be able to make a good enough living at doing what
he truly enjoyed, but for now, this paid the bills and keep
food on the table for his family.

He rousted Vern early and asked him point-blank, "What are you going to do today? You need to think about returning home."

Vern said, "No way. I can't go back. I can't face my folks. Or the police." He covered his head with a pillow as Len left the room. Len suggested to Joyce she get him up and have him do something to help around the house, or take the dog for a walk, but be couldn't lie in bed all day and sulk. And they would call their parents in Sisters tonight, whether Vern liked it or not.

Every day we woke up to sunshine and a cobalt sky. We were thrilled to find out that this would be the day we'd drive out five miles, then on the highway ten miles to Sisters. The small western town looked like it should be in Montana.

We walked by a three-story building called the Hotel Sisters. It had been built in 1912 by a Spanish-American war veteran. The information was proudly displayed on a historical plaque beside the front doors. This nicely modern building boasted hot and cold water in each of its nineteen guest rooms.

The small town had one grocery store. One western clothing store. A general store building called Leithauser General Store built in 1925. In 1950, a newer store had been built just to the west that housed a barber shop. There was a variety store, a yarn mill, and a bakery. Plus, two bars and a gas station. All the buildings had a western façade made of timbers. Even the sidewalks were made of wood.

Our moms would stop at a nice lady's dress shop and at a drugstore that sold kitchenware. Beacham's Clock

Company had really interesting clocks from around the world. We stood watching through the window where a man who wore funny little glasses at the end of his nose sat on a tall stool with a steady hand repairing clocks using miniature tools. There were a few antique shops that looked like junk stores to us kids. Weren't antiques just somebody's old worn-out furniture? We liked the nifty feed and seed store with lots of animal supplies. Harnesses and other horse stuff hung on the walls.

The best place is the Sno Cap Drive-In for juicy hamburgers, salty french fries and creamy homemade milkshakes. Part of the anticipation and our excitement was discovering what flavors were available for the daily special.

Besides my typical order of a cheeseburger and tater tots, I'd be having a chocolate shake with mint chips. Peggy would order the same thing, or maybe switch out for french fries and a chocolate shake with marshmallow. Peggy and I thought the marvy Sno Cap was a cool hangout to watch for boys.

We sat opposite each other in a red vinyl booth. Our legs dangled, not quite touching the black-and-white checkerboard tile floor. If we looked too long it could produce a dizzying effect. Pictures of the building when it opened in 1954 hung proudly on the wall.

Peggy and I took turns reading to each other from trivia cards placed in a square wire basket on the end of the table. Beside it were the salt and pepper shakers, and mustard and ketchup bottles. The first card read that, unlike lots of other Old West towns, Sisters never boomed. Instead the community of ranches and sawmills grew reaching about five hundred people before the last mill closed in 1963, six years earlier.

Camp Polk had been located adjacent to a wagon road which linked the Willamette Valley to Prineville. Because of its location, Sisters soon grew to become a bustling little town. For years it was a sully station for sheepmen who passed through on their way to grazing pastures in the Cascades. Finally, in 1901, Sisters was formally established. People started to drift away. They needed to do something, so the town became known as the "Gateway to the Cascades" and started to recreate itself for summer and winter sports and tourism.

Another card read that Sisters' roots go back to 1865, when Camp Polk was created to protect settlers and travelers from Indians. There were a few minor squabbles spurred more by curiosity than hostility from local tribes who pretty much ignored the immigrants. The fort was abandoned less than a year after being built. A man named Sam Hindman and his family arrived in 1870 to homestead a property near the old camp. He set up a blacksmith shop. Before long he expanded the settlement to include a small store, a livery, and post office. Evidently the U.S. Post Office held a contest to name the office and asked people to suggest names. A farmer suggested Three Sisters, as the mountain peaks had come to be known. The postal service shortened it to Sisters.

Our burger basket lunch orders included tater tots and french fries and were delivered piping hot out of the fryer, too hot to take a bite. Impatiently waiting for his, Will zipped through the open front door, nabbing a tater tot from my deluxe cheeseburger basket. He fled out the back-door before I could even think to yell at him. Peggy and I actually laughed.

The brothers ordered hot dogs and double scoop sherbet cones. One promptly lost the top orange scoop while attempting to balance it all in both hands. Will always ordered the bottom scoop of green, really lime, and top scoop of orange. The orange ball melted in the dirt. "Fiddlesticks, let's get you another scoop," Mom soothed a heartbroken Will.

Mom always had an upside-down banana split, a house specialty. The delicious creation started on the bottom with a layer of bananas sprinkled with nuts, three maraschino cherries, then goopy dark chocolate and whipped cream. On the top were two scoops of vanilla ice cream.

Peggy looked out the window almost choking on a fry. She pointed to two riders on horses. A woman rode a pretty white and speckled brown horse. A man sat straight and proud on a chestnut horse. He wore a cowboy hat. The woman did, too. They each rode off with a vanilla ice cream cone, balancing it carefully.

Marleen felt blessed to work at The Gallery even though it was crazy busy today. In several hours, the long weekend would come to a close. She remembered she needed to call the Sheriff's office. She took a short morning break and stepped into the lounge to make the call.

Deputy Malloy answered. Marleen Brinkley told him she thought the guy in the photo was Rusty Cavanaugh, her neighbor. She wasn't sure if Cavanagh was with a "C" or a "K." Oh, and by the way, she discovered a dead duck in a pillowcase on their front porch when she tried to deliver a pie for the second day in a row. Malloy took some basic information. Marleen gave him her address and a description of the boy's house. He told her they'd be by to see her in a couple of hours.

Malloy told Walker, and they jumped into the car and sped to Sisters. Around 11:15 arriving at Marleen's address, they parked in her driveway. They both noticed how Marleen would have clear vision of the front of the boy's house. Approaching slowly both looked around for clues.

Walker noticed a boot print on the second step and matching prints on the porch up to the door. It had been a cold dewy morning. He saw a tire track in the dirt not on the paved driveway. Clearly a motorcycle. Malloy had the measuring tape out as Walker snapped photos of the surrounding area. Wider tracks on the paved driveway implied a truck. Malloy retrieved the pillowcase and put it into the trunk. The other footprints were narrower and shorter with slightly pointed toes, probably Marleen's.

Already the lunch hour, they decided Marleen would be pretty busy. They parked the Sheriff's office vehicle in front of The Gallery, then walked a couple of blocks to their favorite burger joint, the Sno Cap Drive-In. Both of them were hungry. Walker, the burger addict, always had a cheeseburger and asked them to add three slices of crispy bacon and two onion rings. It would end up about eight inches high. Malloy knew the food was safe here and ordered a regular burger. He loved the tangy dressing they used and always asked for a double dose.

On my last tator tot, I looked at Peggy and pointed at the cashier. There stood my, well our, very own Deputy Malloy. I ran out to tell Dad, tugging on his arm and dragging him inside to he find out what was going on with the case. All Peggy could say was, "Golly, he is a real dreamboat."

Dad greeted Deputy Malloy who introduced Detective Walker. I stood right by Dad, like a statue afraid if I moved or said anything, he'd make me leave. Dad mentioned that he and his family were curious about the happenings since Friday morning. Walker said an illustration of the deceased had been circulated and they had several leads to follow. They determined the murder weapon to be the silver flashlight discovered by Max. Then the dynamic duo picked up their white lunch sacks and walked away.

We were all pretty disappointed more information wasn't available. Dad reminded us it wasn't like "Adam 12," where crimes were solved in a half hour. And that we may never know what actually happened. Mom added that maybe one day we'd read about it in the newspaper.

You never knew what you'd see in this little town. Whyehus Creek flowed at the southern end. Deer were common and neat to see. They didn't seem too worried about us. Across the street a flock of wild turkeys roamed through a neighborhood. They were going from porch to porch of some houses eating pet food.

At one house I saw that same black car with red stripe down the side. I told Mom it looked like the same car in front of the store the morning of the "episode." I didn't want to really call it what it was so decided I'd refer to it as the "episode." Mom said it certainly could be the same car.

I noticed that again today the sky was so bright and clear. The sun slowly reached the highest point in its bright blue home, delivering rays of warmth touching my arms. It felt like sitting in front of the fireplace at home. Warmth seeped in all the way to my bones.

We didn't go to another favorite restaurant called The Gallery. They fixed the best chili burgers in existence. It's called The Gallery because the walls are covered with art from a popular artist. He became world-renowned for his western pictures. His name was Ray Eyerly. He sketched and painted area views that looked just like a picture someone had taken with a camera.

Mr. Eyerly lived in Montana during his teenage years. He served in WWI before moving to Salem, where he worked for the Oregon State Highway Department. After moving to Sisters in 1962, he became a full-time artist, showing his work at The Gallery.

Sitting in the restaurant one could see more than a dozen paintings in different sizes. All were rustic, outdoorsy-looking in wood frames scattered around the walls. One booth in particular was my favorite to sit in. Several times we'd sat directly underneath a pen and ink drawing of a decrepit barn and old wagon wheel in a short stubble field. It looked about to fall over. It was called "Barn and Wheel" and was done early in his career.

Mr. Eyerly wrote his signature always in a bottom right hand corner of each of this works—Ray Eyerly with a C in a circle then the year.

Maybe I could be an artist like Ray when I grew up. Mom painted several pictures in oils. If she had the gift, maybe I did, too. Dad said we'd eat a meal there the next time we came into town.

Before heading back to camp, we drove a few miles toward Bend for some sightseeing. Dad pulled over as we watched a herd of black horses running, with the Three Sisters in the background.

It wasn't unusual for anyone from the Sheriff's office to come in for a meal at The Gallery. However, there were a few raised eyebrows when Marleen went into the empty lounge area with the two men in tan uniforms. They asked her to share her observations and facts of the past several weeks. She chattered on about the boys' recent activities. She shared her personal timeline of letting the cat out and seeing Coop's truck. They asked about odd noises or sounds. She remembered the rumbling sounds not being Coop's truck. The part that spooked her the most had been the dead duck. They thanked her and told her she'd been very helpful. They'd be back in contact with her if they needed more information.

When we got back to camp, we discovered someone left an empty can on the table. It was completely squashed with tooth holes in it. These were not chipmunk, squirrel or bird pecks, but good size bite holes. A few adults suspected a bear might have wandered through. Since we'd all gone into Sisters and left our campsite area empty, there was no one to verify the suspected intruder. Wouldn't somebody from another campsite have seen a bear?

I shared what the owner of the Camp Sherman store said about bobcats being spotted in the area. An adult said the holes in the can were too large for a bobcat. I almost said out loud what I was thinking which was, "How do you know the size of a bobcat bite?" But I didn't want to be disrespectful to my elders. Peggy looked at me knowing what my question was. She heard it too, plus Buck had told us about bobcats on our trail ride.

I really thought the bobcat explanation was much more believable than a bear. Mom tapped me on my shoulder and pointed toward a loopy-eared peaceful looking dog resting under the tree in the campground on the other side of us, and said, "Or that innocent looking culprit."

That afternoon we played a game of softball in the middle of an uneven dirt field. We used pieces of campfire kindling made into the shape of a square for the bases. Dad was always the pitcher of any softball game. He couldn't run due to a WWII injury when a land mine exploded while he and others were climbing a mountain in the Italian Alps. The other dads were outfielders leaving the infield for us kids.

Max batted first. He hit a good grounder to shortstop, Peggy's dad. Max took off for first base as Peggy's dad tossed the ball to Mom who caught the ball in her mitt. Her foot balanced clearly on the base narrowly missing Max's head who slid in. She'd caught it before he reached the base, "HE'S OUT" I heard from somebody. Then magically it bounced out of her mitt. Out became "SAFE."

"Baloney," I exclaimed, not being shy. Being on her team, I wasn't at all happy that she dropped the ball on purpose. Then I thought, well, that's what moms do. She'd likely lost many board and card games over the years to help build our self-esteem and confidence. Max demolished first base. He also twisted his ankle on a mound of hard dirt. He sat on the sidelines the rest of the game. He thought he would like to be a professional baseball player, but maybe not since his ankle hurt a lot. "It doesn't matter what you accomplish, I'll always be proud of you," Mom said. I rolled my eyes, thinking something that shouldn't be spoken.

Max had always been outgoing, friendly, plus kind-hearted. I thought he'd be a good doctor. Then again, he didn't like studying all that much so that probably wouldn't happen. Maybe a fireman; he liked superheroes. He made friends easily waiting in a line or standing on a corner. He won prizes often for selling the most magazines, candy, or wrapping paper products for school fundraisers. I thought he'd be good at selling something, probably anything.

Peggy and I took our youngest brothers, Bill and Will, on a walk to the store. We secretly hoped this might release some of their boyish energy. Both of these boys thought up pranks that probably hadn't ever been done before, in my book. Mom slipped some nickels to Will. I looked at her, raising my eyebrows almost asking out loud, "Why did he get free money and I didn't?" Being almost fourteen, I had babysitting funds. He was seven and did nothing. I scowled then whined something about how being the oldest wasn't always the best. Her smiling reply about his unearned coins, "No one said life is fair, darling daughter." There would be a noticeable disparity of many things between the oldest and youngest child for years.

Coop drove the three hours directly to Madras. Since Sisters was in Deschutes County, he contemplated going to the sheriff there. However, he knew Camp Sherman and the Metolius River were in Jefferson County. Plus, his cousin Clay was a deputy with Jefferson County. He didn't even stop at home when driving through Sisters. On the drive he thought a lot about Rusty's mom, Mrs. K. What could he do to help her in the future?

Late in the afternoon, ashen-faced Coop walked into the Jefferson County Sheriff's Office. He saw Deputy Malloy, his cousin Clay, putting down the phone at his desk.

Malloy just finished speaking with another person calling in to identify their dead man. Rusty. Rusty. They all called him Rusty. Malloy knew this cousin Coop had a roommate named Rusty.

Flummoxed, Malloy's mouth dropped open when he looked up as his nineteen-year-old cousin Coop approached him. Malloy had a sinking feeling in the pit of his stomach just from his hunched walk. No, not Coop, he said to himself.

Malloy grabbed Walker as they moved into the conference room which would now become an interrogation room. Coop told them everything he knew. They peppered him with questions that he answered honestly and as best as he could. He told them about Rusty's bizarre behavior recently. His seething anger when asked the simplest questions. Then the windfall of fifty-dollar bills. Expensive shoes and new leather jacket. He recalled the name Harley. When Coop mentioned the name Harley, Walker glanced at Malloy. They recognized the name Harley. Rusty had gotten in with a bad crowd. A very dangerous crowd. A deadly crowd, as it turned out.

Oregon had several organized clubs. They all were associated with white supremacy groups, prison gangs, and organized crime. Their list of criminal activity had been growing rapidly: motorcycle thefts, prostitution, money laundering, gang violence, illegal weapons, and narcotics. These were groups everyday citizens did not want to be around. They'd heard Harley had established the East Side Outlaw Gang.

They speculated Rusty most likely had become a mid-level supplier, using and dealing drugs. The popular drug of choice was crystal meth. They theorized Rusty decided to skim some from the packages he had been paid to deliver.

Walker asked Coop to think about the attack. Walker told Coop to close his eyes. Leaning back in the wooden swivel chair, taking himself back in time, Coop remembered the odd smell of paint remover or thinner. Maybe on the clothing of the attackers. Then he remembered the cat pee odor. He fidgeted in the chair reliving the confusion of two extra people showing up. They were completely quiet except for groans and moans when Vern or Rusty had gotten a punch in. He felt terrified. The swoosh of the air when he missed his target. He remembered Vern sputtering something—oh yeah, swearing a blue streak. Coop's pulse raced and head pounded. He twitched in the chair.

Malloy felt badly for his younger cousin. The horror of finding his friend in the river. His utter confusion. Coop felt so aware of his surrounding right then, like he was in the fight all over again. He heard the tick-tock of the clock on the wall. One of the attackers might have wheezed or sneezed. He scraped one of them hard with his fingernails.

Malloy realized that soon he'd be removed from this case. A deputy related to a key witness should not be involved in the investigation.

Sheriff Perkins came in, sat across from Coop, and listened for a couple of minutes. He said, "Mr. MacNeill, it would sure expedite matters if we didn't have to wait for a search warrant, which by law we will do. But there's a lot of rigmarole requesting the warrant. It would save us some precious time if you sign this statement giving us your okay to search your place. Then Detective Walker can go immediately." Perkins was asking for a favor. Sometimes things like this happened in small towns—favors.

Perkins slid a piece of paper toward Coop. Signing at the bottom, he had no reason not to let them in. The sooner the investigation got going, the better.

Coop asked about Rusty's mom. Had anyone spoken to her? No, they hadn't. They'd just found out from Marleen and now Coop who the deceased actually was. Several others had called in with the same identification.

Assuming it would be out of the ordinary, Coop asked anyway. "Can I go with whoever is designated to tell Rusty's mom?" In this county, usually the sheriff or detective handled notifying families of issues like this. However, when learning of the update, Perkins instructed Malloy and Coop to go together. Another perk of living in a small town.

Walker said he could go immediately to do the search and called Deputy Foster from Camp Sherman to meet him there. Coop handed his front door key to Walker.

Before going to see Mrs. K, the deceased's body needed to be positively identified. Malloy pulled Walker and Perkins aside. He stated the obvious. Rusty Kavanagh had been beaten to death. His face was mangled. No mother should have to see her son in this shape. Could Coop could ID the body?

Walker and Perkins discussed it. They concluded Coop could do it instead of normal protocol which should be identification by next of kin. No one wanted to put Rusty's mom through the trauma of seeing her only son the way he looked. Their kindness would save her a devastating final memory.

Perkins reminded Malloy of the two tasks, then he was off the case. Malloy nodded, walking out the door.

As the two men walked down the steps to the basement of a spooky funeral home, the older asked his cousin, "Are you ready to do this?" Coop nodded his head. Malloy introduced Coop to Doc V, who'd met them there. The medical examiner removed a glove and shook his hand.

They let Coop adjust to the stark walls in the chilly room, a room where he'd never been before—in the basement of a funeral home. Shoved in a back corner out of the way hung two framed certificates on the wall directly above a gray metal desk. A black rotary telephone and a white writing pad with a pen carefully placed on the top were the only items on the desk. What a creepy office, Coop thought. There were two long stainless-steel tables on wheels. Coop noticed the edges of the tables were curved upward, he guessed to prevent fluids from spilling onto the floor.

It reminded Coop of a surgical room, recalling when he'd had his tonsils removed when he was about eight years old. If he thought about it too much, he could still smell the ether from the plastic mask that covered his nose and mouth causing him to fall asleep.

Another table was full of clean instruments and, on the end, something that looked like an electric power tool.

He overheard bits and pieces from Doc V and his cousin, saying something about a mortician would have a hard time cleaning up the victim to look halfway decent if the family member chose to have an open casket at a funeral. After he received all the blood test results back from the autopsy, he hoped they'd select to cremate the remains.

Coop could hardly believe what he heard, the two men discussing like it was an everyday occurrence. Doc V didn't flip on the bright silver lights. Then he quietly asked Coop, "Are you ready, young man?" Coop just nodded. Coop knew the body on a rolling cart hidden under a white sheet was his long-time childhood friend. He still didn't want to believe it.

Coop sucked air. He steeled himself. He knew why he was there and what he needed to do. It was all explained carefully by Detective Walker.

Doc V lifted the white sheet off the victim stretched out on a stainless-steel table. Tears temporarily blinded him. Now it felt real, tragically real. He quietly said, "That's Rusty Kavanagh." When they exited, he dropped to his knees, hands on the grass, and retched.

———

Coop told Clay where Rusty's mother lived, forty-five minutes away in Sisters. They'd meet at her duplex at seven o'clock. But first he went to speak with Vern's parents. M2 threw her arms around him. Vern's dad's long arms circled them all together in a huddle. They also had seen the photo of Rusty in the Sunday afternoon newspaper and became very concerned. Plus, Vern had taken her Buick and fled to Len's in Canada. They tried calling Len, but no one answered the phone. They couldn't know Len and Vern were both avoiding speaking with their parents for now.

When no one answered the phone at the boys' house, they'd driven over and found Coop's truck was gone. They'd driven over several times after reading the newspaper. They were just getting ready to contact Coop's mother and try Len again.

Coop told them the whole sordid story and that he'd just come from the Sheriff's office and medical examiner. M2 cried thinking about what this unfortunate episode in their lives would do to her son and Coop. She cried harder thinking of Rusty's poor mother. Vern's dad sat next to her on the extra-long sofa, patting her left knee. "It'll be okay, we will all work this out together," he tried to assure her, and himself.

Coop asked them to call Vern so he could speak with him. Coop relayed to Vern that he told a deputy the whole story. He didn't think they were in any big *trouble*, but they needed his version. The longer Vern waited, the more *trouble* he would be in. Coop emphasized the word trouble, saying it loudly. "Fly right, Vern," was his final comment. Vern wanted to stay in Canada. After several minutes of persuasion and Coop raising his voice a couple of times, a reluctantly wishy-washy Vern promised to be home Tuesday late afternoon.

Rusty's mom heard a knock on the door. When she answered, there stood Coop and a deputy in uniform. Malloy saw where Rusty inherited his looks. She had cinnamon hair with gray streaks and stood all of five feet tall.

Malloy temporarily lost his concentration when looking at the surroundings. He felt like he'd stepped into a giant bowl of guacamole. Avocado green kitchen countertops matched the green shag carpet. Two metal chairs with green- and navy-checked vinyl-covered cushions were pushed snuggly under a metal dinette table. It was next to a matching set of an avocado-colored fridge and stove. He didn't know avocado green sinks even existed. Fake wood paneling covered all the walls. The shag carpet wasn't avocado but instead grass green. A lamp sat on the end table with a matching grass green shade. That's a whole lot of green, he thought. Out of the corner of his eye, he saw something gray dive behind a chair.

Her deep blue eyes instantly went from elated seeing Coop, to questioning, then sorrowful, seeing the officer.

Deputy Malloy introduced himself and when he took her hand, he noticed a surprising firm shake. "Mrs. K," Coop mumbled as he shuffled into the room staring at his feet rather than looking her in the eye. They followed her to her compact living room. She motioned them towards the small sofa. She sat perched on the edge of an avocado, turquoise and tawny floral-patterned swivel chair.

Coop nervously picked up the June edition of *Ladies Home Journal* magazine with actress Ali McGraw on the cover. He placed it next to the *TV Guide* on the glass coffee table that separated them. Malloy eased into a gold- and brown-flecked loveseat directly across from her. Coop's legs turned to jelly as he loosely landed on his side of the small couch.

She noticed Coop's face was black and blue with bruises. One on his neck started turning amber and bronze.

In his official capacity, Deputy Malloy started, "Mrs. Kavanagh," he paused taking a breath, "Ma'am, I'm sorry to have to tell you that an incident has occurred involving your son."

Coop's eyes were fixated on the matted down grass green carpet. He couldn't even look at her. She scooched back in the chair and whispered, "Cooper, tell me the whole story." When he summoned the courage to look at her, tears streamed down his swollen face. A gray cat jumped up on Mrs. Kavanagh's lap. Coop told her everything he remembered, not leaving out anything.

When he finished, she asked, "Cooper, are you positive it's my Rusty?"

"Yes, ma'am."

"I should go to my son…," not finishing the sentence. She wasn't sure if she was making a proclamation or really asking for reassurance that she should. Or shouldn't.

Coop's face turned white as a sheet thinking of Rusty's mom seeing him that way on Doc V's autopsy table. It had been horrible enough for him, he couldn't image her doing it. "Uh, no, ma'am, you shouldn't," he matter-of-factly told her.

She told Malloy she felt shocked, but not really surprised. He asked why and she told him Rusty had been giving her extra money lately, paying her in fifty-dollar bills. When she asked how he gotten it, he shrugged and said he was getting paid what he was owed for doing some extra jobs.

Rusty's mom gently removed her cat Cozmo off her lap and took Coop's hands in hers. She looked up into his sorrowful eyes. She reassured him, "This isn't your fault. Thank you for being such a good friend to Rusty. I'm sure it hasn't been easy for you to continue that friendship. For whatever reason, he chose a different path than you and even Vernon. You are not to blame." She finished looking him squarely in his watery eyes. "We have all done the best we could," she ended.

"Mrs. Kavanagh," Malloy said, "can you provide information on any distinguishing marks?" He wrote in his book, a mole on the outside right thigh and birthmark behind the left ear.

Malloy instructed that if she thought or remembered anything that might help solve the case of her son's murder to please contact Detective Walker. He left his card with Walker's name on the green countertop. When Mrs. K hugged Coop, most bones in his body still hurt. The top of her head only reached the middle of his chest. She buried her face into his lightweight jacket. When they left, through the flimsy door Coop heard Rusty's mother burst into sobs.

Coop's cousin asked if he wanted to stay a few days with him. Coop thanked him but said he needed to speak with his mom and tell her what had happened. He'd stay with her for few days. When he arrived at her house, she came running out of the door. He just wanted a long hug from her like he got when he was a little kid.

———

Detective Walker and Deputy Foster showed up about the same time at Coop's rental. Marleen noticed two county vehicles, as did several other neighbors. It was unusual to say the least.

Inside they meticulously went room by room, opening drawers in the kitchen and bathroom. They found nothing in two of the three bedrooms. In the third bedroom, obviously Rusty's, Foster snapped photos as Walker tagged and bagged plenty of evidence. In one dresser, the detective, not really surprised, found a pistol tucked inside a pillowcase. They loaded two brown paper grocery bags of helpful evidence into Walker's vehicle.

———

My brothers gobbled dinner of homemade chili and warm cornbread that Mom baked fresh, in hopes we all could go sooner on a drive at dusk looking for deer. Mom, Dad and I ate at a normal pace. Dad knew these graceful, beautiful animals moved around, usually coming up from the river to bed down in some cushy green brush. That evening we counted twenty-seven, which tallied up quickly because there was never just one alone, but several together.

Back at camp as we did each night, we sat around the rip roarin' fire telling stories. Dad came up with a spooky one: Johnny left a friend's house in the dead of night. He switched on his headlights to see down the creepy county roads. It started to rain. As he drove, he saw a blurry image of a woman. She wore a long, white dress and was walking down the middle of the road. Shocked, he slammed on his brakes. Leaning out the window, he asked if the young lady needed a ride somewhere.

Will interrupted the story, which proved he was actually listening, reminding us that we were told never to talk to strangers. Dad said it was just a story and not to interrupt. Continuing with the story, the woman didn't say anything. She just got into the front seat. Since she was shivering, Johnny put his coat over her shoulders.

They drove in silence for a few miles. The girl motioned to an old house. Without saying anything, she said that she wanted to stop there. Johnny pulled to a stop in the driveway and the girl got out of the car. Johnny unrolled his window to ask for his coat back, but the girl disappeared.

It was a chilly night, so Johnny wanted his coat. He walked to the door of the old house and knocked four times. An elderly woman answered and he explained what happened. He had just dropped the girl off, but he needed to get his coat.

The old woman burst into tears. As she controlled her emotion, she explained that her daughter had been driving to prom when she got into a car wreck on this day ten years ago. Now her body was buried in the cemetery up the road, next to the spot where Johnny picked her up.

A chill went down his spine and had a hard time believing the story. The next day, he went to the cemetery and found the girl's grave. On top of it lay Johnny's jacket.

Jeff's mom had now become our nightly star expert. Again, we were all looking up at the dark sky of twinkling diamonds. She turned our attention to the moon that the two astronauts would land on in a couple of months. Peggy's brother Bill asked if the moon always shows its same face. She explained that our moon rotates on its axis while it orbits the earth, so we always see the same regions of craters and valleys.

She pointed out a bright star named Polaris that stays fixed above the North Pole. It helped captains of boats and ships for navigation purposes. The brightest star in the sky is Sirius, in the Big Dog constellation.

Then she named all the planets in order from the sun: Mercury, Venus, Earth, Mars, Jupiter, Saturn, Uranus, Neptune, and Pluto. She suggested we all memorize the planets in order by remembering this little silly sentence: "My Very Educated Mother Just Served Us Nuts." We were in the most fun star classroom ever.

Maleah got to stay with us again tonight. We played the card game UNO until the flashlight got dimmer and dimmer. I remembered what Mom said often, "There are consequences to your actions." We shut off the flashlight hoping we'd have enough batteries for the next night.

Nothing stopped for construction, so Arlo had worked on what for most was a holiday. He was glad something had kept him busy. He didn't want to fall asleep that night. The dreams were scaring him. This one included the Rose family. They all found themselves thrown into an unending night on the eve of the execution of somebody. But he woke up before he found out who. Harley? Mr. Rose? Himself?

CHAPTER EIGHT

*O*ff To See The Wizard

From his mom's home, Coop phoned his supervisor at the bank promptly at 7:30 knowing he would be there. He explained he was in the midst of a family emergency and needed two more days off. His supervisor said in a concerned voice, "You are an excellent worker and you haven't taken time off in an entire year. Take whatever time you need, Cooper." Coop promised to be in Thursday morning.

Then Coop's mother called the bank manager at her branch. "I won't be in today, Woodie." The manager was stunned. In all the years they had worked together, Mrs. MacNeill had never taken a day off except for vacation time that was requested months in advance.

"No problem, Jennifer, let us know if you need anything." She didn't sound ill so he assumed it must be something very serious for her to call at the last minute like this. She ended by saying, "I will let you know about tomorrow." Now he knew it was something major.

Tuesday, Arlo went to work contemplating his future. He wondered if he should see a doctor. Maybe the wounds on his neck were infected, causing nighttime hallucinations.

Before our daily outing, Peggy and I had the bright idea to help exhaust our high-energy brothers and the other boys —bike races. Several of the boys had their short-frame, sturdy stingrays so we set up an obstacle course for them to complete. They'd have to traverse the gauntlet twice. We shoveled handfuls of soft pine needles over limbs and a log to make a two-foot high jump. We made an X-sign from twigs where they had to do three tight circles around a large tree. Then they must slalom through a course of five trees, over a dirt mound down a dip then speed to the finish line.

We lined them up and gave the youngest ones a two-second head start. Ready, Set, Go! Off they went, dirt flying and dust rolling in their wake. On the first lap, Billy wiped out coming down the backside after the jump. He got back up, dusty but uninjured. The older brothers, Max and Dave plus Jeff, were in the lead with Will trailing a bit. All seemed a bit cautious after seeing Bill take his tumble, except Jeff.

On the second lap Dave got in the two tight circles around the trees and forgot the third—"Disqualified," I yelled. Hot dog Will ran his bike into a deep hole cutting in too close to a tree. One runner stumbled forward, ripping a hole in his britches, his legs so tired they refused to obey.

Max came in first, staying the course, sometimes not as fast as the others, but true and steady and barely ahead of Jeff. For winning first place, I promised him a soft ice cream cone at the restaurant at the Metolius River Resort. I can't say the plan worked to poop them out, but I did hope their appreciation for our efforts might curtail pranks for a couple of nights.

We all piled into our vehicles for the annual visit to Wizard Falls Fish Hatchery. We drove about a half hour through the forest. I rode with Peggy, sitting in the back seat facing out the back window of their station wagon, waving at my folks behind us.

At a stop sign, one of her twerpy brothers yelled, "Chinese fire drill." This meant we all had to get out and run around the car twice, then get back in from a different door. Her elderly parents, probably in their forties, even did it. They were already around the car once as Peggy and I were climbing all the way from the third-row seat. My parents were in our truck stuck right behind us and watched the commotion, laughing the whole time. Maleah and her parents brought up the rear of the procession, also laughing at the entertainment.

Driving across the wooden one-lane bridge, we arrived at the parking lot. I noticed a neat black car with the red stripe down the side, just like the one that had been parked at the store the first morning of the "episode."

I asked Dad, "What's that car?"

He replied, "It's a '64 Ford Fairlane 500. Why? Do you like it?"

"I think it's cool. I'm sure it's the same one that we saw at the store the morning of the——"

"Are you sure?" Dad cut me off saving me from having to say the "episode" word, "That's certainly a coincidence."

Before going into the hatchery Peggy and I locked arms skipping back to the one-lane bridge singing, "I love to go a-wandering, Along the mountain track, And as I go, I love to sing, My knapsack on my back., Val-deri-, Val-dera, Val-deri, Val-dera-ha-ha-ha-ha-ha Val-deri, Val-dera, My knapsack on my back." She couldn't carry a tune but neither of us cared.

Looking upriver, it narrows, cascading over lava. Dozens of vine maple trees with their twisty sprawling limbs line the shaded stream banks. Because we'd been here so many times in autumn, I knew in a few months they would put on a spectacular show, brightening the area with colorful foliage of yellow, amber, tangerine and scarlet.

Scampering down to the water's edge, scooting underneath the maple tree limbs, I noticed the leaves were long, wide and much like the shape of a three-pronged wisdom tooth, with veins at the base traveling through each leaf. They are bright green on top and paler below. Some seeds falling to the ground looked like miniature helicopter propellers.

The cottonwoods had trunks so big that when Peggy and I put our arms around one our fingers didn't even touch. These leaves are deep green and oval to sort of heart-shaped with veins from the stem outward. They are green on top and white below. In the fall, they turn a beautiful yellow which is so pretty with the vine maples colorful show. I picked a couple of pretty heart-shaped leaves and would press them between the pages in my *Flicka* book.

Had we been here a few weeks earlier, we would have seen falling snow, actually cottony seeds floating in the wind. We had the same type of trees at home along the banks of Oak Creek. The cottonwood felt like tiny twigs in my eyes.

The water dumps into a triangle shaped dip creating swirling white edges. A pool of sea green water changes to Windex bottle blue. Then it drops down farther into another big hole and the water is sea green again. It flows under the bridge turning an aqua color. Out the other side racing through the lava bed it turns a brilliant turquoise. Then the river rises slightly higher on both sides returning to navy and sapphire.

We raised our voices because of the sound of the roaring water. The rushing river created a refreshing breeze. An eagle or an osprey flew overhead, too far away to know for sure. Maybe we'd be lucky enough to see it drop in for a meal.

This wasn't really a waterfall at all, but more like gentle rapids. But most people assumed these were Wizard Falls. It isn't true. It's not there anymore. Before the hatchery had been built in 1947, according to the plaque on the wall, there had been a twelve-foot-waterfall about a quarter of a mile upstream. A photo showed the original cascade where the water bubbling out of Wizard Falls Spring poured into the river. By constructing the fish hatchery, the spring had been rerouted to provide water for the ponds, which dried up the falls. The words seemed to imply that it had been a questionable waterfall in the first place.

I leaned against a huge ponderosa. It smelled much like a vanilla candle. The hatchery had its own smell—fish.

Our parents and brothers read the plaques of informa-tion and waited for us to join them. Then the brothers made a beeline for the deep cement tanks. Mom yelled, "Max! Don't get too close to the edge!!" Peggy's mom yelled. "Dave! Don't get too close to the edge!!"

Standing on the other side of the first tank another mom yelled to her son, "Peter! Don't get too close to the edge." The moms sounded just like the repeating mynah bird at the Mountain House. I am positive that all moms sound the same with their momisms.

The other mom was part of a family of six. She stood about five feet tall standing next to her six-foot-tall husband. Then an older brother and the boy she called Peter, who had dark chocolate-colored hair and sparkling blue eyes. There appeared to be a couple of younger sisters, too.

Peggy and I wandered to a separate large pond with some real whoppers. Tiny fingerlings were in several tanks separated by type of fish: rainbow and brook trout, kokanee and salmon, spring chinook and summer steel-head. They were raised here and released into the wild.

Our brothers were already feeding the fish little morsels purchased for a penny from the plastic tubs located along the tanks. When we tossed the smelly fish food into the tanks, lightning-fast fish bubbled to the surface for a snack.

Four western tanagers landed not far from us. Their black wings were set off by their entire body of bright sunshine yellow with a candy corn orange head. Little black-capped chickadees poked through gravel, looking for nibbles. A red-headed sapsucker clung to the bark of a pine tree, pounding noisily.

Canada geese were migrating. They also liked the fish pellets and didn't mind getting a little too close for comfort to me. These are not cute little ducks like the mallards at home. Instead they are giant geese of beautiful coloring with tall black necks and heads but about the size of a wild turkey. We had to watch where we walked because after they ate, they disposed of their meal in the shape of large tootsie rolls.

I discovered something I'd not seen in prior visits. In the corner of one of the long tanks, underwater a fish carved from light wood was lying on its side. It read, "Welcome to Wizard Falls Fish Hatchery" and the little circle below it read "Est. 1947."

Will pointed out a bald eagle with its white head and tail, then a second one. The first looped back to a huge nest. Max pointed out a raccoon across the pond snatching its next meal. Several dippers and kingfishers were wading in the shallow water. Some goldeneye and merganser ducks were swimming in pairs in the large sky-blue pond. The black and white goldeneye truly had a golden eye next to the swish on its cheek. The russet-headed momma merganser had two ducklings enjoying their free ride while sitting comfortably on her tan back.

Peggy pointed out a herd of deer with three babies, all with speckles, on our drive returning to camp. Peggy and I moved the lawn chairs back to our favorite spot in the river to dangle our feet and look at magazines. The slight breeze caused by the gentle river was just enough to lower the temperature by several degrees.

Late in the afternoon, Walker was in the office when Vern arrived accompanied by his dad. The father stood straight and rigid, still keeping his hair short, a military style buzz cut. Vern slumped. He sat with his head bowed in such a state of utter misery that Walker couldn't help but feel sorry for him. The tall kid looked scared and like he was going to upchuck on the spot. Walker decided to wait to put him out of his misery. He deserved to sit there a while and stew about the consequences of fleeing the country. Vern spilled his guts. When he reached the end of the story, Walker point blank asked him, "Vernon, did you kill Rusty?" "I don't think so. I just don't know who I hit."

His story matched Cooper's. Still Walker said, "I think there's a good possibility you are telling me the truth. So, here's what we are going to do. We're not going to charge you with obstructing justice or anything else right now. We've got a lot of work to do to find out what actually happened. Don't ever do anything stupid like this again. And do not leave the area."

Vern had already determined on the long drive home from Canada, his delinquent days were over. He grew up in about five days. He'd be enlisting in the U.S. Army, like his dad. Apparently not for a while though.

———————

Several of us kids did our daily walk to the store for a little treat. This time when we entered, the smiling man behind the counter said to me, "Hello. You're becoming a regular." I told him where we were staying at Riverside and that it was our annual campout with friends, pointing to Peggy.

Will blurted out, "We're the ones who found a guy at the headwaters on Friday." I punched his arm as hard as I could as he yelped, "What?"

The nice man said, "I'm sorry for you and your family." I thought about his comment walking back to camp. I appreciated that he felt sorry for me, well, us. I realized I felt sorry, too. Sorry the young man died. Sorry for his family. Sorry we had been the ones to find him. Sorry I would always have the picture of his feet etched into my memory.

Back in camp sitting in the river, I brushed away a tiny cone that dropped from a limb landing in my lap. Peggy flicked off some pine needles that landed on her head. A little tree frog leaped from somewhere onto the end of the lounger missing my foot by an inch as I let out a shriek. One thing, okay, two maybe, but a frog on the chair?

Then we both heard those two little pesky nincompoops, Will and Bill, laughing in the bushes. I yelled to Mom, revealing their bothersome misdeeds, and her only reply, "Boys will be boys." I would hear that so many times in my life. It already was way overused as an excuse for boys behaving badly.

Dad suggested a stroll while Mom fixed dinner. He drew our attention to a bird with its stocky gray body and long legs. The dipper dropped into the cold river and was sort of flying or swimming under the surface of the water looking for insects. Its eyes flashed white when it blinked. Dad suspected it must have white feathers on its eyelids. Way out in the meadow, he pointed out a herd of Rocky Mountain elk.

Dinner was one of our favorites—Mom's lasagna packed with Italian spices, garlic, ground up hot sausage and hamburger, tomatoes and several types of cheeses, layered between flat wide noodles. I asked Mom where lasagna came from and she said Italy, a country in Europe. Dad mentioned that was where he served in WWII, in the Italian Alps on Mount Belvedere in the 10th Mountain Division. He'd had plenty of Italian food and he thought

Mom's was the best. She'd brought the recipe for Peggy's mom, but I copied it down first.

1 lb. spicy Italian sausage

1 lb. lean ground beef

1 clove minced garlic

1 medium onion chopped

1 can diced tomatoes, 1 lb., 12 oz.

1 can tomato sauce, 15 oz.

1½ T parsley flakes

1½ T sugar

1 tsp salt

1 tsp crushed basil leaves

1 2 lb. carton large curd cottage cheese

½ c grated parmesan cheese

1 T parsley flakes

1 tsp salt

2 tsp crushed oregano leaves

8 oz. lasagna noodles, cooked and well drained

¾ bl. shredded mozzarella

½ c parmesan cheese

Cook sausage, ground beef, onion and garlic until meats are browned and tender. Drain well. Add diced tomatoes. Stir in tomato sauce, add 1½ T parsley flakes, sugar, 1 tsp salt and basil; simmer uncovered for one hour or until mixture is thick.

Heat oven at 350. Mix cottage cheese, ½ cup parmesan cheese, 1 T parsley flakes, 1 tsp salt and oregano.

In oblong baking dish, at least 13 ½ x 9 x 2, layer half each of the noodles, sauce, mozzarella cheese and cottage cheese mixture. Spread sauce over the top, sprinkle with ½ c. parmesan cheese. Repeat. Reserve enough sauce for a thin top layer. Spread sauce over top, sprinkle with ½ c parmesan cheese.

Bake uncovered 45-55 minutes or until cheese is bubbly in the *center. Let stand 15 minutes after removing from oven. Cut into squares. Serves 8-10. Bake night before, cool and refrigerate. Cook 20-30 minutes at 350 degrees before serving.*

Sunset crept around the trees. Standing by Jeff's mom, I mentioned how pretty the colors were. She asked me to describe what I saw. When I replied, "pink and orange," she said, "No, tell me what you see, not just colors. Make it into a story." She knew I liked to tell stories, so I played along. This would be fun.

I told her "As the orb drops lower, the sun is sliced in half by a straight line of a thin layer of clouds. It's dropped below the clouds now causing the sky to turn cantaloupe to tangerine, flowing to cherry and strawberry colors. The cloud layers are trimmed in silver along the bottom. The shiny ball is getting closer to the mountain ridge causing a brighter reflection on the river. The sun is gently disappearing behind the ridge and the color has changed to ruby like a grapefruit. It looks like a gigantic fruit salad of colors created just for us." She said that's exactly what she wanted to hear from me. She suggested I think about becoming a writer.

Around the campfire, while toasting marshmallows, one of the dads decided he wanted to share a story. I knew this meant yet another scary story. Maleah's mom suggested we forego a scary story and several of us wholeheartedly agreed.

Mom suggested Dad tell a lighthearted tale. He shared about growing up in northern Alberta in Canada and his favorite horse named Shorty. Dad sort of seemed transported back to his youth when he talked about Shorty. He clearly loved that horse.

He said, "He was a reddish-brown bay horse with a black nose. He also had black tips on his ears and lower legs, with a black mane and tail. He wasn't as tall as the other horses, so I named him Shorty. He was just the right size and perfect for me.

Every day I loved brushing Shorty, especially his black, shiny, thick mane. When I did, I told him everything that was happening, good or bad. Often, he would nuzzle me and make funny noises. I knew he was talking to me. I brought him carrots that I would sneak from dinner. I didn't like carrots. When feeding the other animals, if he thought I was ignoring him he'd nudge me with his nose. More than once, I fell head over heels in the hay from the unexpected shove. He followed me around like a puppy in the barnyard. Even when doing chores like rounding up Dad's cows, it was fun riding him. When I rode him, it seemed like I was gliding on air or soaring in the clouds. If an animal could be a best friend, he was mine.

My favorite pastime was riding him bareback. I pretended to be a cowboy. I would get him running, slap him on the rump with the reins and he'd kick up his heels and he'd throw me off. One afternoon, some neighbor girls, Eleanor and Ella Lorensen, were visiting my sisters. They were sitting on the fence as I raced across the yard on Shorty. I whacked him on the rump with the reins and apparently he didn't like it as much as I thought. He bucked higher than usual and I sailed straight up right over his head and landed belly-first on the dusty ground right at the feet of the laughing audience. I could tell Shorty was laughing at me, too." And we all laughed, too. A warm feeling surrounded me—love and camaraderie with our circle of camping companions.

We all said goodnight and Peggy, Maleah and I scampered into our safe house for a game of Crazy Eights. We used the overhead canopy light, hoping Dad wouldn't catch us and see that we were wearing the battery down. Before we fell asleep, I announced I would only marry a man with dark hair, blue eyes and a nice smile, who loved the Metolius as much as I did.

Trying to prevent nightmares, Arlo got loaded, drinking six beers without food. He slept soundly the entire night.

CHAPTER NINE

*A*in't No Mountain High Enough

Wednesday morning Duke had gone missing. Could a bobcat have gotten him? Mom followed the muffled barking and located him stuck in the hole of a tree stump, no doubt a badger hole. Dad and Max carefully and gently pulled him out by holding his stomach. He had dirt up his long nose and inside his droopy ears. Even his brown eyes were caked in dust. Mom cleaned his ears with cotton balls, and his nose with Q-tips. She put him in the river to clean off the rest of him. Then we had breakfast.

Since no decisions had been made about the activity of the day, Peggy and I walked the mile to the store for sweet treats. When paying, I pulled out the Canadian quarter. Where did it come from, I wondered.

I flashed back to that morning at the headwaters. I'd seen a shiny coin and picked it up. A heat flash started in my toes rising into my cheeks as I exclaimed to Peggy, "I think I'm in big trouble." When I told her why, she just shook her head replying, "Man, oh man." I had to tell Dad.

Peggy and I almost ran back to camp. When I showed him the coin blurting out my story, he didn't say a word to me. His blue eyes turned steely. He drove to the store and called Deputy Malloy from the telephone booth. Malloy said someone would be out to retrieve the evidence. When Dad returned, he filled me in and pronounced the word "evidence" slowly, implying I never should have touched it.

I saw Walker's car pull up. He had someone else with him. Local resident Deputy Jensen Foster had returned from vacation. He was also now involved in the case.

Walker asked me where I found the coin. I answered his questions. It brought back memories of that morning. I was so relieved he didn't haul me to jail for something like obstruction of justice. Or hiding evidence. Or whatever else they called it on TV.

I timidly asked where Deputy Malloy was. Walker explained a family connection removed him from the case. Walker told Dad a few facts. I found it interesting that a specialized artist had come in and done a drawing from photos of the dead man. His drawing had led to positive identification. The victim had been killed by a blow to his temple. They were interviewing witnesses and would solve the crime at some point. It could take months, he warned.

———

Cooper's mother took another day off work as did Vern's father. Coop and his mother arrived at the Christopherson's home entering as the black kit-cat cuckoo clock chimed eleven times. As a kid, Coop laughed at the silly thing with rolling eyes and wagging tail. The parents had arranged a time for all of them to get together. Vern pulled the door open for Coop's mom. Seeing each other for the first time since the incident, he and Coop stood outside, silent, just looking at each other in total disbelief. "I know, I can still hardly believe it," Vern stated.

They all concluded that neither son would be going anywhere for some time. Cooper still had his job at the bank and Vern would continue working at the golf course. Life would go on until the case was solved. They would be available for anything the Sheriff's office needed. Then the boys could figure out what was next.

Vern mentioned the army again and his mother said, "We shall see, Vern. There is no rush to decide right now, dear." This was a real shocker for Coop to hear about the military idea which Vern had been adamantly opposed to.

Vern and Coop decided they'd stay in their rental house, minus one roommate. Later they would learn from Marleen about the dead duck left on their porch and other tidbits of information. Coop would be kept in the loop by his cousin. Probably. Well, maybe, since Deputy Malloy had been taken off the case.

Walker stopped at The Gallery before driving the forty-five minutes back to the office. He'd been hankering for one of their specialties, a chili burger. While waiting for his order, he looked at some of Ray Eyerly's paintings.

One of his favorites called "Old School House," showed a building nestled in the middle of pines and scrubby junipers and grasses mostly in browns, greens and cream colors. There were two small buildings behind the school. He guessed one might be an outhouse. A wood fence separates the school property from the hills. The porch covered the front of the building held up by four wooden pillars. There was a cupola on top, or maybe a guard tower. Three large windows let in sunlight to brighten the room. He felt like he was standing in the middle of the schoolyard waiting for the teacher to open the door, welcoming the students in for another day of school.

The artwork diverted his thoughts temporarily from the murder case they were all trying to solve. He savored each bite of the fiery homemade chili layered on the burger. He suspected they used spicy pork that added some pizzaz to it. He splurged, asking for extra onions and cheese. There might be heartburn consequences. Hopefully the chocolate milkshake would help.

Our family plus Peggy's decided it was time to hike and conquer Black Butte, sort of a mini-mountain. We put on our sturdiest walking shoes, long pants, and t-shirts, and slathered on sunscreen. I shoved my radio in my pocket hoping for some reception at the top of a mountain. We piled into our vehicles for a half-hour drive. We were in the lead because Dad had a secret.

Black Butte is a smooth cone-shaped volcano with a fire lookout. Dad drove past a marked pullout where a few cars parked at 4,880 feet. In a forest of coppery-barked, old-growth ponderosa pines, it indicated this was where we should begin the hike up. But he'd heard we could go farther up the butte resulting in less walking time. He thought with this tribe, including a short-legged dog, he should drive as far up possible. He parked by a little sign that showed 1.9 miles to the top; that would be 6,378 feet, if we made it.

The dads led the way. Our energetic brothers followed closely. Peggy and me, with our moms, brought up the rear. At first, we walked through low green scrubby bushes with just a few trees in the distance. The hike wasn't straight up and didn't wind round and round. Instead we serpentined back and forth on basically one side of the butte. About ten minutes into the hike I didn't think it was all that bad. Yes, we were walking up but on flat rocks that seemed evenly placed on the dirt trail. Plenty of greenery and trees lined the path.

Turned out that was just on one small portion of the butte. The bushes got sparser with some late snow packed in and underneath bushes and rocks. I thought I heard my Mom mumble something about why we thought this was a good idea.

Poor short-legged Duke. He ran ahead, doing laps around us, running probably five times as many steps as we walked. He found a patch of white stuff and flopped down not wanting to move his little legs. Dad and Mom shared carrying him a few times.

We stopped often to catch our breath, claiming we were actually viewing the gorgeous scenery and mountains. With my Kodak camera, I took a picture of Mount Jefferson miles away sandwiched between two pine trees. With each curve there was a hotter side, then we curved around to the cooler side. Another twist took us higher, stepping over bigger boulders on uneven ground. It seemed the higher we got, the rocky and steeper it became. Kindly, Max offered to help Mom by holding her hand and pulling her along. She preferred her own pace. The youngest boys with the most energy ran up then back down to check on us slow pokes. They ran ahead for some distance again, then back down with reports of what was ahead.

The path wound and climbed sharply over rocks then bigger boulders that we clambered up and around and over. As we curved to a yet another part of the hotter dusty stretch, we understood why some people said that this wasn't an easy trip. Back around we went to the cooler other side then back into the dreaded hot side with more rocks to climb.

I pointed way in the distance at the tall lookout on the tip top of the cone. I thought that fire lookouts were probably like the lighthouses of the mountains, perched at great vantage points providing the best views of the surrounding area. We weren't even close to the top yet. Now the moms were on their hands and knees holding onto the rocks. They were clearly not enjoying this outing.

Peggy's mom announced she was done. Finished. Wiped out. Not a step farther. We probably had about one-third of the way to go. Mom said Peggy's mom certainly shouldn't stay by herself and graciously offered to sit with her.

Peggy and I continued the climb. Max came rushing down and yelled that there was snow at the top and it wasn't all that far after all. The moms heard the announcement and willy-nilly continued on. Almost at the tip top, a couple of us ate handfuls of snow. After swallowing, we were told that probably wasn't a good idea since it had been there awhile.

As we made the final curve Dad yelled out, "Careful, that last step's a doozy." In the ground a wooden T-crossed sign read: "Black Butte Lookout Tower Built in 1935."

Off to the right were five or six giant trees of differing heights with the lookout standing guard. Walking over to the lookout, the sign at the base of the steps read,

FOREST SERVICE
LOOKOUT STATION
BLACK BUTTE
ELEV. 6436

There are six sections that narrow closer to the top. Flights of wooden steps are tucked inside the see-through tower. Decking surrounds the one-story, flat-roofed lookout at the top. As a man carefully and slowly stepped down the questionable wooden steps, we begged to climb to the top of the tower. In unison all four parents said, "No," in about two seconds flat. "Fuddy-duddies," one of the boys grumbled.

Mom had picked up a flyer at the Camp Sherman store about the history. She told us that Black Butte makes an ideal fire lookout site because of its location east of the Cascades. In 1910 one of Oregon's earliest fire detection structures had been built here—a simple "squirrel's nest" platform wedged between treetops. Even though the original lookout is gone, Black Butte has collected a variety of other lookout structures since then: an intact cupola-style building from 1923, the ruins of a collapsed 1934 tower, and then a modern sixty-two-foot tower.

I felt like I could reach out and touch the surrounding mountains. I framed Mount Washington through skimpy pine tree branches. It was easy to tell it apart from other mountains as it rose gently upwards and then into a sharp point forming its top.

Mom read that Mount Washington at 7,500 feet, was named for President George Washington. It stood stately, dressed in a shawl of snow reminding me of a nun dressed in all black with a white collar. It begins smooth on all sides. At the top it sort of flattens then slopes down to the right, then descends downhill.

She continued reading that Mount Jefferson is 10,157 feet in elevation and that Lewis and Clark named this Cascade peak after Thomas Jefferson who, as president, funded their expedition west. The British originally called it Mount Vancouver.

From our vantage point, The Three Sisters gracefully sweep across the horizon with the first two about the same height. The farthest one is much flatter and mostly hidden from our angle. According to the brochure, the tallest is the South Sister at 10,300 feet. There is no official record of who named the three peaks. A popular story is that they are called Mount Faith, Mount Hope and Mount Charity, north to south. They were named Three Sisters by members of a Methodist mission in Salem in the 1840s. Mom nicknamed them Patty, Ardie and Helen, sisters in her family.

We could see so many mountains. Broken Top, its name sort of explains itself with its shattered top, not really coming to a peak and apparently not named after anyone famous.

Three-Fingered Jack has little information on the origin of the name, which dates back to before 1895. One story says it's a namesake of a local three-fingered trapper named Jack.

Way in the distance, Mount Hood, granddaddy of all the mountains, is a whopping 11,250 feet in elevation. It is named for Lord Samuel Hood, some British naval officer who fought in the American Revolutionary War. In 1792, Lieutenant William Broughton, sailing with George Vancouver, named the peak for Lord Hood.

Looking closer, Dad pointed out sort of a hidden mountain—Mount Bachelor. Outside of Bend, it used to be called Bachelor Butte. But local officials changed the name fearing people would think skiing a butte would be considered small-time.

Standing on the edge of the butte reminded me of what Mom often said when I whined, usually wanting to do something, "Well, everyone else is doing it," and her reply was, "What if everyone jumped off a cliff, would you do it, too?" I certainly would not jump off of Black Butte.

After more pleading, both sets of parents agreed we could climb to the third level of the fire lookout. A sign below read 83 feet.

Walking down the butte was much faster and easier, although I slipped and landed on my patootie. We got back into our vehicles and returned to camp. Both moms had a hard time getting out, stretching slowing and bending carefully.

That afternoon Walker and Foster reviewed testimony from Cooper, Marleen, and now Vernon. They were one man down since Malloy could no longer assist. Perkins wasn't available for help either. They needed assistance badly. Malloy couldn't possibly handle all the calls, while two dedicated their entire efforts to solving this murder. Deputy Fountain couldn't help; there was plenty going on in Deschutes County.

Recapping what they had, there was a connection to Canada. Vern had recalled Rusty saying one guy was from Canada. They had a Canadian quarter now from the headwaters and the nickel Walker found in the parking lot. Vern had been to Canada prior to the incident also. Two handkerchiefs or bandanas. A silver flashlight, probably the murder weapon. A tree branch with blood and hair. A cloth bag that held the boxy flashlight of Coop's, and remains of a mostly used joint. Two matchbooks from D&D.

They discussed the need for photos and more information about Harley and possibly someone else. Hopefully they hadn't already fled the area. They needed surveillance of the camp north of Bend. Good old fashion footwork that was time consuming, and they speculated maybe they would need somebody to go undercover to find Harley.

Foster had been working in the region for years and recalled Detective Menetz had done years of some pretty heavy undercover work in the Valley. Perkins offered to reach out to his supervisor to see if they could borrow him. Again.

Menetz had been wondering about the case anyway. He felt vested for some reason.

Sheriff Perkins mentioned not knowing how long this case could continue. There would be unexpected budgetary issues. He didn't look forward to approaching the county commissioners for additional funds. But maybe it would shore up his request for more staffing and funding. He gathered his staff together and said, "Well boys, I have good news and bad news. We can have Menetz, but there's no budget to cover extra expenses."

Savings could come from housing Menetz, a motel bill would add up quickly. Perkins didn't think Menetz should stay with him. Someone coming and going undercover from the sheriff's home could be problematic. Walker had four kids under age ten. Foster lived too far away, almost one hour each way.

Malloy jumped in, offering his spare bedroom where the detective could come and go as he needed; no noise and could sleep odd hours if needed.

Within two hours it was done. Menetz was coming. All agreed it would be fine for him to stay at Malloy's place.

Malloy called making the offer of housing accommodations and Menetz agreed. Malloy gave him his address. He turned to Walker and said, "It's set. He'll be here at seven tomorrow night."

———————

Commotion at one group of three campers not far away caught the attention of all of us. Probably the entire acreage of Riverside Campground heard the hubbub as I caught just a few words from a high-pitched voice, "Hospital. Rabies. My Baby." The cherry red Volkswagen camper van, a double slug bug in our jargon, generated its own dust storm as it tore out of camp.

Three dads went over to see if they could help. When they returned, Dad reported that a rambunctious six-year-old boy named Charlie had been stalking and pestering a chipmunk. He chased it round and round a tree. Evidently the chipmunk had enough and stopped. Charlie nabbed it in his right hand. Having no desire to be petted, the irate chippy promptly bit Charlie in two places on the bottom of his hand. The youngster bawled in agony. Then he panicked because of the sight of blood, coughed and spit which convinced his distraught mother he'd been bitten by a rabid chipmunk and was already foaming at the mouth. Her baby would die from rabies if they didn't seek medical attention immediately. No reasoning or calming comments helped, so the dad piled them in the van and has taken them to the hospital in Bend. Dad could weave a great yarn.

Several hours later a man strolled into our campground and announced he was the father of the boy who irked the chipmunk. He thanked our dads for offering assistance. He conveyed, "The ER doctor was sure it wasn't a rabid chipmunk but had bitten in self-defense. It wasn't the first time this had happened to a mischievous child. He gave my son a tetanus shot; he explained it would prevent lockjaw from a possible bacterial infection that could create spasms in the jaw, which then progress to the rest of his body. A good reminder not to play or chase wild animals. You should have seen my son's eyes, as big as dinner plates, they were. He gave my wife a sedative. It was a peaceful, quiet drive back to camp and both are resting comfortably in our van. Thanks again, neighbors." He chuckled and waved as he walked back toward the double slug bug.

That night we all pooled our meals for a delicious potluck. Again, uncountable stars glittered against a velvety black sky. Sitting around the campfire, we toasted marshmallows and squeezed them between two slabs of four squares of a Hersey's milk chocolate bar, then a half of a graham cracker for the top and the other half for the bottom. S'mores were a real treat.

Even though some of us were beat from the hike, Maleah's dad said he'd heard some snipes the night before and we should go looking for them. Flashlights in hand, he led a mass of us gullible kids around in the pitch dark, shining the light hither and yon looking for the notorious snipes. The search always ended when another dad screamed at the top of his lungs, lunging out from behind a tree. They suckered us in each time.

Jeff's mom dubbed us official stargazers. We waited patiently, anticipating that exhilarating rush of spotting a shooting star. Seeing Sputnik blink, plodding across the dark sky, and viewing craters of the moon was neato. The moon looked about full, even though Dad said it would be three more nights until it was one hundred percent full for this month. The boys burst into scary folklore about were-wolves, vampires, people going crazy, animal attacks, and other ghastly things that could happen because of a full moon. Good grief, where did these imaginations come from?

Peggy and I were bushed from the hike. We fell asleep as soon as our heads hit the pillow, leaving Maleah with her flashlight to read teen magazines.

———

Wednesday, instead of feeling better, Arlo felt worse, physically and mentally. He'd lost his appetite. But knew he needed to eat something. He didn't return to the D&D. Now he was throwing up. That night, he tossed and turned but finally got to sleep. In his delusion, he woke up seeing himself on the little box TV on the dresser, killing somebody, but he couldn't tell who. He woke up drenched in sweat. Standing in the shower, he said, that's it.

CHAPTER TEN

Over The River And Through The Woods

Thursday morning the four members of the Jefferson County Sheriff's Office were back at their corner booth at the café. Drinks came moments later—coffee for Perkins and Malloy, iced tea for Foster, and Walker told Twila, "Milk, please, no coffee for me this morning." The spicy chiliburger from the day before seemed to bother his stomach. Even though technically off the case, being short-handed, Malloy sat in on the casual meeting that would cover more than just the murder investigation.

Walker and Foster reported they were following up on leads, speaking with neighbors. One of them needed to start looking through fingerprint books but hadn't had the time. It would take a while for them to tie it all together. Perkins said Malloy could help look through the fingerprint books, but nothing else.

Both Coop and Vern returned to their jobs. Co-workers at the bank looked at Coop, wondering what in the world happened to him. His face was still black and blue with orange and brown tones. Nobody where Vern worked really cared, they just needed him to work hard and catch up since he'd missed a few days.

Peggy and I tried to ignore the clamoring outside. It was way too early in the morning and especially nippy. We wanted to stay hunkered in our cozy sleeping bags.

The dads had surprised the boys, saying they were taking them fishing at Suttle Lake and would rent a couple of boats. We were thrilled to have them gone, hopefully the entire day.

The three of us girls decided we'd like to walk to the store, stop for a treat, then continue walking down to Allingham Bridge, which would be another mile. Round trip would be four miles. The moms said they'd like to come along.

The scenery didn't change from day to day on the familiar walk. Yet we noticed something different, whether it was a dainty, yellow star-shaped wildflowers on a log, different kids playing in the river, or woodpeckers hammering on a tree.

Reaching the store, we all went in and bought a variety of frozen treats. Mom had her favorite, a fudge bar. I had to decide between an orangesicle or an ice cream sandwich. The thin layers of chocolate cake with vanilla ice cream squeezed in between won out. King Cornets, Eskimo pies, and a Nutty Buddy were purchased.

227

We went across the street, standing on the bridge looking down seeing the large fish that brought in tourists by the hundreds. More interesting to me was the merganser family trying to swim upstream along the bank. Little greenish-yellow pine siskins pecked the ground. Larger and brighter, yellow and black warblers added their song to the sounds of the river.

Mom read about the history of the Camp Sherman Store from a brochure she'd picked up when we were selecting our treats. We'd been to the store dozens and dozens of times but until now never knew the background.

"Frank Leithauser built the first permanent building in 1917 to house the store and in 1922 Ross Ornduff removed that building and constructed the present store.

Rod and Evelyn Foster ran the store from 1925 to 1940. In 1928 the post office became a year-round operation. During the Fosters' 15 years, the store had 32-volt electricity from a turbine across the river that provided power for the store refrigerator, an iron, and a small heater in the house.

Local Camp Sherman resident and builder Luther Metke owned the store during World War II and his daughter Mae Dodd was the proprietor.

The land on which the store sits in Tract G is leased from the U.S. Forest Service, like the cabins along the river."

Walking farther than we'd done all week, we followed the river through tall bushes and under low tree branches. We came to the first Forest Service campground called Camp Sherman. Dozens of campsites were set up with families much like ours.

A young boy stood on a fallen tree jutting into the river. He threw a large stick for his golden retriever to fetch and bring back. She stood there until the boy said, "Go get it,

Autumn." She leaped off the end of tree, swam in four-foot water, grabbed the stick in her mouth, and powerfully swam back against the current. We watched them repeat this time after time. A couple showed up, who I assumed was the boy's parents. I heard the mom say, "Brent, it's time to come back for lunch."

A guy stood in the middle of the river. He wore chest-high waders keeping him dry, with a vest over a shirt undoubtedly full of his equipment. His flexible rod bent back over his right shoulder with the line stretched tight. He casted forward and looked like a pro.

The next campground, called Allingham, is smaller with fewer camping spaces available. It is before the Allingham Bridge, which serves as a dividing line with the next campground named Smiling River. We walked the loop through the third campground where some people were able to back up their campers pretty close to the river. Some tents were pitched along the edge. They were lucky like us to be able to hear the sounds the river made.

Two teenage boys and one girl took turns jumping off the bridge about ten feet into the freezing river. As soon as one hit the water, they yelled something undeterminable. I assumed it must be how cold the water felt or hurt when hitting it. But they did it over and over. Then, in unison, holding hands, they counted, one, two, three, and all jumped at the same time.

Then one boy tossed an inner tube upriver and as it floated under the bridge, the other tried to land in the middle. After several tries the boys continued to miscalculate by jumping too late. Missing again with the tube floating under the bridge, this time the girl turned and sprinted across the one-lane road and jumped over the railing. We followed, watching her land in the middle of the rubber tube. We all clapped. Her friends yelled their approval as she floated downstream. One yelled, "Way to go, Holly."

We walked across the bridge and headed down the opposite side hoping to see some new scenery. The easy path had dozens of bends and curves. We dipped down on the trail jumping over the spring that had created a marshy squishy area. Not wanting to get my shoes wet, I leaped from one side to the other. The moms walked gingerly across a conveniently placed fallen log. They did not want to get dirty.

We came upon the same fisherman now standing on the bank in a different location of the river. Shallower water cascaded over rocks, causing some gentle rapids. His rod bent forward and line tightened, he had a fish! We watched as he worked it to the river's edge by letting it swim freely for a while then reeled in some more of the line. He played with it a few times until the fish came in the shallows. Then he stepped in and bent down and gently removed the fly from its mouth. He held it for a few seconds then released it and the fish wiggled away. I thought, what a kind man to catch and then release this fish. Smart thinking on his part because he'd never catch a limit so he could fish all day.

We all clapped when he released it. As he turned, seeming embarrassed by the crowd that had assembled, he tipped his fishing cap, changed flies and cast again.

We trekked onward back toward Camp Sherman, seeing the campground we'd walked through earlier on the other side of the river. Soon we were weaving not only around trees, but through rustic log cabins and a few homes where a few people lived full-time. Some of the windows of the cabins were still covered and didn't have that lived-in look. The owners hadn't arrived yet for the summer. Some waited until after the crowds of Memorial

Day Weekend returned to their lives elsewhere. Blue lupine grew freely around patios and decks. One home had a slowly turning water wheel off the deck. I wanted to sit on their bench swing, gliding back and forth, gazing up and down the peaceful river but I didn't, knowing I should ask permission first. Little yellow flowers were blooming around the homes and along the river.

Back at Camp Sherman, and after the warm walk, Peggy's mom announced, "treat time" again. We crossed the road to the open window at the Metolius River Resort restaurant. We all ordered ice cream cones, mine being chocolate and vanilla swirl. We sat on the picnic tables enjoying the cold sweet licks before starting the final mile of our hike.

This would be our last walk of the week. I thought about what an out-of-the-ordinary week it had been. Returning to camp while still quiet most of us put a chair in the river, removing shoes and socks to cool off. We lolly-gagged and plotted, knowing soon the fathers and sons would return and the peacefulness would end.

Our motto, "Don't get mad get even," was running out of time. We purposely waited to instigate our revenge until the end of the week, saving us from certain retaliation, but what could we do to get even with our irksome brothers? In a normal situation, the typical shortsheeting a bed, stringing white thread or clear fishing line across a door-way, unscrewing lightbulbs, Vaseline on the toilet seat or any door handles, or clear plastic wrap under the toilet seat would suffice, but not in this setting. Plus, others would be impacted by slippery Vaseline boobytrapping toilet seats in the outhouse. I hated going in there anyway.

Several times a day the boys jumped on their bikes like they were mounting bareback in a John Wayne movie. They'd leave a trail of dust as they tore off somewhere.

It had to be sabotage of their bikes. After brainstorming the possibilities of loosening handlebars or seats, or letting air out of the tires, Peggy took a spool of clear fishing line from her dad's fishing gear box. Now what? Tie up the handlebars. Do something to the pedals? What about the back tire?

We'd not done anything this devious before and had no idea what might happen. What if we tied the back of the front wheel to the fender with the invisible line? What would that accomplish? Or should we tie them all together?

As the boys were elsewhere, Peggy and I looped together fishing line around the front wheel over the fender on each of the four bikes. We left Jeff's stingray be, as he wasn't the bothersome one in this instance. This was all for the brothers. Since they had been gone a good portion of the day and we clearly had access to their modes of transportation, we would get the blame. But we'd never fess up. Nor did we care.

Mid-afternoon the vehicles rolled in. The boys talked all at once about the exciting time they'd had fishing. They'd caught quite a few trout, and enough to cook some for their dinner. Fortunately, no one had fallen out of a boat. But it would have made for a great story.

We sat in the lawn chairs, reading magazines, waiting, waiting, waiting. Then it happened. One of the boys yelled, "Race time!" Max, Will, Dave, Bill and Jeff ran to their bikes, hopped on from the rear, feet on pedals for a rapid takeoff. Because of the distance of the spokes on the wheels, there was just enough give so each went about two inches before impact.

Peggy and I reveled in total satisfaction, watching as each one had a different result. Max lurched two inches then tipped left, still on his bike when he landed in the dirt. Will pitched forward, sliding sideways through the tall handlebars with the bike falling on him. Dave's bike fell on Bill's bike, who had already tumbled over onto the ground with a much bigger Dave landing on him. Jeff shot off like a rocket and wondering where his buddies were, looked back to see his comrades in the dirt. This turned out much better than we ever would have guessed. Success was ours. Accusations flew like the birds. There was no evidence of wrongdoing on our part. We sat in the lawn chairs with our moms the entire time, nowhere close to their bikes. Of course, we got blamed, but never admitted to anything nor would we ever.

We had an odd combination for dinner of grilled trout and sizzling hot dogs, for those of us not appreciating the taste of bland fish. Mom fixed some baked beans and warm cornbread. During an evening stroll before pitch dark, we spotted a family of deer drinking from the river. We roasted marshmallows then stargazed one final time, watching and waiting for anything moving in the dark sky with the almost full moon.

I felt a little in denial knowing the next day we'd head home. Dad wanted to return Friday afternoon to have plenty of time to unpack, using Saturday for cleaning up and getting tasks done so we could relax after church on Sunday. He'd be returning to work on Monday after being gone a week.

That evening Arlo let Suzanne at the front desk know he would be checking out in two days. After a year of being such a good tenant, she felt sorry to see him go. She asked, "How come you're leaving us?" His short reply, "My mum, ummm, mom, is having health issues."

"If you get any mail, where should I forward it?"

"I won't."

She kept it to herself that she'd written down his parents' address in a little book tucked away in the counter drawer.

Sitting at the small table in his room, he wrote a four-page letter to the Jefferson County Sheriff's Office telling his version of the story. He did clobber a guy or two with a tree branch. He didn't think he'd killed anybody.

Now he realized he had delivered some drugs and explained how that transpired. He wrote that Harley killed the kid because he'd cheated him with drug deals. He told them anything he could think of that would help bring Rusty's killer to justice.

He sent three-quarters of his year's earnings, ten one hundred-dollar bills and one fifty, and asked that it be given to Rusty's mum with his apologizes for not stepping in and being a stronger person to stop it.

Yep, he was a loser, after all. A gullible loser at that. He wasn't capable of telling the truth to anyone in person. He feared for his life if he spoke up against Harley. He only signed his first name, "Arlo, Uptown Motel, Bend."

Just after seven that evening, an unremarkable silver Dodge Dart pulled into Malloy's driveway. Climbing out of an old lady-looking sedan was a tanned-complexioned guy with brunette Beatles-length shaggy hair. His mutton chop side-burns matched the color of his thick mustache. The little patch of hair creating a goatee on his chin looked two shades darker. No wonder he normally was bald, Malloy thought, easier to wear fake hair for undercover work.

The swarthy looking man wore a cream pullover under a coffee-colored long-sleeved sweater. The white embroidered PGA stood out on the snazzy sweater. His tan polyester pants flared at the bottom. He oozed money. Except for the car.

Perched on his nose were the wildly popular round John Lennon glasses. He could have easily been the fifth Beatle, just not from England, but instead Italy or Spain. He looked like others Malloy had seen the past couple of years. All were searching for cheap land for real estate or prospective golf course developments.

Malloy wouldn't have recognized this guy if he'd seen him on the street. He thought if any neighbors noticed, they'd certainly be curious about his visitor. Slightly disappointed, he had hoped Menetz would show up in some super cool Corvette or some souped-up flashy wheels like a cool cat would be driving.

CHAPTER ELEVEN

*T*here's No Place Like Home

Friday morning, sadly our week had come to an end. Dad and Mom were reluctantly repacking the truck and trailer, basically reversing the process from seven days earlier. Everything needed to go into its original place, that way everything would fit.

I stood by the river moping about leaving. I thought about what an interesting and unusual week it had been. Mom called to me to climb into the back of the truck and as I turned, I saw a tree limb floating down the river. Although certainly not unusual, except this limb had a man's gray tennis shoe snagged to it. I turned and yelled, "DAAAAAAAAD."

CHAPTER TWELVE

$\mathcal{H}$omeward Bound

One week had transpired, one life-altering week. Friday morning, Arlo gave his foreman notice telling him about a family emergency. After a full day's work, he collected his final weekly paycheck. In cabin #10 he gathered up his few belongings. He walked a few blocks to the Trailways station and bought a ticket for the next morning from Bend to Portland, Portland to Seattle, Seattle to Vancouver B.C. He just wanted to get across the border. He'd figure out the Vancouver to Vegreville portion later.

On Saturday morning he got up early. He cut off one year's worth of long dark hair and shaved off his matching beard and mustache. He didn't leave it in the sink; he cleaned it all up and tossed it all in the trash can. He didn't want to cause Mrs. Rose any extra trouble.

Looking in the mirror he said aloud, "Jeez, I look like Dad, or I look like Mum, from this angle. No, I look like me." He hadn't decided if he really liked himself or not.

He packed up the years' worth of monthly letters from his mum. Each time he got a packet, he felt a tug for home. He didn't want to call it homesickness. Her letters revealed what he'd missed—a new niece that Adam and his wife had, and fortunately hadn't started her first name with an "A." His great grandfather had passed in the winter at age ninety-seven. He was at the church. He knew that this meant a funeral would be held for him when he could be buried in late spring when the ground thawed. That service had been held while Arlo was gone. Adler's Department Store added a new clothing section just for children. The youngest of the five Adler children had been in school with Arlo. A grain silo burned down. They were nervous about the new Prime Minister, Pierre Trudeau, not sure his political views aligned with theirs. The Vegreville Rangers continued in their quest to be the best hockey team in existence, winning another Craig Cup. Life was carrying on without him, it seemed.

In return, Arlo had sent her postcards every other month of Bend, Drake Park, Newberry Volcanic Monument, Three Sisters, Bachelor Butte and one of the historic Crooked River Bridge. He didn't write much just that he was fine and liked this job.

The few clothes he purchased fit easily into the duffle bag he brought with him. He had enough US dollars to buy meals when the bus made a stop. In Seattle, he would exchange the money back to Canadian.

Over the year, June to June, he saved a pretty nifty amount of cash from his hard work and lots of overtime.

His costs were low: monthly room rental, food, his first motorcycle and a little for gas.

———————

The only people Arlo remotely associated with was the Rose family that owned the motel. There were the guys he worked with, but he kept that group at arm's length. His well-meaning supervisor invited him over a couple of times to his place for a barbecue, but Arlo always declined. He politely made up some excuse. The Roses were down-home, hard-working people.

Mrs. Rose, Suzanne, not only worked the front desk but cleaned rooms for incoming guests. She appreciated Arlo as a permanent tenant, not having to clean cabin #10 every few nights. She did offer to clean up for him once a week, which he gladly accepted. She even did his laundry, a small task compared to having to clean it every time someone came in then out.

The husband, Larry, worked hard keeping everything in order. Once a dripping bathroom faucet was fixed as soon as Arlo mentioned it to Suzanne.

Their son, Steve, a young teenager, hung around Arlo after he got his motorcycle. Then the kid hovered just waiting for him to putter on his bike. Arlo had an admirer and didn't even know he'd become an icon to impressionable Steve. If Arlo would have looked more carefully, he would have seen the same admiring eyes from his younger brothers and sister. But he missed it. Steve didn't talk much, which was to Arlo's liking. He learned Steve was smart in school but was sort of a square, just like him. Steve wasn't really into team sports but liked playing hockey on the frozen ponds. Arlo could totally relate to Steve, except for playing ice hockey.

Their daughter Renée, probably eleven, reminded Arlo of his youngest sister Lexie, with lots of smiles, high energy, and always flitting around like a butterfly.

The Roses all had about the same tone of brown hair —milk chocolate. Just like his family all had dark hair.

Arlo lived for riding his bike on the weekends around the countryside. The landscape reminded him of home, especially the cold, dry winter. Hot in the summer, cold in the winter and nice in spring and autumn. When he'd return from his adventures, Steve would appear asking where he'd gone.

One day he told Steve he'd driven north about twenty miles first through Redmond, then Terrebonne and across the tenth-of-a-mile-long, flat Crooked River Bridge, stopping on the south rim. He was surprised the barriers weren't higher on long expanse. Looking down the wide, jagged, rocky wall canyon to the river three hundred feet below gave him the creeps. Despite the natural beauty, he got an odd vibe. Perhaps it had something to do the large yellow caution sign printed in black bold words warning: "300 Ft Cliff Ahead. Supervise children at all times. No Pets allowed beyond this point."

Even though incredibly scenic, it had a horrible history. He heard a tragic saga that several years earlier two women in a love affair decided one's children were getting in the way. Both were found guilty of throwing a boy and girl over the bridge still alive. Authorities found the two deceased children in the ravine. When telling Steve where he'd been, he couldn't shake the eerie feeling about the place. He wouldn't go back there.

Steve almost drooled over Arlo's bike. He would get his own bike when he turned sixteen or seventeen. He had been saving money he earned from working for his dad around the motel. And he mentioned he had also been helping his mom with the accounting and books, which he really enjoyed. He liked numbers. He proudly shared he even found a few ways they could save some money by purchasing items in larger quantities and not making so many trips to the supply house. At Steve's suggestion, they turned a small room into a storage closet. His dad built sturdy shelves to hold all the twenty-five-gallon containers of cleaning supplies they were now purchasing.

The only time Arlo did anything social with the family was when Steve turned fourteen. Mrs. Rose invited him to their private family yard for a barbecue and cake for Steve. Steve beamed when Arlo showed up. He gave Steve a six-piece socket set of Craftsman tools he bought at Sears. The way Steve reacted embarrassed Arlo somewhat; you'd think he'd delivered the moon to the kid.

Randomly, at the family dinner table, Steve would say something enlightening about Arlo: He lived in a small town in northern Alberta. He rode trains a lot. He had lots of brothers and sisters.

Larry asked, "How do you know that?"

"Arlo told me," Steve replied like it was old news.

"You know, he's a little off the wall, but I like him," Renée added.

When Arlo left on May 31, he left his motorcycle parked in his usual spot by the front door at cabin #10. He taped a piece of white paper to the seat. It read: "*For Steve.*"

At 6:30 a.m. he walked away from his life of one year. At 6:55, he sat in a seat on a Trailways bus heading to Portland. He was hightailing it home.

He closed this chapter that started with high hopes. It ended quite differently. He never got to California.

Monday morning Walker opened a thick envelope. Hundred-dollar bills fell onto his desk. And a four-page letter from some guy named Arlo.

Arlo was already back on Canadian soil catching the train to Vegreville.

Tuesday, on his twentieth birthday, one year to the day after he left, Arlo walked back into his family home. He watched like in a slow-motion movie the harvest gold plate slip from his mother's hand, crockery breaking into dozens of shattered pieces. She burst into tears as she grabbed him tightly, hugging the breath out of him. She felt so soft and smelled so good, like home. To her, he looked about the same as when he left except his eyes looked hopeless, dejected. There were some deep scratches in his neck. Everyone wanted answers. He wanted to sleep. It took him an entire week before telling his father the whole story.

Arlo had been home three weeks when his mother handed him an envelope with a return postmark, "Bend, Oregon." Mrs. Rose's letter started with an apology hoping he didn't mind she'd written down his parents' address, copying it from one of the letters his mother had sent. She did it just in case something ever happened to him and she needed to reach his family.

Then she hoped he had gotten home safely. Then it was how much they liked having him around.

Her final line read: "Arlo, the police came looking for you Monday after you left. They asked a lot of questions. They made it sound very serious, so I gave them your parents' address. We can't tell if you are in trouble or not. We certainly hope not. Cordially, Larry & Suzanne Rose."

Arlo thought to himself, I'm doomed. I did it after all. I must have killed the kid. Now what?

Then there was a separate half page from Steve. It was simple.

Hey, Man, I don't know how to ever repay you for leaving your bike for me. It's the coolest gift I have ever gotten or probably will ever get. Please come see us sometime, Arlo. Your friend, Steve.

CHAPTER THIRTEEN

*B*orn to be Wild

Wearing his mod mop-top wig, mustache and chops, and walking-billboard PGA sweater, Menetz sat in the same booth at the D&D that he had for the past eight nights. He did look like a well-to-do golf course developer with plot maps scattered around the table. He had the menu almost memorized, a few entrées that were his favorites. He pushed the circular glasses back up on his nose.

His heart skipped a beat when two men came in. One had bushy brown hair, dressed like a biker. The other had a light complexion with sandy blonde hair. Menetz glanced at the bartender who nodded ever so slightly that no one but Menetz would even notice.

The detective slid a small camera peeking out from under the thick afternoon *Oregonian* newspaper pointing it towards Harley. He took dozens of photos of both men, snapping more than enough.

Menetz headed for the entrance marked "Bath-rooms" and slipped into a third door he knew would take him to the kitchen. He ducked out the back door, walked until he found the only Harley Davidson in the parking lot. He snapped photos of the bike, tires and his tape measure showing sixteen inches on the Goodyear white wall tire. Hopefully it would be an exact match to the tire tracks in the parking lot of the headwaters.

He retraced his steps and sat back down just as meat loaf, mashed potatoes with gravy, homemade yeast rolls and green beans were served. He ate at his leisure as the other two had dinner, too.

Harley sneezed several times. Menetz figured he had a cold or allergies. Didn't Coop say he'd heard one guy sneeze? Vern mentioned it, too. Menetz wrote it on a napkin.

He let Harley and the other guy depart. As he walked to the cash register to pay for probably his final D&D dinner, he picked up the water glass from the booth Harley was sitting at and slipped it into a large bag.

Menetz followed from a distance to the dirt road north of town where Harley and the other biker pulled off. He drove on. Farther down the road he stopped and, using a telephoto lens, got some more photos of the house, barn, lots of dogs and several bikes. There might have been a coyote or two also. He couldn't tell how many bikers lived there. The barn door was closed.

The next day Menetz delivered sharp photos of Harley and his bike to Walker from the restaurant and blurrier ones from probably a mile away. They all slapped each other on the back. And they wanted more and closer photos from Menetz.

Walker headed out on the almost one-hour drive to Sisters to show Marleen the photos. She recognized the biker with brown hair. He'd been at Rusty's a few times. She clearly recognized his face not just hair. He had sneezed a couple of times. He was the one with the tattoo of a skull on his hand she could easily see.

Two other neighbors had seen the man in the photo on their street on two or three different occasions. Coop verified it was the guy he saw pulling away from their house several nights before the headwaters' incident. He was yelling at Rusty. Vern had seen the guy in the pictures, too. No one recognized the blonde-haired biker.

Walker learned long ago to trust his gut and his gut was telling him Harley was their man. But he knew he had to gather more evidence to establish the probable cause needed for an arrest warrant. District Attorney Crespi was a stickler for facts and would not present the case before a grand jury until he felt confident they would return with a true bill of indictment. There could be no lose ends for a potential high-profile murder trial.

He needed the latent fingerprints lifted from the glass Menetz collected to match those found on the flashlight. They had to match without a doubt. They still needed a last name. Plus, just because the fingerprints may match, he knew the DA would want as much evidence as possible.

They certainly had reasonable suspicion; he knew the legal mumbo jumbo, "supported by circumstances sufficiently strong to justify a cautious belief that the facts are probably true." But that wouldn't hold up for the DA or a grand jury. He knew they had probable cause. They already had enough to obtain a warrant for the arrest of Harley, or the issuing of a search warrant, in his book anyway. But it wasn't his book the DA went by. He knew deep down inside that they'd have one chance to get Harley. They couldn't tip their hand with a search or bringing him in for an interview. They needed a criminal indictment to arrest him.

Malloy kept plenty busy with other routine business: writing speeding tickets and covering wrecks, injured and missing hikers, a cougar sighting and consequent attack on sheep, on and on. Their neighboring county, Deschutes, had issues with heavy meth and LSD use and drug trafficking.

Sheriff Perkins met with Sheriff Poe and updated him on the case. They hadn't needed Deputy Fountain's assistance since the morning of discovering the body. That could change quickly.

They had tracked the lead suspect just north of Bend in Poe's County. Poe was well aware of the outlaw camp off Highway 97. The murder occurred in Jefferson County but because of the suspect's residence, Deschutes County was now involved. Poe appreciated Menetz was doing surveillance, charting comings and goings, number of residents and anything else helpful. His deputies were busy with some other serious issues.

Perkins provided photos of Harley and Sheriff Poe promised to show them around at the next morning's briefing.

They still didn't have a last name for Harley. Nor did they know if Harley was even his legal name.

Poe said he'd like to offer more assistance, but they were dealing with two missing persons cases. They'd heard through the grapevine that a Ronald Largo, originally from New York, convicted of tax evasion and perjury, had set up a prostitution ring in the area.

The second, Roger Courtland, was dealing in stolen goods, guns, and drugs. The two hadn't arrived in the area together, but rumor mill sources reported they were acquaintances when living on the east coast.

Still, Poe promised back-up if needed when serving an arrest warrant.

Deputy Fountain, Deschutes County Sheriff Office's teddy bear, drove off following a few leads about some locals who supposedly were in a drug war. Fountain was the most likable deputy in Sheriff Poe's department. When calls came in, most people requested him for assistance. He respected everyone and strived to live by the Golden Rule, treating others as he wished to be treated. His easy-going personality, honesty, fast smile, and sincere respect for all had caused him to become popular with criminals, too.

More often than not, an offender lodged in jail would ask to speak with Deputy Fountain if they'd had any contact with him in the past. He'd been awakened from a good night's sleep more times than he could remember, showing up because the culprits would only spill their guts admitting guilt as Fountain sat there listening and offering whatever assistance he could provide to help them out. He wondered if he shouldn't have been a jail chaplain, if there was such a position. But not in these parts; they were understaffed as it was.

Plus, now his county had two missing persons reports he was checking out. Law enforcement wanted to get the drug issues stopped before they got out of hand.

A man was badly beaten and in the hospital. Fountain asked Chaplain Miller to pay the victim a visit to see if he would open up to a deputy. It didn't take long to hear the answer "Yes." Fountain showed up to speak with the poor cuss lying in a hospital bed. The beat-up man tried to tell Fountain everything he knew. But his broken jaw was wired closed, so he wrote everything down. Fountain asked questions, the guy wrote answers. And he provided a few more names, if they would talk. He would be leaving town as soon as he could walk.

His story described the East Side bikers from north of Bend who were running the drug ring in the area and they were not allowing anyone else on their turf. He signed the three pages, Osborn White.

Fountain showed the man a photo. "That's who about killed me," he barely eked out of his bound-up mouth. It was Harley.

If Fountain had an official partner, it would be Deputy Berg. But it was rare two deputies were in one vehicle as backup; their department was spread too thin. Deputy Berg did go with him to find one of the guys called Raccoon, holed up in a seedy motel. Raccoon had heard about Osborn, who everyone called Ozzie, almost getting killed. He identified Harley in the photo. He'd bought drugs from Harley for the some time. And he recognized the kid in the newspaper photo a while back. Rusty had delivered a few packages of drugs to him from Harley.

Raccoon was a real talker. He told them Harley had come from San Francisco to start a new gang in Central Oregon. Fountain asked if he knew Harley's last name. Nope, he didn't, but wait, maybe it was something like a bird, maybe: Swallow, Robin, Hawk, no not Hawk, Woodpecker, Eagle, nope, none of it sounded right. Raccoon didn't know but he did know Harley would think him a rat fink and probably kill him, too.

They had just gotten more firsthand knowledge of Rusty linked to Harley. But they also knew Raccoon was a fink and unreliable. They discussed whether he told them the truth or if they were being hoodwinked. They agreed he had told them the truth. If he had a lick of sense, he wouldn't be sticking round. This new information about the tie to San Francisco would be a huge help.

After a telephone call to Walker, the ecstatic detective called the downtown San Francisco Police Department. Photos of prints and the drawing by Menetz were going in the mail to Detective Ricketts, their point of contact. Still, they only had a first name—Harley.

During the day and after dinner a few evenings, Menetz sat in his unmarked car with a camera pointed out the window toward the biker camp. Sometimes he used Malloy's Ford truck in case his Dart was becoming recognizable. He moved his car from place to place, never in the same location for long. He parked behind a large pine that obscured him. Dogs roamed around, not the expected pit bulls, just a bunch of strays. And goats, about a dozen goats. He was pretty sure he'd seen a couple of coyotes, but they were very common in this area.

He was almost positive seven bikers lived on the premises at any one time. Most didn't leave the compound. He figured they could barricade themselves in the barn if needed. He had seen a few of them adding sheets of plywood to the exterior siding, like they were fortifying it.

There was a space above the barn with a door open banging in the wind. In his mind he conjured up a gunfight where somebody lying on the hayloft floor was shooting at him from behind the flapping open door.

He knew his job was finished. He had supplied all the information and photos he could. He would clear out of Malloy's house the next day.

Harley knew cops had been snooping around asking lots of questions. He wasn't positive, but he thought somebody had followed him a while back. Somebody was spying on him. He thought he might be paranoid. Intuition told him more cop vehicles had been around than usual. He'd heard from a couple of his buyers that the fuzz had talked to them. Raccoon lied to his face, denying telling them anything.

Two weeks later, Walker received a call from Detective Ricketts in San Francisco. After days combing through thick books of fingerprints, they had a match. Harold Finch. He went by the name of Harley. They would send copies of the entire four-inch thick file to them immediately. It would include his entire record, mug shots, his driver's license and other photos.

Walker prepared a typewritten report of the investigation findings and print match from San Francisco and presented it to Perkins who thought they now had enough to present to the district attorney. They knew protocol, or hoops the DA had to jump through, so it could take days. They were so close to nailing this guy.

They'd wait until the files and photos came from California.

When their regular mailman Cliff came through the door carrying a box from San Francisco, any visitor in the Sheriff's office they would have thought Christmas arrived in June.

Nine days later, after the grand jury of seven jurors convened in the criminal matter, it handed down a true bill of indictment. District Attorney Crespi sent it to Judge Jurgenson to sign the actual arrest warrant.

That afternoon Detective Walker got what he'd been hoping for—a warrant to take Harley Finch into physical custody and present him before the judge. They'd proved they had enough evidence to arrest Harley for Rusty's murder. But the congratulatory celebration would have to wait.

Plans were in high gear and a precision timeline established for the early morning surprise in forty-eight hours.

Tuesday, July 1, it was all-hands-on-deck for the arrest of Harley Finch. They suited up wearing chest protectors and had extra ammunition and guns. They assumed driving into the outlaw biker camp wouldn't be a piece of cake. The quarter mile flat dirt road wasn't exactly camouflaged.

Walker was first in his own vehicle. Malloy and Foster in a second vehicle, drove to the entrance of the road to the camp. Deputy Fountain joined in his Jeep. Sheriff Perkins was in car number four. Two more Deschutes deputies, Berg and Campbell, assisting as back up. Berg drove the last vehicle with Campbell in the passenger seat. There were five vehicles in all.

At dawn, about 5:10, they went in quietly—no sirens, no lights flashing, headlights off. Five cars drove slowly down the quarter mile dirt road hoping not to create a cloud of dust.

Somebody noticed the procession and yelled, "FUZZ." Harley knew they were coming for him. He'd even been sleeping in his clothes lately. He ran to his bike and sat idling in the barn letting them get closer. He revved the engine, raced out the door and charged straight for them, playing chicken, weaving between the cars, gunning it faster and faster.

They all had to turn around while Harley accelerated through the procession. As Deputy Berg spun the vehicle in a three-sixty, Deputy Campbell observed an area with some fresh dirt. He spotted a coyote standing on two soft dirt mounds.

In seconds Harley reached Highway 97, turning north he revved his bike, soon reaching fifty-nine miles per hour. By now each vehicle had turned around. He looked back and could see clouds of dust and them turning onto the road. He laughed at the snake of five police cars from two different agencies trying to catch up to him.

He raced north, now at sixty-five. He flew the seventeen miles towards Redmond. With the population of four thousand he got some distance on the cops as they slowed through the small town, but he didn't. The land was relatively flat and easy to race through. In the two miles to Terrebonne the cops got closer.

He increased power to seventy-five miles per hour. But he wasn't losing the cops after all. They were better drivers than he would have guessed. He knew his maximum speed was 99.4 marked with an arrow on the speedometer. He never needed to go this fast before. What a gas.

Walker in the first car drove ninety almost catching up to Harley. Harley drove dangerously fast, way too fast for him. All sorts of ideas were floating around in Walker's head. Maybe they'd just follow him until he ran out of fuel or he gives up, pulling over somewhere. Or would the cars all run out of gas before the motorcycle? Could Malloy shoot a motorcycle tire at eighty-five miles per hour? Even though he was a sharpshooter, he doubted he was that proficient.

Projecting ahead, Walker figured they could end up in Washington. He didn't want to chase this kid all day, but he would if necessary.

It was one hundred fifty miles from Bend to Goldendale, Washington, crossing the bridge at the Columbia River. From Goldendale it would be another hour to Toppenish. Around here Highway 97 combined with Interstate 82.

Motorcycles did get excellent gas mileage. They would not let him get away. If they got close to the border, he'd radio the Washington State Police for assistance. Harley couldn't keep up this speed that long. Or could he?

Harley felt giddy, almost lightheaded, with lights flashing, sirens blaring, him leading them on a goose chase, a Harley chase. He was screaming down the highway at eighty-nine miles per hour. Behind him they looked like a convoy of five dusty cockroaches. The first and second vehicles were gaining on him.

He glanced down momentarily seeing the speedometer needle climbing. He opened it up to his maximum speed of

99.4, the needle almost touching 100. He would lead them on the chase of their lifetime before he'd give up. He'd drive like hell until he ran out of gas. Then he'd make a run for it on foot.

There was no way he was going to prison for killing that cockroach kid. Or anybody else for that matter.

He reached the beginning of the tenth-of-a-mile-long Crooked River Bridge. The flat road was built above the arch over the Crooked River three hundred feet below. He'd driven it several times going to Washington.

He reached the halfway span as the motorcade of rolling sirens and red and blue lights arrived onto the bridge behind him. He laughed.

However this ended, he relished the thought that the fuzz would be talking about this chase for decades to come and they would certainly remember his name. Harley.

A movement caught his eye. A coyote wandered into the middle of the road almost at the end of the bridge. It sat down. Harley sped closer and closer. It didn't budge. He recalled his grandmother's boding warning, "A coyote is an omen of an unfortunate event of things in your path or in your future."

He dramatically swerved to the right pulling up on the front wheel, easily careening off the low concrete barrier, soaring through the air. He heard vehicle tires screeching to a halt.

In the four seconds plunging three hundred feet to his demise, Harley's grandmother's face flashed before him. Her words had come to pass.

They could not believe what they were seeing unfold in front of their eyes. Running to the edge of the bridge, below they saw one spinning wheel of Harley's bike. Metal parts were scattered on the bank and in the river. A black splotch oozed red.

Malloy stated matter-of-factly, "Well, that's one way of saving the cost of a court case."

Walker noted, "One less drug dealer."

Foster declared, "I'm not going down there to retrieve that body."

Fountain asked, "Was that a coyote at the end of the bridge? Did you see it?"

Berg followed, "Did he kill himself or swerve to avoid the coyote?"

Campbell exclaimed, "Damnation, what a way to go."

Walker concluded, "Naw, he just didn't want to face the music."

Sheriff Perkins looked at his watch, "Time of death, 5:43 a.m."

That afternoon, Walker called Menetz and filled him in.

CHAPTER FOURTEEN

All You Need is Love

After a solid week of stewing about the crime, knowing the police were after him from what Mrs. Rose had reported, Arlo worked himself up into quite a state of mind. His parents were worried because he was losing weight and stayed locked up in his room. He came to this conclusion: He would just turn himself in to the authorities.

Almost suppertime on Friday, the fourth of July, which wasn't a significant day in Canada, Lexie answered the dingdong at the door. There stood a Royal Canadian Mounted Police officer. He asked to speak with Arlo.

"AARRLLLOOO," she nervously yelled up the staircase. They'd never had a Mountie at their home before.

Arlo almost stumbled down the stairs. He blurted out, "I'm sorry, Sir, I did it."

Both parents entered the hallway as the Mountie replied, "Did what, Son?"

Realizing he really didn't know why the Mountie was there, Arlo slightly recovered as his father asked, "Can I help you, Sir?"

"I am delivering a message to Arlo Bortnick from the Jefferson County Sheriff's Office, State of Oregon, United States of America."

Sweating, Arlo assumed it was a warrant for his arrest in his part of the murder, drug trafficking and anything else he'd admitted to before high tailing it back home.

Arlo's mother remembered her manners and invited the Mountie into the living room. He declined a cup of tea.

Handing the worried young man whose hands were shaking the one-page typed letter, Arlo sat down in his mother's threadbare rocking chair and read each word. He looked up at his mother, who was now standing beside the tall Mountie. She bowed her head and closed her eyes like she was praying, Please God, don't take my son.

Arlo's eyes bugged out and surprising all of them said, "It's basically thanking me for my help in documenting a crime. My first-hand knowledge helped them find the murderer, some drug sellers and buyers."

"Dad, I'm not a criminal. They aren't arresting me," he almost screamed.

His teary-eyed mother said, "Read what else it says." Arlo, continued, "The victim's mother appreciates the money I left. It covered the unexpected funeral for her son." He let out the biggest sigh of relief the Mountie had ever heard.

"They are exonerating me of anything I unknowingly participated in," a now thankful Arlo said, "but there's one more paragraph." He read it to himself shaking his head. Then said aloud, "Harley died on July 1."

Arlo's mother softly said, "Canada Day, our Independence Day."

CHAPTER FIFTEEN

$\mathscr{T}$ime of the Season

Friday, the Fourth of July, began our first exciting day of the Albany Timber Carnival, a three-day celebration. I looked forward to the time-honored tradition every summer. We lived in a very patriotic little town, celebrating Veterans Day and the Fourth of July like none other. It was a big deal, a really big deal.

We celebrated every Independence Day focusing on our region's timber industry. The Chamber of Commerce managed it, then the Albany Junior Chamber of Commerce (Jaycees) assumed responsibility of the principal service project. This year they wore a one-piece red jumpsuit with a plaid red and white collar chest pockets, and long pockets from the waist to below the hips. They were known for their zany getups.

There would be logging competitions, a royal court, a parade, and fireworks display. The royal court consisted of princesses from Albany and nearby towns. While successful sales of Timber Carnival buttons were not the sole criterion, the queen was usually the princess who sold the most. Dad always bought buttons for all of us.

Our parade of marching bands, high school drill teams, colorful floral floats, and humongous noisy log trucks made up the parade showing off Timber Carnival themes of patriotism, local businesses, and praises to the timber industry.

Usually men from the Northwest, Canada, the Yukon and Northwest Territories provided the skills and entertainment. But men from Australia introduced traditional chopping events from their country and now were almost locals in our community during Timber Carnival. If we were lucky enough to be at Shakey's Pizza Parlor when some of them were chowing down, it was neat hearing them talk with their cool accents. Max often asked for the autographs making him a favorite.

Sitting in the grandstands in the summer sunshine, sunbeams reflecting off the water, my favorite event was coming up—logrolling on the lake. The women really showed some fancy footwork and balance staying upright on the free-floating log longer than the men. The men's legs bulged with muscles. It didn't take long before one's impressive sprinting, kicking and other foot techniques caused the opponent to fall off, getting drenched. I guessed the saying, "It's as easy as falling off a log" came from this event.

This evening would be the spectacular fireworks show that begins at 10:30. We'd pile into the back of our truck, canopy removed, and when we got to the lake, we'd lie down in the back on layers of blankets watching the night sky pop, glow, and sparkle with noisy, very loud colorful fireworks.

Peggy's family would be joining us in their station wagon. She and her brothers would climb up and sit on top of their wagon. Traditions.

Dad bought the three-day family pass so we could come and go as we pleased for the lumberjack events. I wore sapphire pedal pushers with embroidered white stars, the size of a dime. A cherry red button-down sleeveless cotton blouse and navy Keds. Playing outside the past month had lightened by honey blonde hair and my blue eyes matched my entire ensemble.

My bothers, dressed in jeans, wore contrasting shirts, one royal blue with white stripes and other white with bright blue stripes.

Dad wore a white shirt underneath his Yellow Lions Club vest with all sorts of patches and Timber Carnival pins.

Mom wore multiple shades of snazzy blue paisley print slacks and a crisply ironed white blouse.

My family looked like a jumbled up American Flag.

We had all gotten up early ready to walk with Dad who would join other Lions Club members at Eleanor Park flipping pancakes and sausage at their annual fundraiser. Max was ready to get his fill of pancakes and maple syrup.

The morning edition of the Albany *Democrat Herald* lay on the back steps. Picking it up, Dad opened it and thumbed through quickly while Mom leashed up Duke. Will was tying his shoes and Max finished brushing his teeth as I paced the kitchen floor. Snapping my fingers wasn't working so I loudly said, "Let's go people, time's a wasting."

One article on page five caught Dad's attention. As I headed out the door, "Hold Up, Sis," he told me.

Murder on the Metolius Solved

by Shelton Pugh, *Bend Bulletin*

On July 1, Harold Finch, known as Harley, age 32, originally of San Francisco but living north of Bend for several years, died after a high-speed chase while being pursued by Jefferson and Deschutes County Sheriff's deputies. They were attempting to arrest him for the suspected murder of Sisters resident, 19-year-old Rusty Kavanagh.

Deputies pursued the suspect for 20 miles, reaching speeds over 90 miles per hour through Redmond and Terrebonne. At the speed of 100 miles per hour, Mr. Finch drove his motorcycle off the Crooked River Bridge, plunging to his demise, 300 feet below into the north bank of the river. His body was recovered by Deschutes Search and Rescue Teams.

A family from Albany, Oregon, discovered the body of the victim in the headwaters of the Metolius River on May 23.

"Golly," I exhaled, reaching for the gold cross hanging around my neck.

"That's it?" Max challenged.

"That's it," Mom conceded.

"Well, that's the end of that." Dad concluded.

"Wow. Neato. Let's go to breakfast!" Will demanded.